"I'm a suspect, Cat."

Jay spoke quickly, his words almost running together. "You have to help me. You have to help me show them—"

"Wait. You're a suspect?" How could good, kind-hearted Jay Garrett be a suspect in a murder investigation? The Jay she remembered always smiled, laughed and kissed with lips that could lead a girl into all sorts of trouble....

"Please tell me you're the detective you always swore you would be. You have to help me. I need you."

He needs me. After all this time. "Jay, listen to me. If you're a suspect, what happened? Cops do not go around accusing people—"

"The cops are walking around like their bloody heads are cut off. Sarah's parents are waiting for them to release her body while the police point the finger at me rather than the real killer. I feel trapped, Cat. You've got to come to the Cove."

"I can't."

D1208205

Dear Reader,

I am so thrilled to introduce you to my debut novel with Harlequin Superromance! I am a Brit, living in southwest England and so proud that Harlequin is happy for me to write about British characters living in the fictional seaside town of Templeton Cove, England. I really hope you love this story as much as I do!

Detective Sergeant Cat Forrester is a woman in emotional turmoil from pretty much the very first page. Having lost her father to a drunk driver, Cat has spent the past seven years since his death looking after her grieving alcoholic mother alone, after her brother deserted them.

When she receives a phone call from her past lover and friend, Jay Garrett, telling her their mutual friend has been murdered and he is a suspect, Cat is torn between rushing to his aid and staying home.

Knowing she can't leave Jay to fight the accusation alone, she forces her brother to step up to their joint responsibility and leaves the city for Templeton Cove. The story that unfolds is one of danger, risk, high passion and love...for both Cat and Jay's dead friend and each other.

I received the email from my agent back in May 2012 telling me that Harlequin wanted to contract *Finding Justice*. A lot of screaming, crying and general hysteria ensued. Then I "met" my editor. I am smiling as I write this because I am so happy to be working with such a wonderful lady who makes me feel I can actually write.

I sincerely hope you enjoy Cat and Jay's story and I'd love to hear from you when you're done. Visit me at www.rachelbrimble.com.

Love,

Rachel Brimble

P.S. Be sure to look out for my next book set in Templeton Cove, coming in August 2013 from Harlequin Superromance!

Finding
Justice

RACHEL BRIMBLE

HARLEQUIN® SUPER ROMANCE®

Recycling programs
for this product may
not exist in your area.

ISBN-13: 978-0-373-71835-1

FINDING JUSTICE

Copyright © 2013 by Rachel Brimble

Printed in U.S.A.

ABOUT THE AUTHOR

Rachel Brimble lives with her husband and two young daughters in a small town near Bath in the U.K. She started writing short stories about eight years ago, but once her children were at school, she embarked on her first novel. A small press published it in 2007. Since then, she's had several books published, but securing her first contract with Harlequin Superromance was the proudest day of her career.

An active member of the Romantic Novelists Association and Romance Writers of America, when Rachel isn't writing you'll find her with her head in a book or walking the beautiful English countryside with her family. Her dream place to live is Bourton-on-the-Water in southwest England. And in the evening? Well, a well-deserved glass of wine is never, ever refused.

Dedicated to my wonderful husband, Terry Brimble, without whom I would not have had the courage or tenacity to follow my dreams. I love you.

Acknowledgments

There are so many people I want to thank for believing in me and making this book possible. First, to my wonderful agent Dawn Dowdle, who taught me to write deeper and better than I ever did before. I hope *Finding Justice* is my first thank-you of many.

To my friend and stoic contact, Police Constable Penny Walters, who made the suspense come alive. (All errors are mine.) You are my girl!

Finally, to my fantastic editor, Piya Campana—you could not have been more encouraging or supportive throughout. Thank you for being so great and teaching me so much!

CHAPTER ONE

"GODDAMN IT, he's not getting away with this. Do you hear me?" Detective Sergeant Cat Forrester glared at the circle of detectives watching her with varying amounts of guilt etched across their faces. "He was drunk. He got in a car and mowed down a twenty-eight-year-old mother. That makes him a killer, a murderer. I want his ass on a stick. So get back out there and talk to every damn person who knew him, loved him, hated him and slept with him. Somebody somewhere is hiding his sorry ass."

One of her female officers raised her hand. "No one in his family is talking right now, but I'm pretty sure if I keep up the pressure on the eldest daughter—"

Cat glared. "Is anyone else apart from me taking this case seriously? The guy was drunk, left the pub and got in his car. He then thought nothing about driving through Marlborough Place, past a school right when they were letting out for the day. He killed a mother. A mother of a small child. If that small child hadn't been talking to her friends a few feet away, she would be dead, too. We are going to catch this guy. Do I make myself clear?"

There was a cursory wave of nods and fingers tapping on keyboards in response. "Good. Well, get to it, then. Go. All of you."

The mumbled "yes, ma'am"s and scraping of chair legs against tile grated on Cat's nerves, hitching her stress level up another notch. Turning her back, she stared at the incident board. He couldn't get away with this. Not another drunk driver going unanswerable to his crime.

"Sergeant?"

"What?" she snapped.

"Sergeant." The firm, don't-mess-with-me voice of Inspector Harris echoed around the small room.

Cat grimaced. *Damn.* She turned and planted a smile on her face. "Sir."

He shook his head. "Don't give me that smile of yours, Sergeant. What was that all about? The driver has been missing in action for two days and you're dressing down your team as if he's been on the run for two weeks."

"I want him caught."

He stared at her for a moment longer before he blew out a breath and rested his hip against the gray metal desk behind him. "How much longer is this one-woman mission to end all drunk driving going to go on, Cat?"

The use of her first name spoke volumes. She hated it. If she lost her inspector's respect, and it evolved into sympathy, God only knew what the effect would be on her team if they witnessed it.

She crossed her arms. "It's not a mission, sir. I just don't think it's being given the time or concentration it deserves. This guy left a man alone to raise a four-year-old daughter."

"As your father's killer left you, your brother and mum."

Heat pinched at Cat's cheeks. "That's not the same. I was an adult."

He shrugged. "Depends how you look at it. What will this child remember of her mother? You had years of memories with your dad."

She turned away from him, picked up a marker and

made some illegible and pointless alterations to the board. "This isn't about my dad, sir. He died seven years ago."

"And it's still as raw as yesterday."

Cat squeezed her eyes shut. "You're wrong."

"Am I?"

"Yes."

There was a long silence and Cat inwardly cursed when the words in front of her blurred. She blinked. "Was there something you wanted to ask me, sir? I really should—"

"A call just came through."

Cat put down the marker and turned. "Call?"

He nodded, his gaze locked on hers. "Your mum. She needs picking up."

Shame and embarrassment flooded her body in equal measure and Cat swept past him to her desk. "Where?"

Inspector Harris stood. "The Hunters Arms."

"Fine." Cat whipped her bag from her chair and hitched it onto her shoulder. "If there's nothing else—"

"Cat." He caught her wrist as she moved to brush past him. "She needs help. Professional help."

"I can handle it."

"Not on your own. Not anymore."

She eased her arm from his hand. "I'll be back when I can."

Cat swallowed the humiliation burning like acid in her throat and walked from the room.

When she got outside, she inhaled great lungfuls of fresh air like she hadn't had the God-given pleasure of it in a week. Once her heartbeat slowed and her cheeks cooled, she flicked her hair over her shoulders, slid into the front seat of her police-issue car and drove toward the pub.

Fifteen minutes later, the soles of her shoes sucked and pulled against the sticky linoleum tiles as she walked deeper into The Hunters Arms. The bright August sunshine struggled to penetrate the nicotine-stained windows, and the TV screen hanging above the bar was so thick with dust, Oprah looked as though she was talking through a snowstorm.

Cat narrowed her eyes. Except for the three patrons sitting at the bar with the same early-morning thirst as her mum's, the pub was empty. She met the bartender's gaze as he wiped glasses.

"Where is she?"

He tilted his head toward the closed door of the ladies' bathroom.

She inhaled a deep breath and walked toward the closed door, fighting the nausea in her throat. How many more times would she have to do this? Ten? Twenty? Or was today the day she found her mum dead? Stepping inside, she nudged each cubicle door open in turn, her heartbeat increasing, her hands clammy. Tears threatened and she blinked them back. If her mum was dead, Cat was prepared. She'd been prepared since alcohol became her mum's necessary poison seven years before.

Pushing open the final stall, she stared down at her mum's painfully thin body sprawled across the tiny, tiled space. Patches of red wine stained her sunny-yellow dress; her designer slingbacks were scuffed and torn. Shoulder-length red hair, once so similar to Cat's, lay limp and loose about her shoulders, her long ago luminous skin an ugly shade of gray.

Dropping to her knees, Cat slid her hands under her mum's arms and heaved her upward until her head lay in Cat's lap. "Mum, it's me. Come on. Time to wake up."

She gently tapped her mum's cheek until she coughed, exhaling alcohol-infused breath into Cat's open mouth. Cat gagged, the sound loud and revolting as it echoed around the filthy enclosed space.

"For crying out loud." Cat held the back of her hand to her mouth.

Slowly her mum opened her eyes. After a moment, her gaze focused and she smiled. "Hey, baby. What are you doing here?"

Struggling to keep a lid on her rising frustration, Cat forced a soft smile. "I've come to take you home, silly."

"You're a good girl, honey. Always be there for me, won't you?"

Cat looked away as the usual words of assurance dissolved on her tongue like condensation on a cold bottle of beer. "Let's just get you out of here, okay?"

Hauling her mum to her feet, they shuffled from the bathroom into the bar. Ignoring the glassy-eyed stares of the drunks watching them, Cat tilted her chin and continued forward until they emerged outside. Cat lowered her mum into the passenger seat of her car and snapped her seat belt into place. She slammed the door.

She was a detective sergeant in the U.K. police force, yet she couldn't fix her grieving, alcoholic mother no matter how hard she tried. She sometimes wondered if it would be easier catching her first serial killer than dealing with the criminality of her mum's affliction. Shaking her head to clear the lingering sense of failure hovering around her like an invisible phantom, Cat marched around to the driver's side.

She'd find a way to help her mum sooner rather than later. She had to. The alternative was her brother and her becoming orphans at the age of twenty-nine and twenty-seven respectively. The fingers of the demon drink continued to claw at their shadows. Always there, always threatening to destroy what both of them had left.

Yanking open the car door, Cat slid into the seat and glanced across at her mum. Slumped over, her head tilted to the side, her eyes closed in comatose slumber, Julia Forrester barely resembled the glamorous mother and wife she'd been once upon a time. Cat brushed the fallen hair from her mum's cheek.

"I love you, Mum. I promise I'm doing my best to fix this."

Twisting around in her seat, Cat started the engine and fought to keep a firm hold on her resolve. Everything would be all right. It had to be.

The drive home passed in a blur of radio conversation with her team at the station, the whole time Inspector Harris's accusation of her personal involvement with drunk-driving cases beating her upside the head. She needed to stop reacting so vehemently every time a new hit and run landed on her desk. Yes, they were an open sore to her alcohol-hating heart, each one a sharp cut of remembrance striking her flesh like a knife, but that wouldn't help catch the guilty party.

The driver who killed her father was three times over the limit when he was caught. The Breathalyser reading served as the lock on the door to his prison cell. Others, like her current case, were harder to catch—but catch him she would.

Cat swallowed the perpetual guilt her mother's undoing caused time and again. If her father could see them now, he'd be so angry with her mum, her and Chris. How had their family been reduced to such disconnected chaos in seven years?

Swallowing hard, she tightened her grip on the steering wheel and concentrated on getting home.

By the time they reached the house, Julia was fairly lucid and Cat managed to get her inside and onto the settee without the humiliation of curtain-twitching neighbors asking if she needed any help—again. She whipped a fleece throw from the back of an adjacent armchair and tucked it tightly around her mum's perspiring body, knowing she'd wake shaking and cold.

Satisfied her mum would sleep for at least another hour, Cat left the room and walked upstairs to her bedroom. Physical and mental exhaustion settled over her like a concrete duvet as she fell backward onto the bed. Her heavy lids closed.

"Just for a couple of minutes," she murmured.

The sharp shrill of the phone on her bedside table obliterated her flagging energy, shaking her wide awake. Cat flew across the bed and snatched up the receiver before it woke her mum.

"Hello?" Her gaze darted to the open door.

"Hi. Um…is that Julia?"

"No. This is Cat Forrester, her daughter. Julia can't come to the phone right now. Can I help you?"

"Cat?"

Annoyance prickled at her nerve endings as she fell back onto the bed again, her eyes closing. "Yeah, as in poised to claw someone's eyes out."

His totally masculine burst of laughter sent a shiver down her spine and a loop the loop through her stomach. Her eyes snapped open and she sat bolt upright.

She knew that laugh….

"Got it."

A smile tugged at her lips. His voice was rich and deep, warm when everything else around her felt cold. She swallowed. It couldn't be. "Jay?"

"The one and only. How are you, pretty girl?"

"My God, it *is* you." Her smile stretched to a full-blown grin. "I can't believe this. It's been years." Since her father died.

"It's great to hear your voice again. What have you been up to?"

She hesitated, hating to lie but the alternative was impossible. Jay. Jay Garrett. Childhood friend and confidante. Her one-time lover.

"Not much, really. Work, work and more work." She forced a cheery smile. "How are you?"

Silence.

Cat stood and walked toward the bedroom door. "Jay? You there?"

"I need your help, Cat. I'm in trouble. Big trouble."

The timbre of despair in his voice alerted her to grief. Loss. She heard it loud and clear. It didn't matter whether the speaker was male or female, young or old. When you lost someone before you should, it always sounded the same. She was trained to recognize it—personally and professionally. To listen and help. To alleviate others' pain and hide her own. She stopped pacing and tightened her grip on the receiver.

"What's wrong?"

"It's Sarah."

Her mind whirled back seven years ago to the last time she and her family took their annual holiday to Templeton Cove. A picturesque town situated amongst the spectacular "English Riviera" region of Southwest England. The place Jay and his family had lived for generations.

"Sarah? Is she okay?" Cold dread seeped into Cat's blood, making goose bumps erupt on her arms. "Jay?"

"She's dead, Cat. Murdered."

She sucked in a breath as a lump of stone dropped into her abdomen. "What?"

"You need to come to the Cove. Investigate her death. The police here aren't getting anywhere." His shaky breath rasped down the line. "I'm a suspect, Cat. You have to help me. You have to help me show them—"

"Wait. You're a suspect?" How could good, kind-hearted Jay Garrett be a suspect in a murder investigation? The Jay she remembered always smiled, laughed and kissed with lips that could lead a girl into all sorts of trouble. . . .

"Please tell me you're the detective you always swore you would be. You have to help me. I need you."

He needs me. After all this time. "Jay, listen to me. If you're a suspect, what happened? Cops do not go around accusing people—"

"The cops are walking around like their bloody heads are cut off. Sarah's parents are waiting for them to release her body while the police point the finger at me rather than the real killer. I feel trapped, Cat. You've got to come to the Cove."

Cat felt the color leave her face and she gripped her hair back in a fist. "How did she die?"

"Strangled."

She squeezed her eyes shut. "Oh, God, no."

Sarah. Her friend. Her partner in crime. Memories of their childhood antics crashed into her heart and mind, of tormenting Jay and Chris, Cat's older brother, as they hung around the arcade trying to look cool. Of course, they'd grown up and Jay became the one whom all the girls noticed whenever he walked into a room. Especially Cat.

The seconds passed like heartbeats before Jay spoke again. "You'll come? You'll help me find the son of a bitch who did this?"

Her mum shot to the forefront of her mind on the eternal elastic band connecting them. She snapped her eyes open. "I can't."

Panic poured through her veins. She couldn't leave. She could never leave. "You don't understand—"

"Cat, please. We have to find out what was going on with Sarah before she died. Who would kill her? Everyone loved her. You can't think I would do this. I loved her. You know that."

Love. What was love to any of them? Tears seared the back of Cat's eyes as she strode from the bedroom onto the landing. "You have to let the police do their job. Templeton Cove is miles from my jurisdiction. There's nothing I can do. I'd help if I could, but—"

"Cat, please. It's my fault."

Her heart turned over and she ground to an abrupt stop. "What do you mean your fault?"

"I didn't kill her, but I didn't get to her quick enough to save her, either."

Cat looked over the banister at the open living room door. "You were there?"

"No, but I should've been. I'll explain everything. Just say you'll come. For me...for Sarah. Please."

"Jay..."

The clink of glass against glass halted Cat's words. Her mum had obviously woken and was now wetting her dry throat. Squeezing her eyes shut, Cat swore under her breath. Clearly, she'd missed another hidden bottle on her daily sweep.

"Cat?" Desperation sounded in Jay's voice.

She walked wearily downstairs. "I can't. I'm sorry. I've got a million and one things going on. Things I can't just leave."

She leaned around the living-room doorjamb and anger burned in her stomach. Her mum downed a glass of vodka, the half-empty bottle swinging from her other hand.

"Surely you've some holiday time due." Jay pleaded

into her ear. "I've been distracted for too long. I owe it to Sarah to find her killer."

Cat balled her hand into a fist when her mum abandoned the glass in favor of drinking straight from the bottle. She was due some time off—time off from everything. She moved from the door and into the hall.

"Give me your number and twenty-four hours to see what I can do." She fought the tears of frustration stinging her eyes.

"You'll come?"

"Yes, Jay. God help me, I'll come."

CHAPTER TWO

CAT JUMPED WHEN THE loudspeaker announced the arrival of the train that would take her to Templeton Cove. She glanced at her watch. Right on time. Which meant Jay was already onboard. She tightened her fingers around the handle of her suitcase and inhaled a shaky breath, immediately fighting the urge to gag. The smell of oil and grease mixed with frying bacon and sugar-dipped donuts did little to settle the lurching in her stomach.

Today had been chosen as "Mission: Templeton Cove" day because Jay was passing through Cat's hometown of Reading on his way back from a business trip in London. It made sense for them to travel to the Cove together. Or so Jay said, anyway. Cat felt no surer of that now than she had a week ago.

She fought the self-doubt niggling her from every angle. How could she possibly get on a train to Templeton Cove and leave her brother in charge of looking after their mum? Her brother, who'd left home when their once-attentive mother started coming home drunk seven nights a week reeking of booze and cigarettes. Cat's resentment burned. Would she ever forgive Chris for leaving her alone to deal with the ensuing mess? She seriously doubted it. Tilting her chin, she tried to ignore the tension pulsing at her temple.

She shifted from one foot to the other and hitched her

tote bag higher onto her shoulder. She must be either mad or desperate to be leaving him in charge.

The train came into view. No going back now. This was it. She was about to be reunited with one of the two people who'd made her summers from the age of eleven to twenty the best of her life. The other was now dead. Murdered. Cat swallowed. Possibly at Jay's hands.

She bit her teeth together. No. She wouldn't go there. Innocent until proven guilty.

Cat pulled back her shoulders. She would find Sarah's killer if it was the last thing she did because no part of her believed it was Jay. It couldn't be him. She would spend however long it took proving her gut instinct was right. This wasn't about loyalty, this was about fact. Jay Garrett was no murderer.

She stared at the purple-and-blue train as it rumbled and squealed to a stop. Cat held back as the carriage doors opened and a deluge of passengers spilled onto the platform. She watched with her feet welded to the concrete as one person after another boarded ahead of her.

A week had passed since Jay's initial phone call, and the two of them had spoken half a dozen times between then and now. Despite her insistence she was needed at police headquarters and there was no chance in hell of her boss releasing her for a month, Inspector Harris did exactly that with minimum resistance.

His comments about the bags beneath her eyes and unbecoming weight loss hadn't been strictly necessary, but Cat got the general idea. Apparently, a little downtime away from the city was just what she needed. Her nerves hitched and she shivered at the prospect ahead. Downtime was the last thing looking for her friend's killer would be.

She tilted her chin. She had to keep positive. Not only would she find him or her, some time away from her mum could only be a good thing, too. It would work out best for all of them. It wouldn't hurt Chris to pick up the slack for a while; he was as much their mother's son as she was her daughter. As much as it pained her to admit it, Cat was weakening under the daily pressure of being her mum's keeper. Finding Sarah's killer was something she had to do. She refused to turn away from either her or Jay when they needed her most.

She stepped forward, gripped the bar at the side of the train door and stepped aboard, heaving her suitcase in behind her. She'd figure out what to do next about her mum's addiction when she came home. For now, she had a friend's killer to find and a one-time lover to face.

She made her way down the narrow aisle toward carriage B, where Jay had said he'd meet her. Her gaze wandered left and right, up and down. The carriage was busier than she'd anticipated, and as she slowly made her way through, finding a seat seemed a hopeless task. Jay had said he would find her, not the other way around. She scanned the sea of faces as she continued down the aisle, but no one looked remotely like Jay. Despite the time that had passed since she last saw him, Cat felt sure she'd recognize him.

At last, she found two empty seats separated by a table just wide enough to hold a couple of back-to-back laptops. She hauled her luggage onto the rack above and sat down. Grateful for the window seat, she purposely turned away from people walking backward and forward carrying steaming cups of coffee and bottles of water. Chitchat was not on her agenda.

She pulled her cell phone from her inside jacket pocket and looked at the screen. Was it pathetic to ring her brother already? She'd left him and his fiancée with Mum less than an hour ago. Would he snap at her? Or worse, beg her to come home? She stuffed the phone back into her pocket. Checking in with Chris once she reached the Cove would be soon enough. Her brother was twenty-nine, not nine.

The screech of the guard's whistle hitched her nerves a little higher. If anyone had been sitting opposite her, they'd think her a first-time train traveler rather than a detective sergeant in the Thames Valley Police Force.

The train eased forward, gradually increasing its speed. The concrete-and-chrome chaos of urban Reading gave way to grass, greenery and grace. The emerging English countryside had never looked so beautiful or full of promise. She would take this time to recenter, to regain a sense of herself and what she wanted. With a clearer mind, she could do more good for her mum.

Gripping the arms of her chair, she hoisted herself upward. How was Jay meant to find her among all these passengers? She'd suggested they send each other pictures via their phones but he'd laughed in that toe-curling way of his, telling her he didn't want to frighten her into not coming. Cat sank back down into her seat and shook her head. It was like saying Brad Pitt could morph into Frankenstein's monster over a decade. Never gonna happen.

Jay had possessed movie-star looks even when they were kids. He hadn't been able to do anything to fend off the hormonal attentions of ripe seventeen- and eighteen-year-old girls then, and she guessed it was likely the same with lustful twentysomething ones today. Cat smiled. The truth was she'd been one of those girls herself, once. And for one night, he'd been completely hers.

Her smile dissolved. She'd been a different person then and no doubt Jay had, too. Smoothing her trembling hand over her hair, self-consciousness tripped along the surface of her skin. He was likely as good-looking as ever.

She grimaced. God only knew how much the problems of the last few years had aged her.

Cat squeezed her eyes shut. What was she doing? Why was she even thinking about Jay's looks? He was a murder suspect. A murder suspect who'd asked her to the Cove to find the real killer and prove his innocence, not rekindle a twenty-four-hour romance. She'd agreed to this trip for exactly the same reason.

The scrunching and scraping beside her announced company and Cat stiffened when the musky scent of male aftershave wafted beneath her nostrils. He moved around, lifting something onto the luggage rack, followed by the whisper of a jacket sliding from his shoulders. Cat slowly opened her eyes and surreptitiously watched her new carriage companion from beneath lowered lashes. He stood a little away from her, patting his trousers before pulling a phone from his back pocket.

Jay. Her heart picked up speed.

With his eyes on the BlackBerry in his hand, he slid into the seat opposite her. She couldn't see his face in its entirety, but what she saw still looked good. He was tall and dark, with broad shoulders, and the complete absence of a beer belly set Jay pretty high in her admiration of the opposite sex. Especially considering the specimens she'd endured picking her mum up from various dives.

He lifted his head. "Finished checking me out?"

Her mouth instantly curved into a wide grin. "Still as full of yourself as ever, I see."

He shrugged. "Hey, if a woman as gorgeous as you wants to take a moment, that's fine by me."

Cat shook her head. "Idiot."

They laughed and leaned across the table for an awkward embrace. Cat resisted the urge to inhale the delicious scent of him and quickly sat back in her seat. She must remain professional. As far as she knew, Jay could have Sarah's blood on his hands.

"Well, you're certainly growing old gracefully." She forced a wide smile.

His gaze traveled languidly over her face. "So are you. I can't believe this." He swept the dark brown, gorgeously floppy hair back from his forehead. "I only moved seats because the man opposite thought it was all right to start trimming his nasal hair right in front of me."

Cat laughed. "No, he did not."

"He did. And yes, I took a picture and Tweeted it." He winked. "Only joking. You look fantastic."

She smiled, knowing full well she looked the complete opposite. "Thanks. You look pretty good, too."

Their eyes locked. His intense gaze reflected thoughts that were inexcusable yet totally flattering. Heat burned on her face and in other places. Jeez, the man hadn't lost any of his invisible pull, that was for sure.

She cleared her throat. "So, I'm here. Have you spoken to Sarah's parents? Do they know I'm coming to town?"

He leaned back in his seat, all humor vanishing from his gaze as his jaw tightened. "No. They won't see me or answer my calls. Not that I blame them. Would you if I was accused of killing your daughter?"

Cat swallowed. "No, I don't suppose I would."

"You have to help find the guy who did this, Cat. I would never hurt Sarah. We have to make her parents believe it, too."

She stared at him. Nothing but sincerity shone back. She looked to the window. "If my boss finds out I'm at the Cove poking around in a case I have no business poking around in, he'll kick my butt into next week."

"You have no idea how much it means to me you're here."

Cat turned. There it was again. The subtle change of tone in his voice. During their phone calls over the last week, his voice would be filled with his smile, oozing charm and good cheer, like liquid honey down the telephone line. Then it changed to something so somber and sad, she swore she heard his heart breaking.

Cat leaned forward and resisted the temptation to take his hand in hers. "Hey, I came because I wanted to, okay? One way or another, I'll find her killer and bring him or her to justice. I promise." She glanced at the people sitting across the aisle. "But now is not the time to be talking about this."

He nodded. "I know. I just… This isn't right, Cat. The police are wasting valuable time."

"And I'll try to put that right but you have to be honest with me…about everything."

He frowned. "Of course."

"I need to know everything you know."

He glanced toward the other passengers. "You will."

"Good."

A deep sense of foreboding slipped over her shoulders. Something wasn't right with him. Something deep. Forcing herself into cop mode rather than friend mode, the investigating officer in her rose to the surface, prickling the hairs at the back of her neck.

"So is there anything more you're not telling me?" she asked quietly.

A muscle leaped in his jaw. "What makes you ask that?"

Defensive. Coldness stole the warmth from his eyes. Cat frowned. "I can tell by the way you're looking at me. You want to tell me something but you're not sure how… or if you should. Am I right?"

Their eyes locked before he looked to the window. "I'm

struggling with the fact that I have no clue what was going on with Sarah before she died. If I knew that, maybe she wouldn't be lying in the morgue right now."

Cat studied his profile. Watched for the tell-tale signs of darting eyes and shifting shoulders. Signs that he was uncomfortable, lying, hiding from her scrutiny. All she saw was the slumped shoulders of sadness...worse, failure. She swallowed her burgeoning sympathy.

"Why didn't you know? You and Sarah were friends. Good friends."

He dropped back in his chair, closed his eyes. When Cat had a perpetrator in the interview room who did the same thing, she referred to it as "closing the curtains." She pursed her lips together to stop herself from talking. He needed to fill in the gaps. If she stormed in with a load of uneducated guesses, she could easily end up with nothing but a sticky mess of misunderstandings and excuses.

He blew out a heavy breath and opened his eyes. "Let's just say I've been busy. Busy at work. We lost contact."

"You and Sarah?" She shook her head. "That's impossible."

"Friends grow apart."

She stared. Her gut knotted. He was lying. "Well, if that's the case, why are you looking as though you should be hung, drawn and quartered?"

His gaze darted over her face and the skin at his neck shifted. "I haven't taken a lot of notice of what was going on around me for the last few years. Things I should've cared about. Friends, especially."

"Why not?"

Anger flashed in his eyes. "What is this, Cat?"

"This is me investigating my friend's murder. What you asked me here to do. If you don't like it then I don't understand why you made that phone call in the first place."

She leaned forward, kept her voice low. "I'm a cop, Jay. I view everything and everyone with suspicion until the right person is under arrest."

"Including me."

Guilt scratched at her heart and she slammed the door on her love for the man sitting in front of her. "Including you." She swallowed. "This time last week I was dealing with my own work…and other stuff. Now I'm on a train with one friend I haven't seen in far too long, and another is dead."

An invisible connection hovered between them before he slumped back in his chair a second time. "You're right. I'm sorry."

Inhaling a long breath, Cat exhaled it in a rush. "Let's talk about this when we're at your place. Not here. Okay?"

He nodded, his gaze somber and intense. "Whatever you say, Detective."

Cat resisted the urge to buckle under the disappointment in his gaze. This was going to be fifty times harder than she anticipated if Jay didn't understand that he was equally in the line of fire as anyone else until she knew more.

She dragged her eyes from the dangerously hypnotic power of his and turned to the window. Before she looked away, Cat could've sworn his eyes glazed with unshed tears. Something deeper was definitely going on. The Jay Garrett she knew was bold as brass and far more sure of himself than the gorgeous man in front of her with his shoulders rounded in a classic image of exhaustion. She wouldn't push him. Bigger questions, the personal ones, could wait. The first thing she needed to deal with was Sarah. Jay was alive—and a suspect.

CHAPTER THREE

THE TAXI PULLED TO A stop outside Jay's house and he opened the passenger-side door. Watching Cat over the roof, he smiled as she stared up at the cabin, her eyes alive with awe. He drew in a long breath through flared nostrils. He'd bought the cabin because of her. Cat loved this house. Always had. He leaned through the window and paid the driver. After he'd taken her suitcase from the trunk, the taxi turned around and made its way back down the spiraling road into Templeton Cove.

He stood next to her and gestured toward the cabin. "What do you think?"

She shook her head. "You know exactly what I think. I absolutely love it." She turned to look at him, a smile softly curving her lips. "You must have done well for yourself since I last saw you."

Jay's smile dissolved. "Yeah, well, money doesn't count for anything when one of your friends turns up dead on the edge of your land."

Guilt knotted inside him for chilling the atmosphere so succinctly, but he didn't deserve the admiration shining in her eyes. He didn't deserve her looking at him as if he was anything more than he was. A man who'd gotten so tied up in his own life, he hadn't noticed the trouble Sarah was in.

She looked across the grassy hill running down to the

forest at the edge of his land. "Sarah was found on Clo-ver Point?"

"Yes."

She turned. "I'm so sorry."

For the twentieth time since he'd spotted Cat's gorgeous red hair over the top of the train seat, Jay curled his itching hands into fists. He wanted to touch her as though he needed to make sure she was real. She looked different. Just as beautiful, but different. Far too underweight for his liking and the gray smudges under her eyes told him she could do with staying in bed for a week. Yet she'd come as soon as he called.

"Her body was found meters from my property." He dragged his gaze from hers to stare at the forest. "I'm a suspect because I knew her and she was here. I don't blame the police for jumping on me straight away."

She looked past him to the forest, her cheeks darkening. "What happened with the police? I assume you were questioned pretty much as soon as she was found."

He followed her gaze, wishing she'd look at him. Her eyes were the only window he had into a brain that worked like a machine and a heart that he'd hoped would be his one day. She had to believe him innocent. If she didn't, he had no idea where to turn next.

"Inspector Bennett, the senior investigation officer in Sarah's case, arrived the next day. He questioned me here. He stood on the deck, firing questions at me as though I was the type of guy who could choke a woman to death and then drink his morning coffee without a care in the world." He shook his head, his jaw clenching. "I didn't even know she was dead until Bennett and his team turned up."

She shifted away from him, her gaze turned from his. "What did he say? Do you have an alibi?"

Nausea furled in his stomach. The space she'd opened between them spoke volumes. Jay swallowed against the pain that struck him deep inside. "He goaded me for over an hour, insinuating I had both access and probable cause to hurt her because of…our renowned fall out."

"The fall out you've yet to tell me about."

He watched her profile. Her jaw was clenched and her eyes were narrowed. He felt guilty of everything Bennett accused him of. Having Cat looking away from him scratched at his soul, caused an ache in his heart. "I have an alibi, Cat. Four alibis."

She turned. "Four?"

Jay nodded. Was that relief in her eyes? "I was with some visiting French investors that evening, well into the night."

"So you're no longer a suspect?"

Jay lifted his shoulders. "I have no idea. Bennett took their names and said he'd be in touch. I haven't heard anything from him since so I'm assuming he's happy… although…"

She frowned. "What?"

"Nothing else has been done or said by the cops in over a week. There hasn't been as much as a press conference since. No reconstruction, no information about the killing made public at all. It's why I called you."

"Well, they're hardly likely to tell you what they're doing. If you had probable cause and access, you will be on their radar until someone else is found and charged."

Jay stared, imploring her to believe him innocent. "That's what I thought."

Without thinking, he brushed back some of the thick red hair that blew across her cheek. "You're back where you belong, Cat."

She stiffened beneath his fingers. "No, Jay, I'm not. I'm here for Sarah…and then I go home."

She strode past him to sit on a bench that overlooked the forest. Jay exhaled and followed her. The tension hummed around them like an invisible force field. Sitting beside her, he planted his elbows on his knees and stared ahead. He never could have anticipated the effect Cat looking at him with suspicion in her incredible, ridiculously green eyes would have on him.

She looked amazing despite the sadness he sensed hovering around her. Why the hell hadn't he called her before? Why wait until Sarah's body was found on the grounds of his estate before bringing her back into his life? He yearned to turn back the clock and make everything right in the world. He'd been a stupid, blind, money-hungry dickhead.

He forced his mind to focus on the macabre and faced her. "They found her body in the forest."

She stared at him for a long moment before looking down at her hands. The knuckles showed white. "I was shocked when you called. Scared. Now I feel this is where I'm supposed to be. Right here with you, doing whatever the hell I can to put Sarah to rest."

"Even if it gets you in trouble?"

A wry smile curved her lips. "I'm more used to trouble than you can imagine. I want to find whoever did this as much as you. She was an amazing friend to both of us."

Jay ran his gaze over the face he'd once known so well but hadn't taken the time to watch change and grow. Who was Cat now? Who had Sarah been? His heart kicked painfully.

"Yet neither of us bothered to pick up the phone and call her for God knows how long, did we?"

Irritation flashed sharply in her eyes. "Accusations and blame don't help. Not ever."

"We have nothing to work with, Cat." Frustration sharpened his tone. "As long as the police still think I might have had something to do with this…"

She flicked her long auburn hair over her shoulders. "If we're going to prove your innocence by finding out who killed Sarah, the first thing we need to do is build a picture of who she was before she died."

She believes me. Hope dared to ignite like a flame behind his rib cage. "You believe I had nothing to do with this?"

She frowned but her gaze never left his. "I want to. More than anything. But I'll treat this case the same as any other. We live in a world of innocent until proven guilty, remember?"

Her words were thinly veiled. She wanted to believe him but didn't. Not yet. Authority and linear thinking ruled Cat's world; his was ruled by the next deal, the next pot of money. He needed to focus on the future without looking back. If he looked back too hard, it would kill him.

Yet he needed to look back if he had any chance of proving his innocence and Cat would have to let down her professional guard and look into her heart to truly believe he could never harm Sarah.

There was no other way. Cat didn't know him anymore. No one did.

He turned his gaze to the forest. "I hadn't spoken to her in months. I didn't know a damn thing about what was going on with her."

The seconds passed like heartbeats until Cat spoke again. "Do you think I knew all the murder victims I've helped lay to rest over the years? This blame you're drowning under stops now. People lose touch, grow up, change. Look at you."

"What about me?"

"I look at you and I don't see the boy I shared every summer with growing up, I see…"

He looked at her. Two spots of color stained her cheeks, her eyes wide. "You see what?"

"I see someone older, wiser…maybe a bit afraid there are bigger things out there than even the great Jay Garrett can handle. It makes a welcome change. You've grown up. It suits you."

Unease rippled along his nerve endings. She'd always read him like an open book, but he thought with all the years that passed, she wouldn't know, wouldn't guess. He was wrong. He already felt exposed…ashamed.

"Your coming to the Cove wasn't supposed to be about me, but I'm scared to death you think me capable of murder, Cat. I asked you here for Sarah. The feeling rocketing through me at a hundred miles an hour, telling me you were the best thing in my damn life, is as unwanted as it is unexpected."

Self-hatred simmered in his chest and gut like pools of boiling tar. He leaned forward on his elbows again, unable to bear looking at the wariness in her eyes. "You're right, I have grown up and I want to make up for the mistakes I've made." He stared ahead and then leaped straight in with the question he'd really wanted to ask her since he saw that first flicker of regret in her eyes. "How about you?"

"What about me?"

He huffed out a laugh. "You can't lie to me. I sense something bothering you, too. Something personal."

Silence.

He turned. She stared at the forest, her jaw tight. "Yes, well, the mistakes I've made can't be put right. At least not yet, so I'm going to try to forget about them for a while and concentrate on Sarah."

Jay watched her. He recognized the passing shame as it whispered across her eyes, the way her mouth opened and closed in hesitation. Witnessed her brain and conscience battling with the age-old human need to share. They were special. Cat and Jay, Jay and Cat. Cat, Jay and Sarah, Sarah, Jay and Cat. Every summer they'd been a unit—a whole.

It looked as though two out of three still were. It was impossible Cat didn't feel the out-of-bounds pull between them. Memories of their single night together seven years before crashed into Jay's mind as he stared at the thick red hair he'd finally managed to bury his face in all those years ago. She'd given him the gift of her virginity, neither of them knowing that the following day she'd leave Templeton Cove, never to return.

He followed her gaze toward the forest. "You're right. Sarah is all that matters now."

"Good, because murder starts with the victim every time. We have to find out who Sarah's friends were before she died, her lovers, work colleagues…the list goes on."

"What if we don't find out any of that stuff? Then what? Surely it can't always be the victim that holds the key to their murder."

"It is. Every time."

Jay stared as the blood roared in his ears and frustration hummed through every fiber of his body. He'd done nothing to help Sarah. Nothing to stop her from being killed. Her body was found on the edge of his property. It had to be about the killer…because if it was about Sarah, he was partly to blame. She'd tried to contact him several times when he was using but he'd been too messed up to care. When he got clean, she didn't want to know him. He did something so bad when he was high, she never forgave him. Until the day she was killed and she'd phoned asking to see him.

Sweat broke out on his upper lip and he dropped back against the bench. "She called me."

"What?"

"Sarah. She called me the day she died. She asked me to meet her at Marian's—"

"Who's Marian?"

He turned. The tone of her voice wasn't gentle, it was demanding. His gaze dropped to her full, pink-painted lips and the desire to kiss her shuddered through his body. Always strong, kind and capable, Cat had grown even more so in the years since he'd seen her. Whereas he'd diminished, allowed himself to be taken under by drugs, succumbed to their power and ruined lives. Yet for the first time, someone else's confidence was the balm he needed to soothe his gut-wrenching fear that Sarah's parents, Cat, the entire community, could think he killed one of the loveliest people on the planet.

He drew in a breath, exhaled. "Marian works in a bakery by the beach. I'm in there a lot. I…" He stopped, waved a hand. "Doesn't matter. What matters is Sarah never turned up, but worse, I never went looking for her."

"Didn't you call her?" She frowned.

"Yes, but there was no answer. Now we know why." He shook his head, regret and loss beating hard in his chest. "A few days later I started hearing rumors about her that made absolutely no sense, but we should at least check to see if they have merit."

"What rumors?"

He sighed. "Sex, drugs and rock and roll."

Her eyes widened. "Sarah?"

"Yep."

She tutted. "Well, no wonder you didn't believe them. The Sarah I knew was as likely to take drugs as I am to run naked through Templeton Cove town center."

He managed a small smile. "Hey, never say never."

"In your dreams, Jay Garrett." She shook her head, the hint of her humor in her eyes dissolving. "These next few days are going to be tough. No investigating team or officer is going to appreciate an off-duty cop from a different jurisdiction poking around in a murder case. So both of us need to be our most charismatic, charming and manipulative throughout this entire process." Her eyes sparkled with raw intent.

His gaze drifted over her face to linger at her lips. "I bet a pound to a penny you're still doing your best to look after everybody. I always knew you'd end up being a cop or nurse. One or the other."

"Yeah, well, the intention to do good doesn't always lead to success, does it?"

Jay looked at her bowed head, felt something shift in her demeanor. "Hey, you okay?"

She lifted her head and when she met his eyes, she smiled but her lips trembled. "Sure." She tossed her hair over her shoulders, all business once more. "So come on. Tell me more about Sarah. Where or from whom did you hear these rumors? Her friends? Colleagues?"

The tiniest flicker of pain showed in her eyes, the smallest regret in the timbre of her voice and Jay knew in that fleeting second neither was to do with Sarah. He wouldn't push her. God knows, he had enough crap of his own he intended to keep under wraps. What she told him was her prerogative…even if he did want to fix whatever pain he caused in her eyes a few seconds before.

"It was Marian mostly. She's like the Templeton oracle." He blew out a breath. "Every now and then she said she heard this or that about Sarah. I didn't believe a word of it until Sarah was found dead. Then I started to worry there was some truth in what she said."

"Surely you can't believe Sarah was into drugs?" She raised her eyebrows.

He shook his head. "I don't know. The police haven't stated there was anything in her system when she was found, but it would make it a bit more plausible how someone as good as the Sarah we knew might have been killed. She was a primary school teacher. She helped out in the community, kids and adults loved her. How the hell did she end up in the forest at the bottom of Clover Point?"

Cat's eyes darkened in concentration. "Was she seeing anyone? Any changes at the school you knew about? What about the kids?"

Jay shook his head. The perpetual feeling of hopelessness that cloaked his emotions like a heavy blanket stole back across his shoulders. "I don't know. I don't know anything else."

She dropped back against the seat and wiped her hand over her face. "We will. Things will begin to fall into place quicker than you think once we're thinking along the right lines." She smiled. "Trust me."

Her phenomenal green eyes shone with renewed vitality, twisting Jay's heart in a vice. "Didn't I always?"

They lapsed into silence before Jay looked away, shaken by the sudden need to kiss her. He knew his emotions were running high and to act on them would be selfish. Would be the old Jay.

"The path to Sarah's killer could lie in these rumors, you know." Cat's voice broke through his thoughts.

"Well, I'm glad you think that because I've been sitting here wondering whether I was stupid to expect you to come all this way without a shred of evidence for us to start working with."

"You were stupid."

"What?"

"You were stupid, because from this moment on I'm going to be on your ass expecting you to do absolutely everything I ask."

Jay's gut tightened as her voice turned silky soft. His gaze dropped once more to her mouth as his own drained of saliva. Here was Cat, all grown-up, sexy and success-ful in a career he knew so little about. While he was busy forgetting every friend and foe and concentrating on buy-ing up Templeton Cove, this woman was putting away criminals, killers and rapists.

He was in awe of her.

"You must have it all."

She gave a wry laugh. "I don't think so."

"Men falling at your feet, a hotshot career as a female detective taking down the bad guys. That's pretty hot."

"Yeah, right. I have the dream life."

There it was again. That flicker in her eyes, turning away to look past his shoulder. He couldn't call her on it. He wouldn't question her and risk her bolting straight back to Reading. Protectiveness seared through him. He'd seen the pain shoot across her face, staining her cheeks and whitening her lips. He didn't care to see it again. He'd uncover what was wrong and put it right.

"So, are you—" he started.

"Enough about me." Her gaze told him she was back in cop mode, any intimacy between them vanquished. "What is it you do now? I assume from the trousers and shirt you've given up singing."

He inched back in his seat. Fine. She had every right to hit the ball back to his side of the net. Clearly work was a safer subject for both of them. He could talk about success. Initiatives to earn damn good money he knew inside out. Love. Friendship. Intimacy... They were the things that somehow slipped to the wayside, leaving him as clueless as he was the last time he saw her.

He cleared his throat. "This trip to London? It's rare. I only ever go there for the occasional business negotiation. Most of the time I run everything from Templeton."

"So you're the new man at the helm, right? Your dad passed the baton over to you?"

He smiled. "Dad retired about a year ago. I took over."

"And took over what exactly? The last time I was here, I was twenty years old and thought your dad was the richest man in the world. He owned, what, three businesses in Templeton?"

"About that, but I've added a lot more since."

She raised her eyebrows. "Proud of it, too, I see."

A flash of heat hit his face. Damn his pride. Damn his need to succeed. He'd changed. No more. No more money over everything else.

"I never want to leave the Cove, Cat. I love it here."

She smiled. "Hey, there's no need to explain that to me. How many twenty-year-olds still vacation with their parents? Every time they said they were coming down here, I came. I love the Cove, too, Jay. Always have. Always will. Your dad must be really proud of you."

Now, maybe. But the pain still lingers in his eyes. "He is."

She turned back to the vista ahead of them and sighed. "I must admit, I'm really looking forward to seeing all the places where I spent time with you and Sarah. I didn't realize how much I missed the Cove until now."

Jay watched her profile. Seeing her again was another reminder of what his life could have been if his drug habit hadn't taken over and screwed it all up. Damn it to hell. Why had he let it all go wrong?

He pushed to his feet. "Shall we go inside?"

"Sure."

She stood and Jay took her hands. "You loved Sarah as much as I did. Even though these next days or weeks or how ever long it takes will be tough—"

Her shoulders tensed. "Days, Jay. We'll find her killer in days."

He smiled. "Great. Days. With you leading this investigation, the bastard who killed Sarah will be locked up in no time."

"Or bitch."

He flinched. "A woman? No way."

Her gaze bored into his, a dart of concentration spearing between her brows as she studied him. "Why do you say that?"

He shook his head. "Jesus, if a woman could do that…"

Cat lifted her shoulders. "Why not?"

His cheeks heated. Her suspicion was clear in her eyes. She was questioning him. He was a suspect. He swallowed against the ball of frustration that lingered bitterly in his mouth. "Well, I suppose a woman could…but God, I hate to think any woman capable of such a degree of violence. To actually choke the life from someone?"

She continued to stare awhile longer before she slowly eased her hands from his. "I'm saying these things because we can't afford to dismiss any possibility. Between us, we'll find out what happened. He or she will not get away with killing our best friend." She closed her eyes. "I can see her, Jay. I close my eyes and I can see Sarah laughing and joking on the beach, or running around with her beloved dog, Scruffie. Now she's gone. Dead. No white wedding. No kids. No future."

She opened her eyes and rubbed her fingers at her temples. "Let's go inside."

As they walked, Jay fought the urge to take her hand knowing she was in pain. He sensed her mind was working, her shoulders had yet to drop down from her earlobes. She was a cop. She needed time to think and he wouldn't be the one to disturb her. They reached the front door and he slid the key into the lock and pushed open the door.

"After you."

She laid her hand on his forearm. "I think we need to start with these rumors."

He shook his head. "It's a dead end. When I found out she was killed, I went to the local drug haunts—"

Her eyes widened. "How would *you* know about drug haunts?"

Shit. Suspicion flared in her eyes once more. He lifted his shoulders. "I don't know the places. I just assumed them."

She stared. "Like where?"

"The park. The housing estate toward Marchenton. You know, the seedier places around the Cove."

"Did you find out anything?"

"Nothing. No one claimed to see her hanging around or talking to anyone. I've spoken to people at The Harbor pub, the shopping center, Caroline's Coffee Shop. They all mentioned she might be involved in drugs somehow, but it didn't sound like Sarah at all."

"Why? What did they say?"

"That she was different. Edgy. Jumpy. Losing weight. But no one had seen her high or out of control. I just don't get it. The fact I hadn't spoken to her in months is like a lead weight on me, Cat. I didn't know what she was going through. I didn't know her at all."

She dropped her gaze to the ground between them.

"There's something I should tell you. Let's go inside."
She looked up.

Jay's unease hitched up a notch. Words battled on his
tongue as questions whirled in his mind. Had she gained
access to police information? Did she know more than he
did and purposely kept it from him? Did she think him entirely guilty and intended arresting him? Nausea swirled
in his gut. He gestured toward the open door. "After you."

Cat walked into the open plan living room ahead of
him. Jay tossed the keys onto the table by the door and
then joined her. He inhaled a shaky breath. "Cat?"

She faced him, her face inscrutable. "The day you rang
me asking me to come, I was afraid to commit to anything straight away. I needed time to get over the shock
of Sarah being killed before I could view her death as a
murder investigation."

"And?"

"I started finding out what I could about her life before
she died. I'm glad to say I uncovered—"

"Wait a minute." Jay held up his hand and cut her off
as disbelief stabbed at his affronted ego. "You knew about
Sarah's state of mind when she died and didn't tell me?
We've spoken for over a week, Cat. Why bother pushing me for information if you already knew about her?"

Her green eyes darkened. "I'm doing my job, that's
why. I needed to know I could trust you, needed to believe
you'll be as honest with me as I'll be with you."

Jay stared. "You've been in cop mode this entire time?"

"Jay, come on. Why are you looking at me like that?
Isn't that why you asked me here in the first place?"

Defensiveness raged in her eyes like a gathering storm.
Any intimacy he thought he saw or felt between them was
entirely of his own doing. God, was he that self-involved?
Clearly he was, and clearly Cat didn't see him as anything

more than a mutual friend of Sarah's, intent on avenging her murder. What the bloody hell did he expect? He hadn't called her to the Cove thinking anything would happen between them. It wasn't her fault he'd wanted to touch her from the minute he saw her.

"Jay, are you listening to me? I said I've already made a few discreet enquiries."

Her voice jerked him from his paralysis and icy-cold fingers tip-tapped up his spine. Cat was intelligent, savvy and determined. He had undoubtedly destroyed any hope of her believing him innocent given his past. A past it looked as though she'd known about all along.

"What did you find out?"

"I found out you and Sarah haven't spent any time together for over four years."

He met her questioning gaze but said nothing.

"Why would two friends who'd known each other their entire lives suddenly stop talking unless something major split them apart? Tell me what happened. If you hold things back from me, what am I supposed to think?"

She didn't know about his drug problems.

Tell her. Damn well tell her. Tell her how you ruined your friendship with Sarah while out of your head on cocaine. Tell her how people now look at you in the Cove.

Heat stole through his gut, burning hot and unwelcome. "I... We..."

She closed her eyes for a moment and when she opened them, her gaze was softer, more concerned than accusatory. "I'm not here to cause you grief... God knows, I'm not even here to relive a time when I felt my whole life would be like a summer holiday forever. All three of us were so young then. I grew up, Sarah grew up. I thought you had, too, but the way you're clamming up now..."

The insult to his maturity struck at his pride like a

knife through weakened flesh. He shook his head and gave a wry laugh. "Do you think I've had everything given to me on a plate since you left?"

"What? No, I—"

"Dad didn't give me any different opportunities than he's given every other employee, Cat. If you think differently, you don't know him at all."

She squeezed her eyes shut. "Jay, for crying out loud. This isn't about you. This is about—"

"I learned the business from the bottom rung to the top. There were never any shortcuts as far as Dad was concerned, and now I understand why. You cannot understand the wants and wishes of people around you unless you've walked in their shoes. That's the bottom line."

When she opened her eyes again, they blazed fiery green with anger. "Well, you haven't walked in mine or Sarah's, so why don't you cut the crap and tell me what was going on between you and her?"

Jay stared at the two bright red spots of color flaming her cheeks as heat burned in his own. Her breasts rose and fell with each breath and her hands were balled into fists at her sides. Fine. She wanted to know about walking in people's shoes? He'd damn well tell her.

"If we find out Sarah was involved in drugs, I've not just walked in her shoes, I've hiked in them. Up until four and half years ago, I was a coke addict. You name it, Cat, I took it."

CHAPTER FOUR

"WHAT?" CAT STARED and fought the panic running through her veins.

He closed his eyes. "I'm sorry. I didn't want to blurt it out like that."

"You…you're an…" Cat clutched a hand to her throat.

"Well, look who we have here."

The booming, jovial voice came from behind Jay, making Cat jump. She snapped her gaze over his shoulder, her heart pounding. *George. Oh, God, not now.*

Trembling from the shock of Jay's admission, she forced a wide grin onto her face. "George. What are you doing here?"

He opened his arms. "Well, I work for Jay now. His father is off around the world enjoying his retirement, so Jay here makes good use of me instead."

"I don't believe it. You're Jay's handyman now?"

His expression changed to feigned insult. "Of course. Do you think this boy could find anyone else to match my caliber? I think not."

Cat forced a laugh, words lodging in her throat as tension hummed on an invisible cord between her and Jay. George was clearly oblivious to the shockwaves ricocheting from the walls around them. She glanced at Jay and his eyes lingered on hers for a heartbeat before he turned and moved away to stand at the fireplace.

She snapped her gaze back to George, her smile wobbling. "It is so good to see you."

He beamed. "Little Catherine." He stretched his arms wide. "What a sight for sore eyes you are."

Cat stepped into his embrace and closed her eyes. It had been far too long since she smelled George's comforting combination of tangy, old-fashioned aftershave and the mint lozenges he perpetually had tucked into his cheek.

Nausea burned hot in her stomach while fondness for George swelled her heart.

Jay was a recovering addict.

Her blood boiled hot in her veins as confusion, hurt and disappointment rushed through her heart and soul, branding her with Jay's betrayal.

George pulled back and held her hands at arm's length, an expression of soft adoration on his face, tufts of silver hair shining at the sides of his otherwise bald head. Whenever she'd spent time at Jay's family home, George was her summertime guardian, a man who made her feel just as loved as her father had. She forced a smile once more. "You look wonderful. You haven't aged a single day."

He chuckled. "Well, you have."

She pulled her face into an expression of mock offense. "Don't you know it's rude to say that to a lady?"

He immediately reddened. "Oh, no, I meant you're all grown up and not the girl running around with her hair hanging out of its ribbons all the time."

Cat laughed and cupped her hand to his jaw. "I know what you meant, silly. It's great to see you looking so well."

His blue eyes sparkled. "You, too. I couldn't believe it when Jay told me you were coming back home for a while."

Warmth furled in Cat's stomach. He called Templeton Cove her home in the same easy way Jay had. She glanced at Jay. "I'm not so sure about the Cove being home, George."

She turned back and George's smile faltered as he looked from her to Jay and back again. He opened his mouth to say something and then shook his head. "Hmm… well, whatever you might say, you know as well as I do this is where you belong."

They lapsed into silence and the tension permeated the room. After a time that must have been moments but felt far longer, George cleared his throat. "So, how's Julia?"

Cat stared. "Um…fine. She's fine."

He cocked an eyebrow. "Just fine? The woman I remember was full of life, running around after you and Chris but always managing to look so damn glamorous." He sighed. "Yes, a gorgeous woman who should never have been left a widow at such a young age."

Cat swallowed as tears lodged in her throat. "She's carrying on as she always did. You know Mum, strong as an ox and just as stubborn."

He laughed. "She had to be, with you lot trying to run circles around her. I remember the time you swore you never pinched that makeup from her bag and then came in with it all smudged around your eyes. Lord, I had to leave the room so she could tell you off without me standing there fit to burst with laughter."

Happy memories rushed into Cat's heart. "She didn't miss a thing back then, did she?"

"Nope. She had your cards marked, you and Chris, both." He winked. "As we all did. The pair of you couldn't get anything past me, either. No matter how many times you tried."

Cat continued to smile, her heart aching with the heavy weight of her mother's demise bearing down on her chest. George's intelligent gaze wandered over her face as though looking right inside her. She looked to the floor. "I've missed you."

"Hey." He put a finger to her chin, forcing her gaze to his. "While you're here we'll find time to catch up properly, okay?"

She smiled, warmth spreading through her. "I'd like that."

"Good. But right now, I must get on." He pressed a kiss to her cheek. "I'll see you soon, my darling."

Cat smiled, not wanting him to leave. No part of her wanted to be left alone with Jay. "See you."

George moved to step away and then stopped. His canny gaze fell on Jay and his brow furrowed. "Cat got your tongue?" He laughed. "Did you hear what I said? Cat got your tongue. Cat. Catherine." He shook his head and swiped a hand under his eye. "Lord, I make myself laugh sometimes."

The tension hitched up a notch, the silence heavy and awkward.

George's smile dissolved and he looked from Jay to Cat and back again. "Right…well, I'll leave you to it, then."

He shot Jay a meaningful glare before ambling from the room and out toward the kitchen that lay beyond. Alone again, Cat met Jay's stare.

"I…" She shook her head as any words to sum up how she felt escaped her. "Just show me where I'm sleeping."

"Cat, we need to talk."

Anger rose in a hot flame scorching her heart. "Not yet. I can't…I can't even look at you right now."

He squeezed his eyes shut. "I told you the truth. Surely that's better than lying?"

"The truth?" She trembled. "How about you telling me

the truth, the *whole* truth when you picked up the phone and summoned me here like some damn innocent, huh?"

His eyes snapped open, their brown depths shining with what looked like unshed tears. "What?"

Anger blistered through Cat's sympathy. "You heard me. Now, I said show me where I'm sleeping." Her breath rasped painfully against her throat and her chest grew tight.

After a long moment, he threw up his hands. "Fine. Follow me."

He brushed past her toward the stairs and she followed. Stopping at the third door along a long gallery landing, he pushed opened the door. "I've put you in here."

"Thank you." She stepped inside and slammed the door.

She waited with her forehead against the wood until his hesitant footsteps disappeared. Only then did she release her held breath.

"No, no, no." Cat's words whispered out on a breath of barely contained despair.

An addict. Jay was an addict. An addict like her mum… and possibly Sarah.

She pushed away from the door and faced the room. She shook her head. How had he afforded the cabin? How had he managed to get sober and look so damn good while her mother festered in her own destruction? The room and its opulence swam in her blurred vision as she stumbled toward the four-poster bed.

Cat willed her heartbeat to slow. How could seven years pass and a man still smell the same? His lingering scent of musk and man infuriatingly teased her nostrils as it had before. When she'd sat next to him in the taxi, the smell had risen between them. She inhaled, actually smelled him like she was Hannibal Lecter savoring his next meal, for crying out loud.

He's a suspect. A suspect. A recovering addict. An angry man, a selfish man, a dishonest man...

Although she saw the peach satin-finished wallpaper and the thick, cream carpet pile, her mind still reeled with Jay's news and what that now made him in her mind. Cat dropped backward onto the bed and covered her face with her hands as bitterness scorched her throat. *Is that why he called me? Does he know about my mother and assume we'll have some sort of affinity? Is any of this about Sarah?*

She groaned into the silence of the room. She couldn't even leave, couldn't run away despite the urge rising in her on a tidal wave. The possibility of Jay being a suspect stuck hard in her mind. Yes, he'd loved Sarah back then, but four years was a long time. A lifetime for an addict. Had Sarah given up on him? Or enabled him? Had she been selling drugs rather than using? Cat's mind whirled with a kaleidoscope of heartbreaking possibility.

How had all three of their lives spun so completely out of control? Drugs and alcohol had seeped into their once-innocent lives and completely obliterated their dreams of what was real and what wasn't. Sitting up, Cat swiped angrily at her cheeks. No tears. No self-pity. She stared at the closed bedroom door.

She had to give him the benefit of the doubt. Had to seek out the evidence and assess it logically and unemotionally. The reality was that Jay had turned things around and surrounded himself with luxury. She was happy for his success. He had managed to get on in the world, and even though Cat hadn't done too badly in the intervening time, she had little more money now than she had when she was last at the Cove.

Her mum's stealing, spending and drinking it away had seen to her lack of savings. Swallowing against the pain of what had happened to her family, Cat pressed her hand to her stomach, willing the gnawing shame away.

She and Jay lived different lives now. Lives tainted by toxic substances—but different lives, all the same. The fact she had left her mum in Chris's hands and came to the Cove still felt liberating. She'd shown both of them, in no uncertain terms, that she gave priority for certain people and certain circumstances. She drew in a shaky breath. It would take a while for the guilt skimming over her skin to disappear, but despite the short time since she and Jay had been reunited, some of her responsibility was already subsiding.

This trip, even with its sickening cause, would allow the perspective and space she needed to figure out how to help her mum and herself from falling into the abyss of hopelessness that grew wider every day.

Tears threatened and she snapped her eyes open, determination heating her blood. Jay couldn't have killed Sarah. He would never be capable of locking his hands around her throat, squeezing and squeezing until no breath came from her. But if he had been high...

She shook her head vehemently in an effort to banish the ugly consideration from her mind. Her thoughts were born from her perpetual doubt about everything. Nothing more. She needed to put his addiction to one side. She needed to think clearly and professionally.

Maybe her coming to the Cove was God's great plan. She might have been sent there to learn enough from Jay that she would return home with the inner strength to put her mum into rehab. Who was to say her mum couldn't emerge a success story, just as Jay had? Cat's chest tightened as she tried and failed to bring forth some faith, some belief it would all come right in the end. She gripped the silky-soft bedspread beneath her. It had to be possible. She had to believe Jay's intentions had been nothing but honorable when he'd asked her here. She had to. The alternative was unbearable.

Her thoughts turned to Sarah. For her friend, it was too late. Drugs or no drugs, Sarah was dead, her life over. The one thing Cat knew for sure, even before uncovering a single thing, was that she and Jay owed it to Sarah's memory to solve her murder and live the best lives they could.

She had to work from the foundation that Jay was innocent until proven guilty. She would put all her energy into finding the killer without closing her eyes to the truth. It was out there waiting to be uncovered. Cat Forrester never left anything uncovered.

She pushed to her feet and marched into the ensuite bathroom. Jay might have suffered problems in the past seven years, but so had she. Whatever those problems, they didn't make him a killer.

She'd shower and change and then phone Chris to see how things were at home. Trying to act as though the lavish silver-and-gray-tiled bathroom—complete with silver faucets and thick gray towels stacked on chrome shelves—was the norm for her, Cat stripped off her clothes and stepped into the open shower. The hot water slid in torrents over her head and down her body. Closing her eyes, she soaked her hair as she relived the anger and self-hatred in Jay's eyes when he confessed his addictions.

God knew there would be plenty of time for them to talk during the coming days.

She opened her eyes and reached for the shampoo. This wasn't a time for accusation. It might be the perfect time for a few revelations…from both of them. But asking him about the drugs and how that affected his relationship with Sarah was vital, whether he liked it or not. There was a very real possibility the drugs were the reason for their estrangement. Addiction killed friendships like arsenic killed people.

Digging her nails into her scalp, Cat scrubbed her hair as though scrubbing out the turmoil, shame and disappointment of not being able to "fix" her mum. Jay didn't know her mum as anything other than glamorous Mrs. F., as he used to call her. Telling Jay about her deterioration brought a harsh sense of fear and betrayal to Cat's conscience. She feared his reaction to her as well as to her mum. Added to that was the horrible feeling that if she shared their family secret, she was talking behind her mother's back. Painting her in a way Julia would rather die than Jay know.

Cat squeezed her eyes shut. She couldn't tell him; it was too hard. Shame wavered inside her. Shame for her mum and herself that their lives had changed so completely upon the demise of just one man—her father. Jay was clearly braver than she would ever be. She respected him all the more for it.

Twenty minutes later, with her hair wrapped in one towel and her body in another, Cat padded barefoot into the bedroom. She sat down on the bed and pulled her tote bag toward her, fumbling inside for her cell phone. Finding it, she dialed home.

Chris picked up. "Hi, Sis. How's it going?"

Ignoring his question, Cat drew in a breath. "How's Mum?"

Silence.

Cat frowned, annoyance prickling at her nerves. "Chris?"

"She's okay. She's had a drink and gone to bed."

"In what kind of state?"

"Coherent, laughing, wondering if you'll have sex with Jay Garrett again."

Cat's eyes widened. "What? She said that?"

He laughed. "Yep, kind of wondering the same thing myself."

Feeling as though she was in a parallel universe where she was the only one not finding their mum's alcoholism amusing, Cat glared into the empty room. "Looking after Mum isn't a game, Chris. She'll try to lull you into a false sense of security. You don't know what it's like—"

"Listen, I've thought about everything you said…or shouted last week. You're needed at the Cove. I can take care of Mum until you get back…but when you do, things are going to change."

Cat rolled her eyes. "Yeah, right. Didn't you say you and Melinda have set a wedding date? What are you going to do, ask Melinda if it's all right to move Mum into your new marital home for a while? You really think one night of dealing with Mum and you know what's what?"

"No, but Melinda is on board with this and no one is moving in with anyone. Mum is moving out."

Cat swallowed and pressed her hand to her stomach. Rehabilitation. "What are you talking about?"

"Just concentrate on what you have to do there and leave Mum to me, okay?" He blew out a breath. When he spoke again, his voice was softer. "You're there to find your friend's killer. I can't do that. Only you can. Please. Just let me do the bit I can help with because there's absolutely nothing I can do to help Sarah."

"Don't try to distract me, Chris. You want to put Mum in rehab, don't you?"

"Yes."

Cat fisted her hair back from her face as the habitual feeling of helplessness stole over her, the same as it did every time she heard the word *rehab*. She couldn't do it. She couldn't fight the feeling if she put her mum in rehab, she was turning her back on the woman who did everything for her children until the day her husband died.

For twenty-two years, Julia Forrester loved her children, cared for them and held them. What did they know about losing the love of their lives? Chris loved Melinda and would, by God's grace, have her for the rest of his life, and Cat…Cat hoped to have her own love one day, too.

"Cat, I know what you're thinking." Chris's voice cut through her worry.

"No, you don't. Do you think I haven't tried that route?"

"I don't know, have you?"

"Yes. Nowhere will take her until she admits there's a problem, and she won't do that. You can't just drive by and kick her out of the car in the hope a kindly doctor will pick her up, brush her off and deliver her back to you once she's clean."

"I know that."

"Do you? Do you know what it's like to beg the woman who brought you up to admit she needs alcohol like most people need water?"

"Cat, stop."

"No. I won't stop until you start taking this seriously."

"I am. I feel like shit for leaving you so long, okay? Let me sort this out."

Cat said nothing as fear of the unknown washed over her, twisting her self-confidence into a ball and kicking it through the window. She stood and paced the room. Her heart raced and panic seeped into her veins. She needed to leave. To go home and be with her mum. It had been the pair of them alone for so long…

"Cat? You still there?"

Tears spilled over her lids as she nodded. "Yes."

"It's my turn. I love you. Now get off this phone and find the bastard who killed Sarah."

"But—"

"I mean it. Go find him."

The line went dead. Cat snapped the phone closed and tossed it behind her onto the bed. She swiped at her cheeks. She wanted to believe Chris could find a place where their mother would be well looked after and treated with as much respect as Cat gave her, but he didn't have the slightest clue what he was talking about.

Cat hauled her suitcase off the floor and onto the bed. Fine. If he thought he could do it, let him. Unzipping her suitcase, she forced her mind once more to Jay's past addiction. It wasn't the fear her broad shoulders couldn't take anymore, but rather the more he told her about himself, the more obligated she felt to tell him about the mess of her own life. That wasn't why she came. She was there for Sarah…and to think about what to do next at home. Not to cry on the shoulder of a man she'd once loved.

Inspector Harris had agreed to four weeks' leave of absence. Would it be enough time to find Sarah's killer? Either way, it had to be enough for Cat to make a decision about her mum. She sometimes felt her life slipping through her fingers, a life just as precious as the one so brutally taken from her friend.

She wouldn't waste it. Not anymore. She and Jay had some serious work to do.

Minutes later, she headed downstairs. When she reached the bottom step, she halted and stared around in wonder. The open-plan lower floor of the cabin was enormous. She had walked through it in a dreamlike state when they arrived, Jay's revelation of his drug abuse had blocked out the sight and sound of everything.

The massive space was breathtaking. A crisscross network of beams and posts added strength and character, as did the russet-and-gold oversize couches and cushions. Cases and cases of books and a plethora of candles, framed photographs and paraphernalia added an abundance of color and comfort.

It was a man's place, but also one where any woman would happily lie on the settee in Jay's arms. Cat's face heated and she hastily looked around to check Jay wasn't silently watching her as he so often had since the train. She released her held breath. She was alone. Wandering farther into the space, she headed for the living area and stood in front of the huge black wood burner and stone fireplace. It was the focal point of the entire bottom floor.

Smoothing her hand over the hammered metal surface, she smiled with pride at what Jay had achieved. In spite of his problems, Jay Garrett had survived and then some. Her stomach clenched and a strange tingle swept across her skin as the sensation of his thighs clamped between hers on that single night rushed through her.

She snapped her gaze to the staircase. What the hell was she thinking? She struggled in vain to shift her mind to the only reason she was there. To find Sarah's killer. She knew enough about victim psychology to know her association with Jay and the feelings it caused in her had nothing to do with attraction—and everything to do with the need to go back to a time when she was so happy.

A time when her dad was alive and her mum drank nothing more than the occasional glass of wine with dinner.

Cat shook her head. Jay's sobriety, lifestyle and access to money couldn't be further away from her life of alcohol dependency and its effects. Regret washed over her. He called her successful. Beautiful. A cop with a blossoming career, yet she felt like none of that. All her time and self-confidence was wrapped up in that five-feet-five-inch package known as *Mum*. Her mind rarely strayed from working out how to find her mum the help she desperately needed before the woman she loved with every inch of her heart ended up dead.

"Cat?"

She jumped at the sound of his voice and when she spun around, her breath caught. He'd showered, too. His damp hair was swept back, dark and unruly...and impossibly sexy, dressed in black shoes, black jeans and a crisp, pale blue shirt. Cat swallowed the ball of attraction that tugged at her chest.

"Hey." She smiled, hoping the tremor in her bottom lip wasn't visible from across the room.

"Are you okay? You look great, by the way." He walked toward her, lighting candles with a long-stemmed flint as he came closer.

"Thanks. You, too." Cat tried and failed not to stare openmouthed at the sight of his pretty impressive pecs beneath the shirt, and the incredibly grabbable ass as he leaned up and down, reaching the shelves holding votives and pillar lights. Her anger at him for not telling her a week before about his addiction wavered.

He abruptly straightened and turned. Her face burned as if he'd turned the flint on it. She was ogling him like a teenager in heat. He winked before continuing with his walk around the room. Years had passed since she gave Jay her virginity on the sands of Cowden Beach, but as she watched the light dance and flicker over his face, Cat knew he'd been the right man to take it. He was a good man then and a good man now—and God only knew she'd had enough experience personally and professionally of the bad ones.

Please, God, let him be innocent...

Cat looked to the floorboards, afraid to face him lest the sudden urge to kiss him break free. "If I didn't know you better, Jay Garrett, I'd swear you bought this cabin just to torment me."

"How so?"

Cat warmed hearing the smile in his voice. She met his eyes. "You know damn well how many times I said I'd buy it when I won the lottery and moved out here."

His eyes gleamed brighter than they had since she arrived. "I always knew one day you'd see sense and come back to live with me."

Cat's heart kicked.

A long moment of silence followed and she prayed he said nothing else. Left the subject of them well alone, in the past, where it had to stay no matter how tempting the urge to relive it. He was a suspect in a murder investigation—and even if he wasn't, there was no way she would drag his newly successful and happy life into the mire of hers.

He took a step toward her and she resisted the impulse to step back.

"Are you glad it's mine, though?" he asked, his gaze wandering over her face. "I bought it as soon as I could so nobody had the chance to take it from me."

"I can't think of anyone better living here. Except me, of course."

He laughed. "It makes me happy to hear you say that. I didn't want to make another mistake."

She frowned. "Another mistake? What do you mean?"

"From now on things are going to change."

Cat stiffened. Was he talking about Sarah? "You said something like that on the train. Do you want to tell me about it?"

He glanced away toward the French doors leading outside. "I lost touch, Cat. Got so embroiled in the business, I lost touch with what matters."

"Like what?"

"Like Sarah, my family…you." He faced her.

His pain was palpable. Not sure she had enough strength to soothe him, Cat moved to create some space between them. "Sarah's death has shocked you, catapulted you back to a time when we were all safe and happy. You can't dwell on what-ifs and maybes. We all have to face what life throws at us or it will win and we'll lose."

Images of her mum lying on the bathroom floor with her cheek in a pool of her own vomit filled Cat's mind. Another of Cat manhandling a vodka bottle from her hand and hurling it out the back door into the garden. The noises, the anger, the chaos whirled inside her mind. She swallowed the lump in her throat.

"You don't have to tell me about mistakes, Jay. Stuff happens. It's what we do about it that matters." She exhaled, forcing the rare resentment toward her mum from her body. She only became the bitter person she was so ashamed of when she thought of the Cove or Jay. That was why she never made contact with him. What was the point of fixating on the possibilities that could have occurred in her life had her father lived?

His gaze lingered on her mouth before grazing over her hair. "I guess you have things to tell me and I have things to tell you."

Trepidation skittered along the surface of Cat's forearms. Did he know? Did he know just by looking at her that she was hurting? Of course he did. As she did him.

"This isn't about us. This is about Sarah."

"That means we can't get to know each other again?" He shook his head. "While you're here, I want you back. All of you."

The implication, the verve of his tone hitched Cat's heart. The look in his eyes was open and hungry. Her skin tingled as need and entirely selfish desire rushed through her veins. She couldn't let him get too close. She stepped back again, afraid she'd succumb to the simmering need to fling her arms around him and hold on, begging him to never let her go home and face reality.

She was a bona fide coward with a secret and it pained her just to look at him. "You're tense, I'm tense. The sooner we get things moving with this investigation, the better."

He closed his eyes. "I should've been there for Sarah, I wasn't. The fear I'll make the same mistake with you scares the hell out of me. Don't shut me out of this, okay? Don't shut me away from you."

She released her held breath. "I won't. Of course I won't."

He smiled. "That's all I need to hear. We need to talk, but let's eat first. Once I tell you what I've been up to your appetite might disappear."

"Jay—"

His smile faltered. "Please, Cat. Let me feed you, then we'll talk."

The sadness in his gaze and the stiffness of his shoulders weakened her resolve to get the ugly out of the way as soon as possible. She nodded, forced a small smile. "Okay."

"Pasta, basil, cherry tomatoes and fresh green salad, washed down with Templeton's very best bottled water. How does that sound?"

She grinned. "Perfect."

"Well, then…" He offered her his elbow. "Shall we?"

She slipped her hand into the crook of his arm and let him lead her outside. Something wasn't right. Something deep and dangerous ate Jay up from the inside out. He mentioned guilt with Sarah. She hadn't turned up when she was meant to. It didn't make him the guy who clasped his hands around her throat.

His intense need to find out who murdered Sarah could be a smokescreen for something Cat didn't want to contemplate. His calling her there, knowing she once loved him, could be his only defense. She was a cop. A detective. Which meant that to her he was a suspect the same as anyone else. She didn't know him anymore. He wasn't the same carefree boy he was before. While she was in the Cove, she'd leave no stone unturned…no matter how heavy.

Please, God, give me proof he had nothing to do with this…and give it to me tonight.

CHAPTER FIVE

JAY WATCHED CAT SUCK the last morsel of raspberry pavlova from her spoon, her gaze fixed out across the water, her features relaxed and content. They'd been sitting outside for an hour, yet neither of them had brought up a subject of any real importance. They skirted around their families, their jobs, even their damn hobbies. Jay picked up his glass and drank.

His addiction and this whole life Cat knew nothing about hung between like an invisible barrier. He had to tell her. Damn, he wanted her to know. How could they progress past this superficial closeness until both of them filled in the last seven years? Something lingered in her past, too. If there was one thing he'd learned how to do in rehab, it was recognize pain and shame in people's eyes. He saw it deep and scarring in hers.

She turned, her smile bright even in the semidarkness. "You okay?"

Here goes nothing. Jay stood. "Shall we go and sit on the grass? Watch the sun go down?"

Her smile faltered and her brow creased for the briefest of seconds before she smiled again. "Sounds good to me."

"Great." He forced a smile. "I'll go and grab a couple of blankets."

Leaving her sitting but feeling the intensity of her gaze on his retreating back, Jay hurried inside and whipped two fleece throws from the living-room couch. His heart hammered and his throat was drier than his liquor cabinet.

"Come on, Garrett, you can do this," he said, quietly. "It's Cat. She'll love you no matter what."

Heading back out, he prayed that sentiment was true. Friends forever, they had said. He, Cat and Sarah, the summer before he turned eighteen, had sat on Cowden Beach, all a little drunk on beer and youth, vowing to always be friends no matter who went away to college, committed a crime or got married. They'd always be there for each other through thick and thin.

Now one of them was dead and the other was waiting outside to hear all about his two-and-a-half-year mistake.

He stepped outside and his smile slid into place. "Let's go."

She turned and smiled, flipping his stomach all the way over. Beautiful, courageous, kind and caring Cat. Pulling up to his full six feet two inches, Jay took her hand and led her across the veranda and down a narrow set of steps onto the grass surrounding the cabin.

He walked to a spot that had a fantastic view of the horizon, day or night, and flicked out one of the fleeces. Spreading it on the grass, he gestured for her to sit. She did, leaning back on her elbows, which resulted in her breasts thrusting forward. Jay averted his gaze and let the other blanket drop from his hand to the ground. His attraction to her was insane after all this time, but it burned with a passionate yearning he hadn't felt for anyone since. He wanted to be close to her.

Swallowing, he refocused and lay down flat on his back on the blanket beside her. He stared at the salmon-pink and lilac sky. "I suppose this is the perfect time to tell you all about it."

The night was quiet and he heard the subtle changes

in her breathing, the soft hitch and exhalation. After a rustle and swish of material she lay down, too, the heat of her upper arm lingering at the point between his biceps and elbow.

"I suppose it is."

Jay closed his eyes. "It's probably easier if you start with a question and have me answer it. Knowing where to start when you messed up for more than two years is hard."

She exhaled a shaky breath. "Okay, but first I want to apologize for my reaction when you told me about the drugs. I didn't know what to say, think or feel when you threw it out there like that. I wasn't... I'm not judging you, okay?"

Jay turned his head, his cheek brushing the fleece. Her eyes darted over his face, lingered at his lips and slowly raised upward. Her eyes were the darkest green imaginable, almost black in the fading light and Jay suddenly wanted to drown in them.

"You don't have to apologize."

She turned away and looked back to the sky. "So, let's start with a question. How does the man I once knew, Jay Simon Garrett, confident, masculine, hungry for the taste of whatever he wanted at any given moment, end up hooked on a class-A drug?"

He followed her gaze toward the sky. Typical Cat. Straight for the jugular. He'd expected nothing less and it made it so much easier to speak. "Earlier you asked about my singing. Remember?"

"Uh-huh."

"I failed."

The telltale shuffle of clothes again and Jay knew she watched him. He didn't look at her, didn't want to see her eyes. He needed to get everything out in the open in the shortest time possible.

"I left town after a year of getting no further than gigging in the local pubs in and around Templeton. Dad told me it was time to give it up, they'd supported me long enough. I look back now and can't believe he didn't say it sooner. God, if any kid of mine was still living at home without a job and thinking he was the next big thing at twenty-four, I'd like to think I'd kick him out on his ass. I was a jerk back then and didn't realize the opportunities my family could give me."

"You weren't a jerk. You had a dream that used to eat you up. Your singing was everything to you. Money or no money, when you feel like that about something, it should be your focus."

"Yeah, well, like I said, nothing was happening, so Dad said it was time I grew up and did something worthwhile. To him, that something was following in his footsteps. At the time it was like asking me to stand in front of a firing squad."

"So you left."

"So I left. Eventually I hooked up with a band. We had the enthusiasm and talent but never did more than support bigger bands, but still small-time. We all wanted something bigger, acknowledgment we were good, but not a single producer gave us the time of day." He blew out a breath, as the memory and feeling of his youthful arrogance reeled up inside him like an ugly stain, seeping into his blood and making him want to sink farther into the grass.

"So then what happened?" Cat's warm, soft hand stole into his, and Jay's breath shuddered out as he closed his fingers around hers.

"Someone in the band convinced me the only way to

keep the momentum going, to keep the belief we'd make it in the industry, was to snort half a gram of coke up my nose every time I felt myself waning." He finally turned to look at her. "For the following two years I thought it was working."

She raised her eyebrows and met his eyes. Incredulous disbelief shone in the darkness of her eyes and her mouth dropped ever so slightly open as though she wanted to say something but had no idea what. Jay stared back, disbelief he could handle, but disgust and disappointment like he'd seen from his family, and Sarah, was a whole lot worse.

"If coke does nothing else, it makes you believe you're capable of anything." He swallowed. "The trouble is, the only thing you're really capable of is hurting people."

She closed her eyes and Jay's heart sank in his chest like a lump of lead. Was she shutting him out? Unable to look at him? Both were justified. Unease rippled through his body. What should he do next? Keep talking or keep his mouth shut and let her process the gargantuan fact that he wasn't the man she thought him to be? Not the man she once trusted enough to sleep with, to give her most intimate gift to and give it gladly.

Shame seared his face as he opened his mouth, closed it, opened it again. She brought his hand to her lips and pressed a lingering kiss to his knuckles. Her strength and forgiveness absorbed silently into his skin.

The rare heat of tears burned his eyes and he squeezed them shut. "I've made some really bad choices, Cat." His voice came out low and deep, revealing every emotion battling around inside him, but there was no one else he trusted his vulnerability with. "One of the biggest is believing that working my ass off, making more and more money for the family business would somehow fill the bullet wounds every gram of coke I took made in my parents' hearts."

She tightened her fingers around his. "Jay, look at me."

He turned.

"You're clean. You have to let go of the past and move on. If you continue to beat yourself up over what you did or didn't do, the drugs still control you. Surely that's one of the first things they taught you in rehab."

He stared deep into her eyes. He wanted nothing more than to yell, "You're right, I'm clean!" It wouldn't be the truth. He wanted to smile and agree and revel in his success, but he'd never be free of his addiction—wasn't sure he wanted to be—because once he claimed he was, then the narcotic knuckles could quite easily come knocking at his door once again.

"I wish I could say that, but an addict is never clean. If they're stupid enough to think differently, that's the first step back."

She released his hand to clasp hers together at her abdomen. Her face seemed to shut down. Her jaw grew rigid. She met his eyes and her unshed tears glistened beneath the lights on the veranda above them. Her breast rose and she exhaled. "Tell me what happened after you realized cocaine wasn't the road to success."

A new tension radiated from her and Jay turned his gaze back to the sky, apricot now bled into orange. She had every right to her anger and disappointment. Templeton in summer was beauty personified, yet Jay felt as though nothing but ugliness surrounded him. "I didn't realize anything about the cocaine. I just got worse, taking more and more until the other band members kicked me out."

"They kicked you out after one of them introduced you to it? God, I'd like to kick their asses."

He huffed out a wry laugh. "I'm the only one to blame here. It was me who lost control, whereas they believed they could handle their use. Some nights I couldn't string a sentence together, let alone sing." Her hand slid over his and he held on. "I came back to Templeton, high as a kite and disappeared into the abyss."

"The abyss would be the drug haunts you know about?"

"That's where I spent pretty much every second for three weeks and two days after coming home. Before George rang my father telling him exactly where to find me. Dad hauled my ass into a rehabilitation center—"

"Wait. George found you? How did he know where you were?"

Jay turned away, as shame encompassed him like a familiar and debilitating cloak around his shoulders. "I'll get to that part in a minute." He swallowed. "Anyway, Dad hauled me into rehab quicker than I could put up a fight. Left me there. No visitors. No calls. Nothing."

"For how long?"

"For as long as it took."

"Which was?"

"Four months, two weeks and five days."

"Wow."

Jay grimaced. "Yeah, wow. I took the stuff for two years and it took me that long to even start the journey of staying sober. So you asked how George knew where to find me…" He blew out a breath. "Sarah told him. Sarah told him because I was with her. I did something really bad, Cat. Something that severed Sarah's and my relationship completely."

He closed his eyes. "She saved my frigging life and I never had the chance to thank her. She called George, rather than my dad, to come and get me. She called George rather than the police. I owed her so much but she refused to see me after what I did. Refused to answer my calls, so after three months of trying, I left her alone."

She slowly pulled her hand from his and the hook in his chest pulled tighter. He opened his eyes and turned. The concern in her gaze had changed to wary accusation. "Sarah loved you. You were her best friend. What did you do?"

Guilt and shame twisted in his gut like the spikes of a claw hammer, scraping and ripping his pride and self-worth to shreds, leaving the regret to bleed inside of him where it would never escape.

"I went to her work."

"You went to the primary school?" Her eyes widened and she put her hand on her forehead. "You were high when you went there? Where there were kids?"

He clenched his jaw, pursed his lips and nodded.

"Why? Why would you do that? What did you want?"

"God knows. I can't remember going there or seeing Sarah. When I tried to contact her once I was sober, she wasn't having it. So…" He let the sentence drift off as the helplessness he felt when Sarah hung up on him time and time again rose like a bitter pill in his throat. A sharp reminder he would now never be able to atone for putting her through the professional and personal stress of dealing with a drug addict in front of kids no older than seven or eight.

He met Cat's eyes, and her shock and disappointment blazed hard and hot in the semidarkness. "She must have been terrified, Jay. Terrified what you were going to do. She might have thought you had a gun, were violent, capable of hurting her or any one of those kids."

"I know."

"I can't do this."

He turned. "What?"

She pushed to her feet. "Have you any idea what that sort of humiliation and fear can do to a person?"

He scrambled from the grass. "I do now, yes, but then—"

"Stop. I can't listen to it. It's too much like my... It's just too much." She fisted her hands into her beautiful red hair and turned her back on him.

Jay trembled with the effort it took to not wrap his arms around her. Tell her to stay, not to leave. To look at him like she had when they were having dinner, to touch his sleeve and wink and playfully tease him.

She turned back around and optimism surged into his heart that she'd come back to him. Come back and sit and talk and...forgive. She shook her head.

"I have to go to bed. Have to absorb what you've told me. How could you..." She stopped, held up her hands. "I'm going to bed. I love you. Always will. It's just when I think about what that must have done to Sarah..."

Her voice cracked and she put her hand over her mouth. It was too much. He couldn't leave her standing there when he'd tipped her entire world on its axis. Jay stepped forward with his arms outstretched. She hesitated, tears streaking silver down her cheeks before coming forward. She reached her arms around him and the breath left his lungs. Her warm tears soaked into his shirt and Jay stood immobile as her anger and disappointment joined those of so many other people he hurt. It spread a pool deep in his soul that he hoped one day he'd be ready to lift the plug from and let drain away, drop by drop.

"Will you take me in?" Her voice broke the silence.

He pressed a kiss to her crown. "Sure. We'll talk more tomorrow."

She straightened in the circle of his arms and cupped

her hand to his jaw. Gratitude pushed the air from his lungs. She smiled softly.

"I'm not turning away from you. You do know that, right? I'll still be here in the morning and we'll find Sarah's killer. This is just a lot for me to deal with…"

Her words trailed off and turning his head, Jay kissed her palm, eased down her hand and held it tightly.

"I know. It's a lot. I've done a lot, but doing that to Sarah was probably the worst. I tried to apologize, tried to make it up to her, but she never forgave me."

She shook her head. "She did. She called you right before she died. She needed you. Don't you see what that means?"

His eyes scanned her face, her beauty, her fire, and hope burst behind his rib cage. "Whatever was going on with her was serious enough to forgive me and get me back in her life. Quickly."

She nodded. "Exactly. She was into something so bad it got her killed. Whatever both of us have or haven't done in the last seven years, from now on that's our only focus, okay? Once we get whoever killed Sarah behind bars—"

"You'll go home."

She closed her eyes. "Jay—"

"So I have to talk about this, Cat. I want you to know. I don't want any secrets between us."

Her eyes snapped open and something akin to panic shot across them before she took her hand from his and focused on the cabin. "I need to sleep. We'll talk in the morning…after I've had my visit with Bennett."

Surprise catapulted him upright. "You've managed to get an appointment with Bennett?"

She nodded. "Nine o'clock. I need to sleep."

She took off before he could stop her, but Jay followed,

marveling at her ability to make anything possible—and wondering what inside her caused such fear to appear in her eyes when he'd said he wanted no more secrets.

CHAPTER SIX

THE TAXI PULLED UP outside the front double doors of the Templeton Cove police station and Cat delved into her bag for her wallet. She extracted a ten-pound note and handed it to the driver.

"Keep the change."

She got out of the car and slammed the door. The facade of the tiny station looked almost quaint compared to the city station back in Reading. Yet it wasn't quaint. It was a place that dealt with the same crimes, murders and thefts as anywhere else. She drew in a deep breath and tried to clear her mind.

Still vibrating from the shock of Jay's revelation last night, it was an impossible task. First the drugs and then his cruel breaking of Sarah's trust.

Cat had woken at seven and gone around the cabin like a burglar, tiptoeing around his house, desperately trying not to wake him. She'd snuck downstairs, trying and failing to avoid creaking floorboards as she'd walked to the kitchen. Once there, she'd taken a glass from the cupboard and then fumbled with it, thankfully finally managing to catch it like a clown at a kids' circus, before it crashed to the floor.

Jay. Her Jay. Sarah's Jay.

Aware of cops and civilians walking around her, Cat wandered away from the entrance. She was half an hour early despite killing time asking fruitless questions about

Sarah at the convenience store and coffee shop. She pulled her cell from her bag and feigned interest in the blackened screen. Jay and what he'd done bounced around inside her head like a Ping-Pong ball.

The reality of his going to Sarah's school while high on drugs told her just how tightly his addiction had gripped him. The worst Julia had done was to turn up at police headquarters carrying a dilapidated bunch of daffodils, demanding she see her sergeant daughter on her birthday.

Cat's birthday had been a month before.

She looked at the ground and waited for the memory to abate. Humiliation and fear of what her mother would do next had been paramount that day. No doubt the same emotions swept through Sarah at a more terrifying rate than Cat could contemplate. How could Jay have done that to her?

She shook her head. No. Jay wasn't Jay that day. She had to remember that and find the strength to listen to him. Jay was in recovery and had shared the explanation she demanded from him almost as soon as she'd see him. Instead of listening and acting like a friend and professional, she'd run like a coward because it was too painful, too close to her existence.

Hitching her bag onto her shoulder, Cat tilted her chin. She wouldn't do that again. Turning, she marched back toward the station entrance, continuing resolutely forward until she pushed open the door and headed for the reception desk. The duty sergeant greeted her with a smile warm enough to melt an ice-cream sundae and once more, Cat remembered she was no longer in the city.

"Can I help you?" he asked.

She smiled back. "I have a nine o'clock appointment with Inspector Bennett. I'm Sergeant Cat Forrester visiting from Reading."

"Well, nice to meet you, Sergeant. Take a seat. I'll go let him know you're here."

She sat down on one of the four plastic chairs lining the wall behind her and waited. She was impatient to get started, anticipation and hope jumped along her nerve endings. The early-morning sun shone through the vertical blinds beside her, lighting parallel lines across the gray tiled floor. The pale beige walls were scattered with posters telling Templeton residents to Stay Safe, Be Aware of Stranger Danger and Not All Visitors Are Nice Visitors. It was friendly, safe, trustworthy and Cat guessed Sarah's murder was the first one the Cove had seen for years...possibly ever.

The click of a side door opening turned her head and she immediately stood. The man coming toward her was tall, around six-three, maybe four, with short sandy-colored hair, pleasant, shining eyes and a nice smile. He held out his hand.

"Sergeant Forrester, Inspector Bennett. Welcome to Templeton Cove."

She took his hand and his fingers clasped around hers firmly and with just the right amount of expected authority. She dipped her head and smiled. "Thank you, sir. I wish the circumstances were happier, but it's nice to meet you."

His smile faltered as his eyes wandered over her face. Cop eyes. She knew what he was doing and instantly liked him for it. A new face was always one to be learned about. Who was the person behind the mask?

After a moment, he gestured her toward the open door. "Shall we?"

He led her through the busy but not particularly bustling station, past walnut-veneer desks scattered with loose papers and neatly stacked trays. As they walked, they passed several uniformed and non-uniformed officers who eyed her with curiosity before resuming their conversations or telephone calls. They reached his corner office and Bennett shut the door behind them, providing some semblance of quiet.

"Have a seat, Sergeant."

The sudden and colder change in his tone alerted Cat to the reality of Bennett's feelings about her being there. His friendly greeting appeared to have been little more than a smokescreen when they were in reception. Smiling inwardly, Cat sat down. That was fine. They could play this however he wanted, but she would definitely leave knowing more than when she arrived.

"Thank you, sir."

He lowered his admirably fit and athletic physique, considering he must have been in his late forties, into the seat behind his desk. He stared at her expectantly. "So I understand you knew our victim and want in on the investigation?"

Cat sat up straighter. "I'm not here to step on anyone's toes, sir. I'm here to help."

"Is that so?"

"Yes, I've known Sarah since—"

"Yes, you said on the phone. You came here for how many summers?"

"Eight. I was twelve the first time."

"You spent a lot of time with Miss Cole every year?"

Cat smiled. "All the time."

"I see."

He stood and Cat turned in her swivel chair to watch him walk to the windowed wall of his office. He stared out at his team. Her gaze slid past his shoulder to the incident board of Sarah's murder pinned up in the far corner. Impatience hitched up a notch inside her. Now she'd seen it, Cat could barely sit still for wanting to tear out of the office and devour what information his team had accumulated.

When it appeared that Bennett wasn't going to add anything else, Cat cleared her throat. "A close friend of Sarah's rang me asking for my help, sir, and I couldn't ignore it." She hesitated. Should she tell him that close friend was also one of his suspects? Not yet. Deciding to wait to see how this meeting panned out, Cat continued. "I knew Sarah. I know I can offer something to this investigation others can't. If you're willing to let me see what you have, I'll do everything I can to help solve the case."

He turned and one eyebrow arched in blatant disbelief. "You really expect me to give you free reign to start poking about in an investigation you have zero authority to be a part of?"

She swallowed as Mr. Friendly Inspector well and truly disappeared under the cheap carpet tiles at her feet. She raised her hand as though taking an oath. "You have my word I will work entirely *with* you. Anything I find out, no matter how small, you'll be the first to know."

With his gaze still locked on hers, Bennett walked back to his desk and sat down. "If you came here for eight years since you were twelve, pardon me, Sergeant, but you're knocking the wrong side of twenty-five, so I'm guessing you hadn't seen our victim for a while."

Ignoring the jibe at her appearance, Cat lifted her shoulders. "I hadn't seen Sarah for seven years, but that doesn't make my involvement obsolete. The mutual friend who called me for help knew her forever and Sarah rang him the day she died."

His color darkened and his gaze darted over her face. "Is that so?"

Cat tilted her chin at his belligerent tone. "Yes."

He leaned his elbows on the desk and threaded his fingers. "Well, that's very interesting because we checked her land and cell records and spoke to everyone she rang that day. There are no friends unaccounted for. So who is this friend exactly?"

Here goes nothing. "Jay Garrett, he lives—"

"At the top of Clover Point, at the top of the place where the victim drew her last breath. You've been talking to a bloody suspect."

Cat flinched. "But surely if you had reason to still suspect him—"

"He was the first person we paid a personal visit to, Sergeant…and for your information, he failed to mention any phone call."

Why hadn't Jay told them about the phone call? She struggled to keep her expression impassive. "The only reason I can think of that might explain why he did that is because he feels he could've saved her life."

Bennett huffed out a laugh. "Oh, that's why he'd keep the information from me, is it?"

Cat straightened her spine. She'd deal with Jay's failure to tell the police everything he knew the minute she left the station, but there was no way in hell Bennett was going to dismiss her from Sarah's case. "She never showed up at the place she asked Jay to meet her and he didn't follow up with her. He didn't do everything possible to contact her because it was the first time she'd gotten in touch with him in years and he assumed she changed her mind. He didn't see it as important." Cat swallowed the horrible taste in her mouth.

Another eyebrow lift. "Didn't see it as important? Even when her body turned up at the bottom of his damn garden?"

Unease rippled through Cat's bloodstream. "No."

He shook his head. "Unbelievable. Then enlighten me, Sergeant. Give me a reason why I shouldn't get one of my officers to track Garrett down right now and drag his ass into custody."

What have you done, Jay? Why the hell didn't you tell him? Cat steadfastly met his gaze. "Sarah said she needed his help and asked him to meet her at a bakery on the beachfront."

"Marian's?"

Cat nodded, marveling once again at the small-town intimacy. She couldn't decide if it was nice or just plain creepy. "When he got there, Sarah never turned up. Now, of course, we know she was in trouble and maybe felt Jay was the only person to trust. He couldn't do anything then, but he can now. He called me to help you with the investigation, sir, because he had no idea what else to do. So, I'd appreciate you letting me prove to you he's innocent."

"Innocent? So you want in on this case having already written off your friend as a suspect without evidence?" He smiled. "Well, of course you're in. Why would I think it's a bad idea you working on the case?"

Irritation at his sarcasm mixed with the harsh truth of his words. She wasn't giving him the best first impression. She wasn't acting like a damn cop. She closed her eyes. "Look, maybe I want to think him innocent but that will not undermine my determination to find the true killer. If it turns out to be Jay…I'll prove it."

"Is that so?"

"Yes."

"Hmm."

"They were best friends, I'm finding it hard to picture Jay choking the life out of her, but that doesn't mean I won't arrest him if he did. I'll want him serving life behind bars as you will, believe me." The horror of that reality beat through Cat's blood turning it icy-cold.

"You never come across a friendship gone wrong in your career, Sergeant? A domestic dispute that ended in murder? Until I have cause to think otherwise, your friend Mr. Garrett will remain a suspect."

She nodded. "I understand."

He narrowed his eyes, carefully watching her. "How do you explain him not telling us about Miss Cole's phone call? Doesn't that strike you as unusual?"

Defensiveness for Jay rose up in Cat's heart. Innocent until proven guilty. Whether misplaced or not was yet to be proven, but belief for him, in him, burned like fire in her blood. She tilted her chin. "I wonder whether you'd have believed anything he had to say considering his drug use. Maybe he assumed the same."

Their gazes locked. After a long moment, Bennett turned his concentration to some papers on his desk. "Well, apart from the friendship blinding you to reality, you're not giving me any reason to let you in. You didn't know the victim when she died, you don't know who she was seeing, what the drug connection is or what the hell she was doing at Clover Point that day."

"Drug connection?" Cat's gut twisted as a shot of adrenaline rushed through her. Jay mentioned the drugs as a possible rumor, nothing more. Now here was Bennett... "What drugs, sir? Sarah wouldn't have taken drugs."

He stared at her and a faint flush stained his cheeks. He brought his hands together on the desk. "Nothing was found in her system, but we've had mention of Sarah possibly handling drug money."

"Handling...but that's crazy."

He leaned back in his chair and stared at her. "How

would you know after a seven-year absence? You didn't know Sarah at all anymore."

Cat's hackles rose like the hair along a dog's back. "Excuse me, sir, but—"

"But nothing. Bloody hell, even I knew Sarah better than you. This is my case, my jurisdiction. Why—"

"You knew her?"

He met her eyes and something akin to loss or distress flashed across his face before he pulled it back into professional place. "Yes, I knew her. Who didn't in Templeton? She was a lovely girl, one who should have been looking forward to getting married one day, not lying in a morgue waiting for someone to catch the bastard who did this."

Cat closed her eyes. "I didn't think."

"Clearly. You come in here expecting us to be some kind of second-class police force because we're close to the damn sea rather than in an office block. You're not the first to make that mistake and you won't be the last."

She opened her eyes and met his. His gaze blazed with anger. Cat pulled back her shoulders, refusing to apologize for not understanding the complexities of this small town.

"That's not it at all. I have the utmost respect for any headquarters, wherever they might be. But I'm here for Sarah. I want to help. I have to help." Cat leaned forward. "Sarah was killed in cold blood. I'm a cop. How can I walk away and do nothing?"

His gaze wandered over her face and Cat practically heard the cogs working in his brain, the good cop/bad cop playing out in his mind. He had to let her in. If she didn't know how far along the police were with the investigation, it could easily add a week, maybe more to her and Jay's efforts as they went over ground the Templeton team had already covered.

"Why should I trust you'll share what you learn with

me?" Bennett stared. "You're cozying up with a suspect, for crying out loud."

"A suspect you clearly don't have enough on to charge. I can help. I know I can. Jay provided an alibi, why do you still suspect him?"

He narrowed his eyes and curled his lip back from his teeth in blatant distrust. She suppressed the shiver that ran up her spine. Bennett was no pushover. She had to get in on the case.

"The only thing I can give you is my word and my honor as a cop." Cat pressed a hand to her chest. "I won't do anything to jeopardize your trust. I wouldn't dare, judging by the way you're looking at me right now."

A glimmer of a smile brushed over his lips and then vanished. "What if you find out Sarah had a whole other life going on, a life where she was in trouble up to her eyeballs? What then? Would you cover it up for her sake? Her parents' sake?"

Cat frowned. What the hell was he suggesting? "Of course I wouldn't. Sarah was a grown woman. A responsible woman. If she was involved in something illegal, then she clearly made some wrong choices along the way, but whatever she was involved with, good or bad, I'll never believe she deserved to have the life wrung out of her."

This man was capable of cold, hard policing. Their eyes locked. "Am I in?"

Bennett swiped a hand over his face and looked at her again. His exhaustion showed. For all his front, it appeared he was as invested in the investigation as she and Jay were. Living in a small town had its downside with regard to interference and gossip, but it also brought with it a community that would wrap its arms around you or fight in your corner whenever necessary.

"You have friendship, nothing more." Bennett interrupted her thoughts. "I need more than that to include you in this."

Irritation prickled along Cat's skin. She refused to let this golden opportunity slip from her grasp. If he wanted to play hardball, that was fine. She could show the same kind of ruthless challenge.

She stood and planted her fists on her hips. "Fine. Yes, Sarah was a good friend, but first and foremost, I'm a cop with an unblemished record. Every murder case I've worked on, I've pinned the killer. Every burglary, I've gotten the intruder, every rapist…" She paused, shook her head. "You get the idea.

"I loved Sarah, and there is no way I'm walking away from her. I will find who did this, sir. That I promise you."

He glared. "If I say you're out, Sergeant, you're out."

"If this was one of your close friends we were talking about, one who was strangled and left to rot in a forest that happened to be situated in another jurisdiction, would you take no for an answer by the SIO and walk away? Walk away and keep your promise to mind your own business?"

His ruddy cheeks turned scarlet and his eyes flashed with intelligence. The minimum Cat wanted was a look at the board. Her mind whirled, scrambling for the right thing to say to him, the words that would be her gateway in.

"Sir—"

"Shut up, Sergeant."

Cat flinched.

He leaned forward on his elbows and clenched his hands tightly together. "You're in, okay? I decided you were in the moment you said you knew the victim, but I wanted to see how much fire you had in your belly first."

"What?" Cat dropped her hands from her hips.

"You heard me. If it was just a flicker, no chance. But

you have a damn inferno burning inside you and if I don't let you in, I might well have a cop meltdown on my conscience as well as a murder."

Cat pushed out her held breath in a rush and smiled. "Thank God for that. I was running out of ideas."

A small smile lifted his lips. "If you're as good at policing as you are loyal to your friends, I think you'll be useful, but I refuse to put my own neck on the line justifying your involvement without knowing I can trust you first."

Cat's smile dissolved and she gave a curt nod. "Absolutely."

"Good. Then in that case, I want Garrett to know none of this. He's a suspect and until either of us proves otherwise, he'll remain one. Understood?"

Cat swallowed. "Yes, sir."

"Are you staying at his home while you're here?"

"Yes, sir." Cat kept her face impassive, wondering where Bennett was going with this. Would he want her to move out of Jay's?

"You're to stay there. Keep your friends close, your enemies closer."

"Jay will never be my enemy, sir."

He lifted an eyebrow. "Really? Not even if he killed Sarah Cole?"

Damn it. Why had she said that? She pulled back her shoulders. "I mean if Jay did this then my heart will be ripped out because I would have lost two friends that mean the damn world to me."

He studied her and Cat stood immobile. He had to believe her. He had to understand....

At last, he nodded. "Right. Now we're getting somewhere." He pushed back his chair and stood, coming around the desk to stand in front of her. "I'll let you see the board and relay all the information we have so far. In return, you'll tell me anything and everything you think, feel or find out about this case from here on in. Me first. Not another officer. Not another civilian. Do I make myself clear?"

Excitement churned like a million jumping beans in Cat's stomach and her hands shook. She was in. She was really in. She nodded and couldn't quite stop her smile. "Yes, sir."

He glanced toward the window. "I don't want that lot out there knowing who you are or what you're doing. You're the victim's friend and a police officer. Nothing more. Anything you want to talk about concerning this investigation, it goes no further than me and you."

"And Jay...Mr. Garrett is still a suspect? Even with an alibi?"

"Yes."

Cat stared. "Why?"

"Gut, Sergeant. There's a lot to say about an inspector's gut."

Cat swallowed. The determination in Bennett's glare could not be ignored. He knew more about Jay than he was telling her. She resisted the urge to grab his lapels and demand to know why Jay's alibi was in doubt. Why Bennett hadn't crossed him off as a suspect. Instead, she nodded.

"Fair enough." Unease rippled through her. It had to be more than Bennett's instinct keeping Jay in the frame. Was she not seeing the facts? Addicts were the best liars in the world. Cat swallowed. Everything had just grown ten times worse.

"Right, let's get on with it."

She tilted her chin. "Yes, sir."

Cat followed him to the door and they walked out into the noisy humdrum of the working police station. Ringing telephones, chairs scraping tiles, the odd shout above muted conversation filled the room. Cat drew in a breath, inhaling its familiarity like a lifeline. Her work was the only thing that kept her going in the long, alcohol-dominated years of her life. Her time in the Cove was work. Jay's face appeared uninvited in her mind's eye. Work. Nothing more. Nothing less.

"You've got three minutes to take it in," Bennett said under his hushed breath. "Then you disappear."

She nodded.

He led her to the board and stood silently beside her. Cat shut her eyes, drew in a shaky breath and then opened them.

Sarah's body lay on the dark, almost black, foliage covering the ground, her skin stark white in death. One arm was thrown above her head, her legs were apart. Cat blinked against the hot tears pricking her eyes like sharpened needles. Sarah wore a white blouse and black skirt that had ridden—or been forced, high onto her hips revealing a flash of white panties. A set of silver bangles glinted at one wrist, a black wristwatch was on the other.

Cat's gaze flitted back and forth over the photo. To the left of it was the map of Clover Point and its immediate surrounding areas. The lake and adjacent roads could easily have served as escape routes and were marked in red on either side. A close-up picture of the log cabins closest to the forest had been blown up and pinned beside the map.

Cat leaned closer to Sarah's picture and concentrated on memorizing every tiny detail. The picture of her friend could be deemed seductive if it wasn't for the dark purple bruising around her neck and uneven line of dried blood beneath her left nostril. The killer, or Sarah, had closed her eyelids, leaving her looking as though she slept in peaceful slumber. Her blond shoulder-length hair was spread around her like a golden halo.

Several feet of area surrounding the body had been photographed. There wasn't a lot to see apart from trees and foliage. Cat closed her eyes, the familiar prickling skittered across the back of her neck. A new case. This time murder. This time personal.

Sarah would have known Jay's cabin was just a few hundred feet away, which meant she was more than likely hoping to meet him. After not turning up at the bakery, had she been planning to drop by? Or run to his cabin for help?

Even in her current state, Sarah's beauty shone through. High, defined cheekbones, strong jaw, flawless eyelids covering vivid blue eyes and full, full lips that every boy this side of the Atlantic wanted to kiss when they were teenagers. Cat opened her eyes.

"Okay. I've seen enough."

Half an hour later, Cat stepped outside into the bright midmorning sun and hurried down the stone steps in front of the station. Swallowing the lump in her throat, she rushed across the parking lot, praying her tears didn't break. Her heart ached for her dead friend and her mind reeled with the information she'd gained at the tongue and allowance of Inspector Bennett.

The man was a cop; there was no doubt about that. Steady, distant and professional, yet when he said he knew Sarah, it meant the case was personal for him and all the other officers involved, too.

"Cat?"

The sound of footsteps to her side had her turning. Her stomach tightened at the sight of Jay's concerned expression as he hurried toward her.

"What are you doing here?" She resisted the urge to fall into his outstretched arms. Suspect. Liar. Lover.

"You told me your meeting was at nine o'clock. Where else would I be? Are you all right?" He cupped a hand to her elbow and stared into her face, his brown eyes questioning and dark with concern. "I'd hoped you'd want me to come here with you. What time did you leave?"

Why didn't you tell him about the phone call, Jay? What else are you hiding? "Early. I didn't want to wake you."

He continued to stare, a muscle jumping in his jaw. She'd pissed him off. Instead of berating her, he gestured toward his Mercedes glinting like liquid silver in the sunlight.

"Let's get in the car. You're shaking."

He slipped his arm around her shoulder and Cat leaned into him. She couldn't help it. Just for a moment, she wanted to feel his strength against her. Wanted to remember him as he was seven years ago and not as a man she could never love again. *Not as a possible killer.* He led her to the car and helped her into the passenger seat.

She dropped her head against the headrest and closed her eyes. His door opened and he slid into the seat. Sensing him watching her, Cat prayed he possessed enough patience to give her a moment to regain her equilibrium.

Thankfully, he did.

The engine purred to life. "Hotel California" blared from the speakers and the alloy wheels crunched over the graveled parking lot before he pulled onto the smooth Tarmac of the main road. His silence only lasted to the end of the song.

"Cat?"

Turning her head on the headrest, she opened her eyes. "She's dead, Jay."

He frowned and faced front. His hand left the gear-shift and covered hers where it lay on her thigh. "How bad was it?"

She tightened her hand around his fingers. "Bad. It wasn't until I saw her picture, saw her lying there in the grass, that it truly hit me."

His jaw tightened. "I'm sorry you had to see that. I couldn't imagine seeing Sarah that way."

Cat stared as he faced front. Would she suspect every word he said from now on? Every look? Every caring gesture he offered her? She turned to the windshield as regret wound tight inside her. Bennett had ordered her to tell Jay nothing, but instinct told her that letting him know certain things could help her eliminate his guilt. Doing that was rapidly becoming her priority. If she could trust Jay, the burden would be so much lighter.

"The first thing we need to do is go back to Clo-ver Point. Back to where she was found." She stopped. "Damn. I forgot to ask Bennett who found her." She looked at him. "Do you know?"

"The press said she was found by someone staying at the holiday park adjacent to the forest. Apparently, the guy was walking his dog in the forest. No name was given."

She reached into her bag and extracted her phone. "I'll make a note on my phone to call Bennett later. See what they found out about this dog walker. I can only assume there was no suspicion, because I'd like to think Bennett would have told me otherwise, but then again…" What did she really know about Bennett's generosity at this stage? About as much as he knew about hers. The prom-ise to exchange new information wasn't going to be easy and they both knew it.

"So what did he tell you?" Jay asked.

Cat looked up from her phone, her heart picking up

speed. "Not much. His reception to my involvement was as frosty as I expected."

He glanced at her. "So going to see him hasn't helped us at all."

Feeling like a fraud but not having any other choice, Cat shook her head. "Not really, but that's okay. We'll do this on our own if we have to, right?"

He nodded and stared ahead. "Right."

A few seconds passed in silence as Cat looked out of the side window. He would've heard the lie in her voice as clear as day. It couldn't be helped. The last thing she wanted was to give Bennett a reason to bar her from the investigation.

Jay coughed. "Do you want to head straight back to the Clover Point now?"

Cat turned. "Soon. Do you think we might grab something to eat and drink first? I ran out of the house—"

"Yeah, you did. Why?"

Heat assaulted her cheeks. His irritation was palpable. She lifted her shoulders, forcing breeziness into her voice. "I couldn't sleep so I went out for a run. When I saw the time, I thought it was easier to get a taxi than wait for you to get showered and dressed."

"Liar."

Damn it. Denying the accusation was futile so she said nothing.

He stared straight ahead. "You were avoiding me. Admit it."

She grappled to find a plausible lie that might have a chance of appeasing him, but couldn't. Jay was the person she'd always struggled the hardest to deceive and now it seemed that, even with all her police training and experience, her poker face was as effective as a toddler lying to her mother.

"Fine. I'm lying. I left because I wanted to do this alone without a big recap about our conversation last night to distract me. Okay?"

He lifted his hand from hers. "I wasn't accusing you of anything. I'm not surprised you don't want to talk about it. I'm just happy you're talking to me at all."

Guilt seared like a brand across her chest. She was more than talking to him. She still suspected him. An overnight think on their conversation had left Cat's sheets knotted around her body from the constant tossing and turning. He'd shared something so painful, so full of misplaced responsibility, that her anger had soon abated and become something worse. Fear. Fear that if Jay was brave enough to tell her his secrets, he would expect her to do the same.

The thought of telling him about the current state of her mum sent chills down her spine. She didn't want his pity and she certainly didn't need him to take on the role of understanding ex-addict. Which was exactly what he'd do. He'd want to help her mum, and Cat. She drew in a shuddering breath and released it.

"Jay, listen to me. There are things—"

"Do not say there are things we all regret. I know you mean well, but I'm a million miles away from platitudes and understanding. I wanted you to know how I let Sarah down and how guilty I feel about not being able to make it up to her. That's it. I don't want your sympathy."

Cat swallowed her confession with difficulty, but managed it. "Right."

"The most important thing is that you know how sorry I am and that I will never ever let anyone down like that again. Not ever. Especially you." Their eyes locked. "Do you understand?"

She nodded. "You'll always be there for me. I get it."

After a moment, his brow smoothed and he smiled. "Good, because now we're back together, Miss Forrester, there's little chance of you disappearing from my life again."

Her heart kicked. "What do you mean back together? We're not back together, we're friends who are looking—"

"If you want something to eat and drink, I know just the place."

Any further words dissolved helplessly on her tongue. She silently berated herself. Coward. Turncoat. Selfish, borderline masochist. Cat fumbled her fingers along the door panel beside her and pressed the button to lower the window. She inhaled deeply. The air was cool against her hot face and slowly her heart rate slowed.

She concentrated on the passing view as Jay maneuvered the car farther along the sunlit promenade of Cowden Beach. The glorious white-gold sand of the beach with its stacked charcoal-gray rocks sent a barrage of memories and emotions from happier times surging to the surface. Smiling, she sat straighter in her seat to watch the kids tossing balls and Frisbees back and forth, dogs running and playing, and couples walking hand in hand along the shore.

Cat turned away as a rush of longing rose inside of her. A longing for days gone by when she was oblivious to the heartbreak of her nearby future.

"Where are we headed?"

"We need a pit stop at Marian's."

Cat smiled. "Ah, the famous Marian."

He turned and winked. "The one and only." His grin was wider than the ocean.

"You really like this woman, huh?"

"I love this woman, and so will you. Guaranteed. She's my savior, the one Dad put me working with when I first came out of rehab. There was no way I was going to stray from the straight and narrow path with Marian watching my every move. Believe me."

Cat snorted. "You sound almost scared of her."

He glanced at her. "Laugh all you want. You haven't met her yet. Once Marian wants something from you, she pulls out one of her lattes with a honeycomb muffin on the side…" He blew out a low whistle. "Then you're hers."

CHAPTER SEVEN

JAY GLANCED AT CAT AS they walked toward the bakery. The distance between them was tantalizingly close but no matter how strong his urge to take her hand, he wouldn't. He meant what he'd said in the car. He had no intention of letting her go or letting her down now they were reunited. It had been hard telling her about his appearance at Sarah's school, the estrangement between them and his ensuing journey down hell's path, but the relief it was out there lifted a ten-ton weight from his shoulders.

His breath flowed easier from his lungs and his optimism soared for the first time in a long time. Cat was still there, and even better, she was talking to him. Anything less and he wouldn't have blamed her. Her silence would have just been another blow he deserved to suffer.

Ten years ago he'd told his mother he'd marry Cat Forrester, and now she was back in the Cove, all his feelings for her came crashing back. From the minute he saw her on the train, he'd struggled to keep his eyes off of her, wondered if he'd ever take her in his arms and kiss her again. It was pathetic and fruitless. He saw the suspicion in her eyes—sensed her distance.

He would be stupid to think or expect differently. At least, for now.

Once they found the real killer, maybe some of the love in her eyes would return. Maybe she would trust him again. Give them a chance. One thing Jay was sure of, he wouldn't let her leave without telling her how he felt. His life would not veer off-kilter in such a massive way, as it had a year after she left. God willing, in time, he'd get his girl and they'd be happy.

Jay smiled as he watched her denim-clad butt sashay closer to the bakery. She made him feel amazing, capable of anything and, more important, capable of making her happier than she ever imagined. Okay, so he hadn't been happy to find the guest bedroom empty when he woke that morning, but since when had Cat ever done anything he'd expected? Never. It was just something else that attracted him to her. Her independence and strength made her sexy as hell.

But now was not the time for dwelling on rekindled love affairs. They had a job to do. Looking around, Jay pondered the lunchtime rush of people that entered Marian's Bonniest Bakery like an endless stream of hypnotized ants. He had no idea how Marian would react to Cat or vice versa. With two women as fiery and strong as they were, it could mean a whole lot of trouble.

When Cat stopped outside the open bakery door, Jay stepped beside her and leaned toward her ear. "Ready?"

She turned and arched an eyebrow. "She's one woman. One woman who runs a seaside bakery that you happen to own. What's the matter with you?"

He huffed out a dry laugh. "I own this place on paper only. Marian runs the show. If I so much as tried to exert my authority, she'd yank down my trousers and spank my ass without giving a damn who saw her."

Her disdainful expression changed as her mouth stretched into a gleeful grin. "I'm liking her already. Seeing your ass being spanked is way up there on my to-do list."

He winked. "Hey, anytime you want to spank it, just shout."

She shoved him playfully. "Very funny. Clearly the woman scares you to death. As for me? I'm used to entering crime scenes. One woman and a bakery aren't going to scare me."

He opened his mouth to protest when her cell phone rang. Lifting a finger to his lips, she pulled the phone from her pocket. "Number withheld." She pressed the talk button. "Cat Forrester."

A dart of concern shot between her eyebrows and her finger slipped from his mouth. Her gaze flew left and right along the street. "You've got my number? What's that supposed to mean? Who is this? Hello?" She snapped the phone shut and fisted her hand into her hair. "For God's sake."

"What's wrong?"

"It's started."

"What has?"

"Our first crank call." She looked around again as though scanning for watching eyes. "I'd better let Bennett know."

"What did he say? I'm assuming it was a man?"

She met his eyes. "Yep, but I very much doubt it was the one we're looking for. It's probably nothing." She paused to look around once more. "What I don't understand is, I haven't advertised I'm a cop and I've only been here two days. If that was Sarah's killer, which I doubt, how the hell does he know I'm here and how did he get my number?"

Not caring whether it earned him another shove, Jay slipped his arm protectively around Cat's waist. "I don't know."

She gave a soft smile. "Hey, I'm used to this sort of

thing. Don't worry about it. The likelihood is he saw me coming out of the station and thinks I'm some kind of specialist Bennett brought in."

"You going to ring Bennett now?"

"Uh-huh." She stepped away from his arm and dialed. After a moment, she shook her head and mouthed "voice mail." She cleared her throat. "Inspector Bennett? Sergeant Forrester. Just had a crank call and thought you should know. Some idiot saying he had my number and I'd be hearing from him again. Clearly, he watches far too many cop shows on TV. The number's withheld but I'm betting it's a throwaway phone of some sort. The voice was muffled, amateurish. No techno stuff. I'll try you again later."

She shut off the phone. "Hopefully Bennett will ring me back soon, but I doubt it will lead to anything." She slipped her phone back into her pocket. "This may well be the first of many, so you can stop looking like you want to punch someone." She smiled. "It wasn't our man, Jay."

Jay stared as he uncurled his hands. His knuckles throbbed. "How can you be so sure?"

She lifted her shoulders. "Instinct. Come on. I can't wait to meet the woman who has you scared of her." She stepped inside the bakery.

Jay shook his head. The woman's spine looked straight enough to snap in two. This wasn't good at all and if she thought for one minute he'd let anyone come within ten feet of her, she was wrong. However, now wasn't the time to tell her he wouldn't be leaving her alone anymore or that he wanted her sleeping in his bed from now on. She'd more likely check into a bed-and-breakfast to prove a point.

He inhaled the smells of freshly baked bread, sugar

icing and fruit jam of every imaginable flavor as they walked farther into the shop.

"Oh. My. God," Cat murmured and pressed her hand to her stomach. "What is that smell?"

He smiled, pushing his concerns to the back of his mind. For now. "That, my dear, is the sweet smell of heaven."

"God above, if I worked here, I'd be rolling back home every night, not walking."

He laughed. "Which is exactly why Dad started me working here after I came out of rehab."

"As punishment?"

"No, because if I could concentrate on work here, I could pretty much concentrate anywhere."

Her green eyes pierced him to the spot. "You really worked here? I thought you were joking. I can't picture you behind the counter in an apron. Whatever you've done."

"Well, you'd better picture it because it's the truth. Marian and George are a phenomenal couple. Between them, they helped save my life."

She pressed a hand to his chest. "Wait. George and Marian are a couple? Wow, the naughty old dog."

Jay would've paid a hundred thousand pounds just to keep her eyes shining the way they were right then. "It all happened after…after your dad died. They got married about five years ago, after meeting each other when George was visiting one of his army pals in Bristol. He came back with Marian and the two of them lived in separate places while they…courted." He smiled. "Got married two years later."

She grinned. "That is so sweet. Well, good for George."

"Exactly. They're funny as hell together but their love is obvious. Nothing gets past them. George took me straight home to my dad after Sarah rang him, and when I came out of rehab, Marian took me under her wing and worked me from the bottom up." He pulled his shoulders back with pride. Her gaze tipped to admiration—a welcome change from the lasers of disappointment they'd shot at him last night. "I swept the floors and baked bread, cleared tables and served behind the counter. It wasn't until I could ice a birthday cake fit for a king that Marian told Dad I was ready to move on to something else."

She grinned. "I love it. Jay Garrett learning the ropes." She looped her arm through his and the contact sent a bolt of electricity straight to his gut. "Maybe I need to repaint my growing picture of you."

"Was it that bad?"

Her smile wavered and she looked away across the shop. "Not bad. Safe."

"What do you—"

"Forget it." Yanking on his arm, she pulled him toward the counter. "Come on, I want to meet my new friend Marian."

Hope vibrated inside him and he tried to keep a handle on it, but her insinuation that she was protecting herself spoke volumes. He smiled. She sensed the renewed attraction between them. How could she not? It was strong enough that neither of them could possibly ignore it.

Almost every one of the eight booths was taken and another ten or so people waited to be served. The cottage-style bakery, with its pine tables and chairs set with navy-and-white gingham napkins and tablecloths, drew people of Templeton Cove like bees to honey. Marian rushed from the ovens to the counter, shouting out good-hearted reprimands to anyone not waiting their turn, while two young girls helped serve.

Cat wore an expression of pure astonishment as she

watched Marian work. Jay's smile stretched to a grin. He knew exactly what she was thinking—how was it possible for someone to move their hands so fast they actually blurred?

"Meet Marian Cohen née Ball," he whispered against her ear.

Cat's smile faltered. "She looks like the mother every kid dreams of."

Jay frowned. She sounded so wistful. The impression he got of the adult Cat was all work and very little play but the hunger in her gaze as she watched Marian had nothing to do with work. She looked envious. No. Sad. Wanting.

"Hey, you okay?"

"I'm fine." The skin at her throat shifted. "She looks friendly enough."

"She is. Sometimes." He shifted his gaze from the top of Cat's head to Marian. "I suppose seeing Marian is a shock for someone who has the mother all the Templeton teenage boys grew up fantasizing about…even if, personally, I was more into the daughter."

"Yeah, well, that was then, this is now. Things change but Marian looks like the type who would stay…I don't know, constant."

He had expected a quick comeback to his teasing, looked forward to the normal, sharp-tongued Cat Forrester response. This reaction was new. Something wasn't right and he was sure that something was connected to Marian's motherly appearance.

She met his eyes. "Did Marian know Sarah, too?"

Jay studied her for a moment longer before facing Marian. "Not like George did, but Sarah came in here as much as everyone else in the Cove."

"They liked each other?"

"Sure."

Her jaw tightened as her stare remained fixed on Marian. Jay followed her gaze. Cat was right. Marian epitomized motherhood. With her steel-gray hair caught up in a net, her ample bosom encased in a floral blouse, flour and vanilla frosting spattered across a once-white apron, she could be every kid's favorite cartoon mum. He glanced at Cat. Why would that put such a look of longing on Cat's face? Julia Forrester idolized her kids, always had.

"Well, good morning, Jay."

Marian's voice broke through the raucous noise of the happy customers. Jay turned. Marian's miss-nothing gaze shot from him to Cat—and lingered. After a long…long moment, she tipped Cat a wink before turning back to the ovens.

Jay smiled. "See? She likes you already."

"Yeah, and she just managed to make me feel more noticed than my mother has in years. Now, what about that coffee and muffin you promised me?"

She walked across the white tiled floor and slipped into a booth by the window, turning her face away from him and Marian to look outside. Jay frowned. What just happened? He remembered Julia openly saying to anyone who would listen that Cat and Chris were the center of her universe—well, after Cat's father, of course.

Now Paul Forrester was dead.…

Was it grief for her father putting that look on Cat's face? Jay berated himself for going on about his dad and not once acknowledging and commiserating with Cat for the horrific way she lost hers the autumn after her last holiday at the Cove. Julia never accepted any of the ensuing invites to come back to the Cove the following three summers. By year four, Jay was missing in action and the families drifted apart.

"I am such a selfish bastard," he muttered.

"Yep, that's simply the way some people are born."

He snapped his head round. Marian grinned at him from behind the counter, her brown eyes shining with undisguised mischief.

"Do you mind?" He closed the few feet between them in four easy strides. "I was having a private conversation with myself."

She gave an inelegant sniff. "Well, I suppose it's better than being lonely." Her gaze left his and moved to Cat. "Who's the girl? She's a looker."

Jay's heart kicked. He couldn't agree more. But he wouldn't give Marian the satisfaction of telling her that—at least, not until he knew what Cat had going on with Julia. He still loved her, but it was based on so much more than a burning attraction. It was based on experience, trust and the simple companionship between them.

He just hoped to God she trusted him as he trusted her and would tell him what was going on back home. He thought his confession about his drug addiction and estrangement from Sarah had slammed the door on any hope of Cat still wanting him, yet every now and then her eyes betrayed something deeper. Something that brought joy to his heart and gave him hope.

"Hey, dreamy-eyed boy. I asked you a question."

Jay started and dipped his head to meet Marian's unwavering gaze. At five foot two, it went against human nature just how intimidating Marian could be. Her deep brown eyes should reflect the softness of her homely figure, but when she wanted answers, Marian's stare belonged in a prison cell eyeing up her roommate.

"She's a friend." Jay folded his arms.

"Friend, my backside. Complete rubbish." She walked around the counter, wiping her floury hands on her apron.

Once she stood in front of him, she opened her arms and Jay wrapped his around her. "Do you know something?"

Jay pulled back and held her hands at arm's length. "What?"

She stared at Cat. "I predict that girl's going to knock you right into shape, Jay Garrett."

He darted an anxious glance toward Cat who was now busy pretending to read the menu as if it was the spiritual guide to eternal peace rather than a list of buns, brownies and beverages.

"Look, do me a favor and let her get settled in before you start with any matchmaking. She only arrived a couple of days ago."

"So? Love is love. Sex is sex. You're a fool if you wait around and let someone else swoop in to take that beautiful girl away."

She might as well have punched him in the gut. The wind left his lungs in a rush. "No one is going to swoop in—"

She grinned. "Got you worried now, haven't I? So this is the girl George hasn't stopped talking about?"

Jay smiled. "Yep."

"George loves the bones of her. Says she's everything to him." She cocked her eyebrow. "Maybe you should stop working 24/7 and concentrate on things a bit more personal."

"I couldn't agree more. I have stopped. Sarah's death woke me up."

Her smile slipped and her eyes turned glassy. "Well, that's good to hear. Life's too short. No one could have predicted that poor girl was in so much trouble. If only I'd known..." Her voice cracked and she quickly tilted her head in Cat's direction. "You going to introduce me to this young lady, or not?"

"If you promise to behave." He took Marian's hand and squeezed. "I wasn't lying when I said she's not my girlfriend. Cat's here in a professional capacity so don't be surprised if she has a few questions for you."

"What sort of professional capacity?"

"She's a detective. She's going to help me find Sarah's killer."

Marian stared at him, her brown eyes wide. "A detective? From out of Templeton? This murder must be messier than we thought if the police are bringing in outside help."

Jay sighed. "They didn't. I did."

"You? Why?"

"Because I had to do something to prove my innocence, that's why."

She frowned. "They still think you've got something to do with this? Even after they questioned you?"

Jay shrugged and exhaled a long breath. "I don't know. I haven't heard anything from them since, but there was something about the way one of the cops looked at me... like he didn't believe a word I said."

She rubbed her hand up and down his arm. "Hey, I believe you. You'd never hurt that girl, not ever."

Jay gave a halfhearted smile. "Maybe you do, but I went through this town on a mission for drugs and little else. Lots of people wouldn't put murder past a guy like that. You know it, the police know it and—" he looked at Cat "—others are most likely thinking it. I've got a horrible feeling the police aren't going to get to the bottom of this for a long time. That isn't good enough. Sarah was a special lady who deserves the best. That's exactly what Cat is."

"The best, huh?"

He turned. "The best. She's a friend from way back.

Her family came here every summer and the three of us hung out together all summer long. She's…"

"I see. And now you're grown-up playmates." Marian winked.

"Will you stop?"

Marian turned to study Cat, her eyes narrowed. "A detective. Well, now I'm more intrigued than ever." She walked toward her.

Jay uttered a curse before following, managing to reach the booth in synch with a now-beaming Marian. He held out his hand. "Cat Forrester, please meet the lovely, if incredibly pushy, Marian Cohen, baker and cake-maker extraordinaire."

When Cat lifted her head from the menu, her smile was in place, but it didn't light her eyes the way it usually did. Her gaze screamed an unexpected insecurity that completely threw Jay off. Whatever Cat meant by referring to Julia earlier, Marian was the catalyst to the new emotion storming in her green gaze now.

"Nice to meet you, Marian." She held out her hand.

Marian brushed the offered hand aside and gestured for Cat to stand. "Come out of that booth, young lady. A handshake is not the way for me to meet one of Jay's new friends."

Cat's gaze darted to Jay's to Marian's and back again as she slid out of the booth. The moment she was out of the booth, Marian enveloped her in a bear hug. Jay grimaced. Cat stood ramrod straight in Marian's arms, her eyes closed.

Jay's mind whirled with questions of what she thought and felt in that moment. Another second or two passed before Marian released her.

"So." Marian gripped Cat's shoulders. "Jay says you're a detective. But knowing him, he's just saying that because he doesn't want me to know you two are courting so I won't tell you what he's really like."

He cleared his throat. "Well, there will be plenty of time for that another day. Right now, we're in and out of here. Coffee needed pronto."

Dropping Cat's shoulders like they were burning rocks, Marian turned on him and fisted her hands on her hips. Jay noticed Cat took the opportunity to slide back into the booth quicker than Marian could blink.

"Excuse me, Jay Garrett?" Marian glared.

He raised his hands. "Fine." He looked past her to Cat. "If we've got any chance of getting out of here this side of Christmas, you need to tell her your national insurance number, address and bra size. Now."

Cat laughed and Jay grinned…until he looked at Marian. Her expression could frighten the birds from the trees. His smiled dissolved. "Cat lives in Reading with her mother. She has one brother and worked her way up the police force faster than anyone else ever could."

Marian turned. "Is that right?"

Cat nodded. "Not so sure I'm the fastest. It's nice of Jay to say so… But for the record, Jay and I are not courting."

"And your father?"

Jay didn't miss the shift of Cat's throat or the flicker of surprise that swept across her eyes. Part of him wanted to stop the interrogation, but he wouldn't. He wanted to hear what she'd say.

"He was killed by a drunk driver seven years ago."

The clang of trays and the hum of conversation surrounding them faded into the background. Jay's heart twisted. Cat had idolized her father. Despite the steady way she held Marian's gaze, the hurt, loss and anguish stormed like an eddy in her eyes. The sudden strike at his gut hitched the instinctive feeling that Cat's pain went deeper than natural bereavement. He sensed much more going on inside her.

Leaning forward, Marian squeezed Cat's hand, which lay frozen on the table. "Well, I'm sorry to hear you've lost your dad, sweetheart. It explains that big old burden you're carrying around."

Cat glanced at Jay before she huffed out a nervous laugh and sat straighter in her seat. "Burden?"

Marian nodded. "All hunched over with it, you are. Oh, you stand tall like Jay but you're both carrying stuff that will end up breaking you down and burying you alive if you're not careful."

A rush of color leaped from the neckline of Cat's T-shirt all the way up her neck. She looked panicked. "I don't know what you mean."

Jay cleared his throat and pulled back his shoulders. Cat needed him and needed him right now. "Marian, come on now. Enough with the questions. What's a man got to do to get a couple of frothy coffees and two honeycomb muffins around here, huh?"

Marian looked at him and arched an eyebrow. "Well, some manners might be a start."

"Please, may we have two of both…to go?"

Cat sprang to her feet as if a bomb had gone off under her perfect behind. "Yes, to go. Perfect."

Marian looked from one to the other, her eyes narrowed. "I'll get your muffins. Hell, I'll get your coffees, but if you two ain't courting, I'm a damn supermodel."

Cat choked out a laugh, her eyes shining. Jay's heart warmed for the first time since they stepped inside the bakery. He fought the urge to smooth the fallen hair back from her face. After a long moment, he turned. Marian still stood right beside them, watching their every move like a tabloid reporter. Jay frowned.

"Coffees?"

Marian sniffed. "In a minute."

Cat laughed again and touched Marian's arm. "I promise you we're not courting. I'm here to investigate Sarah Cole's murder."

"Hmm. That detective inspector what's-his-name is heading up the investigation, isn't he? George and I saw him talking about Sarah on the news last night."

"Detective Inspector Bennett, yes," Cat said.

Marian nodded. "That's right. Bennett. Don't trust him. Beady eyes."

Cat smiled.

"Are you going to find the man who did this?"

The pain on Marian's face scratched at Jay's heart. Sarah had come into the bakery as much as everyone else in the Cove, and when he'd worked the counter, they'd spoken a bare minimum of words, but Sarah and Marian had talked and laughed for half an hour at a time, regardless of the waiting customers.

He slipped his arm around Marian's shoulders and pulled her close. "I brought Cat in to get the job done, remember?"

"Shouldn't you being letting our police deal with it?" She tipped her head back, her worried gaze darted over his face. "Do you know something they don't?"

"No, it's just…" It was just what? Gut instinct? Stupidity? Guilt? He shook his head. "I just know Sarah would've wanted Cat here. We were friends. Close friends. If I couldn't be there for her when someone was choking her life away, maybe both of us can now."

Marian's eyes glazed with tears and she clutched Jay's hand. "You're a good boy. Getting better every day. I knew to keep the faith in you even if everyone else said different. I knew you wouldn't always be such a selfish son of a gun."

Cat's burst of laughter did nothing to appease Jay's affront. He lifted his arm from Marian's shoulders and raised it in surrender.

"Marian, please, can we just have the coffees so I can leave here with at least an inch of male pride left?"

"What? All I'm saying—"

"I know exactly what you're saying and I can't hang around here listening to it all day. Do you know what? I give up. Don't worry about the coffees."

He gripped Cat's hand.

She sucked in a breath. "Jay, what are you doing? Wait."

Jay ignored Cat's protest and marched toward the door. He was trying his hardest to change, to make up for all the mistakes he made and didn't need Marian reminding him of everything he'd done wrong. He wanted a better future for himself, for the Cove, but more than anything, he hated the way the barbed wire ripping through his chest felt strangely like fear. Fear that he hadn't changed. Despite wanting Sarah's death avenged, the truth was he wanted Cat to stay with him like he wanted air to breathe.

Didn't that make him the same selfish man he'd always been?

Anger coursed through him, ignited by panic that Cat would turn away from him like she had last night. His inability to stop that from happening did nothing to lessen his shame.

CHAPTER EIGHT

CAT FLINCHED WHEN JAY slammed her door shut with such force the car vibrated its indignation. She had no idea what just happened but certainly intended to find out the cause of Jay's uncharacteristic U-turn. The driver's door opened and he sank into the seat, exhaling a heavy breath.

"She doesn't know when to stop talking. Never has. Never will."

Cat stared. His jaw was set so tight it could've been sculpted from marble and his shoulders almost reached his earlobes. "What was all that about?"

His eyes stormed with anger. "She never lets me forget the mistakes I've made and despite loving her, it really pisses me off."

"She didn't mean—"

"You don't know her. She means plenty." He glared out the windshield. "She's like that with me and she was like that with Sarah."

He gunned the engine and they pulled away from the curb. Cat frowned. The afternoon was bright and sunny but the atmosphere inside the car was Icelandic. She drew in a breath and released it.

"So that was more about Sarah than you? Is that what you're saying?"

"Yes."

"I don't believe you."

He shot her a glare. "Then don't, but I'm telling you."

Cat laughed. "What's gotten into you? The poor woman was teasing you, that's all. She didn't deserve to have you drag me out of the bakery midconversation. You were singing her praises until five minutes ago."

"Mistake number one, don't think there's anything poor womanish about Marian. She knows everyone in this town inside out, despite only living here five years. She turned that bakery around from making barely enough to warrant it being open to making a damn fortune. She is comfortable and clever."

Cat raised her eyebrows. "Okay…and the place is yours, right? So I'm guessing you should love the lady for making you a nice cut of the profits. What I don't understand is why you just bit her head clean off when all she was doing was trying to find out if we're a couple or not."

"That's not all she was doing." He curled his fingers around the steering wheel. His knuckles turned white. "Later on, I'm going to tell you every damn dirty detail of what I've been up to since coming out of rehab in case someone else gets there first, because they will, believe me. I've upset enough people that as soon as they see me happy, they'll no doubt take acute pleasure in ripping me back down to size."

"I don't understand. What have you done wrong since getting clean?" *What did he mean since?* Unease prickled along the surface of her skin. "You have a great house, drive a flashy car and earned thousands of pounds in profit for your family business. I'd say that's pretty admirable."

"Yeah, but it's business that has taken over my life. I've worked nonstop to the point it could have helped in killing one of my best friends."

Cat stared. Suspicion about the man Jay was now rose

up inside her once again. Dark and unwelcome, her instincts turned to red alert. "What do you mean?"

He glanced at her. "You don't have to look at me like that. I know what I've done. That's not the problem."

Cat swallowed as her blood ran cold. Was he going to confess? Tell her he wasn't entirely honest with Bennett? That there was so much more going on here than a missed assignation? "What have you done, Jay?"

His jaw set as he glared through the windshield. "I let her down. Not once, several times. The last time was the worst. If I'd been at the bakery when she asked—"

"What?" Cat's heart leaped into her throat and lodged there.

His cheeks darkened. "I mean—"

"You said you were there. You said she didn't turn up." Her heart beat hard and her throat drained dry. "Did you lie to me?"

"Yes…no…"

She curled her hands into fists. "Which is it? Yes or no?"

"Look, you're not the only one struggling with the knowledge you should be sharing things, okay?"

"This isn't about me. Don't try to turn this around—"

His jaw tightened. "You've talked about your mum twice and not in the 'I love Julia' kind of way. I want to know what that's about, too, but you haven't expanded on it, have you? Well, I'm having the same trouble with admitting that until the day I found out about Sarah's murder, I was a money-hungry, cold and determined workaholic. I went from drugs to work. Once an addict, always an addict."

"So you thought you'd lie to me about it instead?"

He pulled to a sharp stop at a red light and turned to face her. His eyes were glazed and his jaw set. "Yes. But now, goddamn it, I'll tell you the truth. I'll tell you everything. The question is, Cat, will you do the same?"

She opened her mouth to protest but then slammed it shut as Jay shot the car forward. Emotions waged a war inside her. He'd lied. To her face. In the middle of a murder investigation. Bennett still suspected him. Cat pressed her hand to her stomach. What next? How could she believe a word that came out of his mouth from there on in?

"You lied to me. Actually lied."

"I was scared, okay? Scared you wouldn't come. I'm innocent. I didn't hurt her. I promise."

Cat stared, her heart beating fast. "You tell me absolutely everything you know. Do you hear me? Everything."

He glanced at her, his gaze wandering over her face. "I will. But I want you to do the same. What's going on with Julia?"

His gaze caught hers for a long moment before she snapped her head to the window. "Nothing."

"Right."

The derision in his tone was rife. If she knew Jay at all, he'd find a way of making her talk—like looking at her with those gorgeous brown eyes of his until she told him every damn thing about the mess of her home life. Wait. Gorgeous brown eyes? The guy was a suspect in their best friend's murder and she was thinking about his damn eyes? What was wrong with her? This was Jay's fault. He'd always been able to glide his way into her mind…and body.

Well, not anymore. She was a cop. A detective. There was no way he would slide under her radar if he was guilty. No matter how much she wanted him to be innocent.

The tension inside the car grew. Silence stretched like

an invisible blanket, covering them with its heavy weight. Cat sensed Jay was waiting for her to say something. She would not tell him about her mum. It was none of his business. Sarah was their business. The only business they would ever share. She'd find the killer and then go home. Case closed.

"What's going on, Cat? Talk to me."

She turned, prayed to God her face was impassive. "Mum's fine. I don't know why you think she isn't."

Their gazes locked. The dangerous intensity of Jay's eyes burned into her, pinning her with accusation. He turned back to the road. "Fine. Later I'll tell you about Sarah's phone call and you can tell me about Julia…or not. Entirely up to you."

Cat snapped her gaze back to the side window, hating him for making her afraid to talk, loving him for wanting to listen. "This is about Sarah, not me. You should tell me everything because it's morally right that you do. What I choose to tell you is entirely my decision because it's personal."

Silence burned as distrust grew. How was he supposed to understand that to tell him anything about her mum would mean betraying her? Jay's memories of Julia would be forever tarnished. He still remembered her as the beautiful, generous and model-happy mum who came to the Cove each year. A big part of Cat didn't want that to change, not after everything he'd done to reclaim his life after the horror of addiction. It wouldn't be right to thrust him back into that world.

Sitting straighter in her seat, she cleared her throat. "Let's go to the forest. I want to see where she was found." *And your reaction to being there.*

They traveled the rest of the way to Clover Point in silence. The journey gave Cat the time she needed to get her emotions under control and refocus on the professional challenges ahead. They were about to see where their friend was killed. Would it help the case or just stir up bigger and deeper pain? Either way, she needed to see what Sarah saw, try to get a feeling or a theory about what brought her friend there that fatal day.

Fifteen minutes later, Jay pulled to a stop outside the cabin and they got out of the car. His gaze met hers over the roof.

"Do you want to go straight down there?"

Cat looked down the hill toward the forest and the location of Sarah's murder. "Probably best. No part of me wants to do this, so delaying it will only make it worse."

He gave a sympathetic smile and gestured her to come around the car. "Come on. I'll hold your hand."

She glared. "I don't want you to hold my hand."

"Well, I do, so too bad." He frowned. "Let's get through this part together and then we'll talk about the phone call. No more lies. But, for God's sake, let me be here for you when we do this."

Need for his strength pressed down traitorously on Cat as she walked around the car. She slid her hand into his and it fit like it always did. Their gazes met and as much as she wanted to hold on to her anger, Cat felt it falter. He had to be innocent. He just had to.

Together they began the descent toward the forest. The heat of his skin against hers and the warmth of familiarity hitched her heart. She was walking to the site of her friend's murder with the only man she'd ever loved. The cruelty of it prickled at the back of her eyes.

They walked on, the only sounds the crunch of grass beneath their feet and the cry of the occasional seagull overhead. All too soon they came to a stile separating the edge of Jay's land and the publicly owned forest at its edges. Cat's mind rushed with images of Sarah as a young girl chasing waves and screaming happily along the Cove's sandy beach. Another of them sitting side by side toasting marshmallows on the veranda of the holiday home Cat's family rented every year. Another with Sarah leaning close to her ear and asking if she thought one of them would end up marrying their hunky friend, Jay Garrett.

Sadness threatened and Cat blinked, forcing herself to refocus. "How far in was she found?" Her gaze centered on the thicket of trees in front of them, darker than night and twice as cold.

"A good way," he said, quietly. "I couldn't have seen anything from the house."

She squeezed his fingers. He squeezed back. Drawing in a long breath, she pushed the hair back from her face with a trembling hand. She was angry with him and he with her. More and more, Cat's emotional resources drained away and if Jay was innocent in all this, he deserved so much more than she had to give. Whatever happened, she and he would never work.

"Once we find her killer, we'll both feel stronger."

His quiet confidence whispered between them and Cat met his somber gaze. Her fingers itched to touch his face and her lips suddenly wanted to feel his, warm and soft against hers. She closed her eyes.

"I just wish I'd come back to the Cove before this. Come back to see Sarah…and you. To have you both near me again. Time is so precious."

"Then stay."

She snapped her eyes wide open. "What?"

"Stay after we nail the bastard who did this. Take some time off and spend it with me. I want you here."

She slid her hand from his and turned her back to him

to stare at the forest. "How can you say that to me now? After everything…" Cat crossed her arms and the view blurred as injustice bounced from the trees surrounding them. "I might have wanted you to be more than my one-time lover once upon a time, but that was over seven years ago. Even without Sarah's death, things are so different now. For both of us."

"And because of that, it's wrong to explore what might or might not have happened if you had come back after your dad died? Or if I had come after you?"

She shook her head and prayed the tears in her eyes didn't spill over. "We're both in an emotionally raw state and any attraction either of us might be feeling has a lot more to do with a longing for a time gone by than with anything real or lasting. Our friend has been murdered, it's understandable that we would look to each other—"

"How can you say that?" He came behind her and cupped her elbows. "It's always been us. Time got in the way. The tragedy of your father's death meant you never came back, but neither of us wanted what happened to stop at one night. We're meant to be…"

He stopped and the weight of his chin rested on the top of her head. Cat closed her eyes. A lone tear escaped over her cheek. "We're meant to be what?"

"We're meant to be Cat and Jay. Jay and Cat."

She smiled and swiped at a fallen tear, her heart aching. "That's not enough, and you know it." She turned around and tipped her head back to look into his eyes. She touched her fingertips to his jaw. "Right now is Sarah's time. When this investigation is over, we're going to say our goodbyes and go back to our normal lives, content in the knowledge Sarah can rest in peace, okay?"

His gaze bore into hers before dropping to her lips. "If you think we can really do that, kiss me."

She pulled her fingers from his face and stepped back. "What?"

"I didn't think so. You're more scared of what could happen if we kissed than you are of going in that forest. You're more scared of this feeling between us than you are of catching a killer. I'm innocent, and I don't believe you really think what is between us is so unfounded it can be ignored."

"Jay—"

He held up his hand and nodded toward the forest. "So, let's do this. Let's take this next step to finding justice for a girl who meant so much to both of us. Then maybe you'll be ready to talk about you and me."

Fear, mixed with a strange joy that he still wanted her, skittered along the surface of her skin. Try as she might to quash it, Cat relished its sensation for the briefest time before reality crushed it to dust. Even if he was innocent, he was an addict. How could she contemplate a relationship with an addict when her mum was already destroying every ounce of love in her heart? But knowing she meant something to him mattered so much. She could go back to Reading and replace a little of her self-esteem at least.

As they walked deeper into the forest, the year-round smell of rotting vegetation, pine needles and damp assaulted Cat's nostrils. The second the darkness enveloped them, her cop instincts rushed into her blood, pumping adrenaline through her veins, putting her conversation with Jay to the back of her mind.

Beneath their feet, the foliage grew thick and then sparse in places. Above them, the trees' branches were a near-solid canopy of every shade of green, punctuated by pinholes of bright light from the afternoon sun. Her hand slipped from Jay's as she turned three hundred and sixty degrees. She scanned the circumference.

"Bennett puts the time of death between six and nine in the evening," she said. "It wouldn't have been pitch black in here during that time. It would've been half-light even if it was closer to nine. I can't imagine anyone coming in here at that time of night unless the prize was incredibly worthwhile. Or they were doing something illegal or immoral."

"Or both."

"Exactly." She met his eyes. How much did she tell him? The shaky barrier between them wobbled. She needed to see his eyes, read his thoughts. The only way to curb the ugly thoughts of Jay being capable of murder was to feed him tidbits of information and watch him react. She blew out a breath. "Bennett suggested something about a drug connection, but not in the way we thought. Sarah wasn't using but he thinks she might have been handling money."

He stared, his eyes wide with disbelief. "Drug money? That's no more likely than if she was actually taking the stuff." He fisted his hands on his hips and glanced around. "What the hell had she gotten into, Cat?"

Cat searched his face for that glimmer of knowing, a hint of guilt. Something. Nothing but disgust looked back at her. Jay didn't believe Sarah could be involved in the drug world any more than she did. Or at least, didn't want to.

She followed his gaze. "We have to take this drug connection seriously. First there were the rumors, and now with what Bennett says, it seems as if there could be some truth to them. We have to find out who she knew who used, bought or sold drugs."

Silence. His back was turned and Cat's nerves trembled. "Jay?"

"What?"

"Where did you hang out when you were using?"

He tipped his head back and huffed out a laugh. "Do you know how much I hate hearing you ask me that?"

Cat reached out to grip his forearm. The muscles tensed like twisted rope beneath her fingers. "Jay, look at me."

He dipped his chin. "What?"

"I'm not asking you to insult you or bring back memories you'd rather forget. It's somewhere for us to start, somewhere Bennett might not know anything about. Your experience could give us a head start. I want Sarah's killer found by whomever, but it would be closure for us both if we found him."

"I get that."

"Then tell me. This is a murder investigation. It's not fair to make me feel unable to ask you questions, not when Sarah's killer is out there and you want me to believe your innocence." Guilt scratched at Cat's conscience. Her questions weren't entirely steeped in Sarah but in him, too. But this was necessary. She had to do this.

"Although the possibility grows less and less likely every day, her killer could still be here. I need to ask you about the drugs. It's one of the best leads we have. If the cops are right about Sarah's involvement, you know more about her world than any of them. You've been there."

His face flushed. She didn't like doing this to him but she had to—this wasn't about them as friends…or lovers. The tension was palpable and the sudden insane urge to lift onto her toes and kiss him flooded through her, negating her previous thought. Her gaze fell to his lips. She wanted to take away his pain and him hers.

"Jay—"

His mouth came down on hers so roughly she staggered back, his arms wrapping around her waist, thick and strong. Just for a moment she'd let this happen. She closed her eyes and drank him in as if he were an oasis in the desert. His tongue found hers and together they grappled for supremacy, for a demonstration of who controlled the kiss. She dug her nails into his wide muscular shoulders, holding on to him like a lifeline.

A low guttural moan escaped from deep within him, vibrating into her mouth, making her shudder and cling harder. His skin smelled masculine and true and entirely Jay. She breathed him in, kissed him and held him before gasping for breath as they parted.

She stared. His eyes were wide and hungry, his mouth reddened. Cat pushed her hand through her hair, holding it there.

"That was…that was…"

"Necessary." He laughed.

Cat smiled, looked to the ground. "And entirely inappropriate."

Their gazes held for a long moment. "The last thing I want is to hurt you, Jay. This is going to be hard. The whole process. I'm here to catch her killer. Our emotions can be dealt with when we have him, or her, locked up. In the meantime, we push whatever is happening between us to the background. We have to."

"Maybe."

He walked forward, pulling her deeper into the forest. Cat shuddered out a heavy breath. They were both surviving, no matter their different stories. That's what the frenzied intensity of that kiss said to her and she could deal with that if she remained focused. So why then was she looking at him from the corner of her eye and wondering when they'd kiss again?

CHAPTER NINE

THE RUSTLE OF THE LEAVES above them and the snap of twigs beneath them serenaded Cat and Jay's progress into the forest. Eventually the air was punctuated with what Cat recognized as the flapping of police tape as it rose and fell on the increasing breeze. They came to a standstill. Both staring ahead, Cat sensed Jay's heart beating as painfully as hers.

The scene had been swept for DNA, Sarah's body taken, leaving behind the remnants of a police investigation by way of trampled bracken and the eerie silvery-white remains of fingerprint dust. Nothing else was there to reveal the horror that took place. Everything was still and quiet except the crudely cut, bright yellow tape snapping and pulling from the four huge oak trees to which it had been tied. Their trunks stood like corner markers around the spot where Sarah's young life had been cut brutally short.

Cat trembled. Jay's arm felt heavy when it slipped across her back; his fingers clasped her shoulder, firm and secure.

"What was she doing here?" she whispered. "It's so damp. So cold."

He didn't answer and she hadn't really wanted him to. She focused on what clues the seemingly empty crime scene could provide. It would provide. They always did.

She narrowed her gaze, centered her mind. "Is coming

through the meadow from your house the only way into the forest? Or is there—"

A child's playful shouting cut through the tense and macabre silence. Cat jumped and cold sweat burst onto her forehead. "My God, are kids allowed in here?" She whirled out from beneath his arm and turned toward where the incongruous sound came. "This isn't a freaking playground."

"It's fenced off. They can't get in here."

"Are you sure? That scream sounded close."

He came to stand beside her and gestured in the same direction. "The other side of the forest backs onto a holiday park, remember? You, Sarah and I used to sneak in there to play on the zip wire and climbing frames."

"Tetherton Holiday Park? That's where those kids are?"

"Yep."

"Jesus. He didn't care, did he?"

"Who?"

"Whoever killed Sarah. What are we? A hundred, two hundred yards from the park?"

He took a couple of steps forward and pointed in the opposite direction. "Over that way is near the outskirts of Funland. That's why I'm convinced someone must have seen something."

Cat looked around. "This couldn't have been the first time Sarah and her killer came here. When I spoke to Bennett, he said there haven't been more than half a dozen phone calls from people offering information. None of then added substance to their enquiries. This is a holiday spot. It's August, and when you have a highly publicized murder like this, people remember things. Especially when something happens when they're away from their home towns. Parents are more alert. They watch their kids more, stay together in family groups."

He planted his hands on his hips and looked first toward the holiday park and then Clover Point and then Funland. "You're right. There are three possible ways into the forest and whichever way Sarah came, she came in willingly and without a fight."

Cat studied him. His brow was furrowed in concentration, his eyes clear. No trace of anything but determination showed in his face. "I think she knew her killer, Jay. I think people were used to seeing them together."

"Like a couple."

Their eyes met and Cat nodded.

"She had to have been seeing someone." His excitement at an imminent step forward lit a flare in his gaze and with it the mistake so many rookie cops made on their first few cases—and so many parents made when their kids went missing. A link. An anchor. Something to hold up and say, "We've got something. We're going to catch you."

"Don't get your hopes up." She sighed. "If there was no boyfriend, it could've been a friend, an associate... anyone she knew, really." *You.*

He lifted his shoulders. "Maybe. But it's more likely she came here because she was seeing someone out of bounds. A married man, a school governor, even a parent of one of the kids she taught. It makes no sense to meet a *friend* in a damn forest."

Cat watched him, waited to see if he noticed the accusation in her tone. Waited to see if he turned away from her, opened the distance between them. He did neither. She drew in a breath, released it. "You're right, it doesn't, but until we know why she came here, we have to keep our minds open to every possibility. Every scenario. We assume nothing at this point, okay?"

"But Sarah didn't have enemies. Everyone loved her.

She was known for her generosity, her affinity with the kids, her patience."

"Yes, but she had her limits." She met his gaze directly. "She didn't want to see you for close on four years, remember. Sarah knew her mind and stuck to what she believed was right."

He narrowed his eyes and then his cheeks darkened. "Got it."

The silence stretched until Cat looked away, hating everything about the situation. The distrust between them and the fact that someone had taken their friend's life hung like an evil barrier between them. She moved away and stared around the forest.

"I think she was trying to help whoever killed her. Trying to help them out of some sort of trouble. Why else meet in such a place? Why else call you after all this time? She must have needed you. Saw no one else she could turn to that she trusted. Sarah most likely knew that, despite your estrangement, you were the only one she could rely on."

"Which means I could possibly know this person, too."

"Or the whole town could." She turned to face him and adrenaline started its familiar hum in her blood. Once she and Jay talked about him not telling Bennett about Sarah's call, Cat hoped the threads keeping her grounded in suspicion of his guilt would snap. She wanted him fighting to find this killer right beside her, in the inner circle rather than the outer.

She cleared her throat. "You're right. Sarah was a popular teacher, yet she arranges an assignation where no one will see them…or her friend does. I think whoever killed her is known in Templeton. Known and possibly liked. Sarah was protecting them."

"And doing so got her killed." He squeezed his eyes shut. "If it turns out I know her killer, I'm going to…"

He opened his eyes and their gazes locked. Anger stormed in the deep brown depths of his eyes and a muscle jumped at his jaw. Cat gripped his forearm and the muscles tensed beneath her fingers.

"You're a good man, Jay. There's nothing you could have done to help her, because you knew nothing…right?"

Lifting her hand from his arm, he took her hands and pulled her into the tight circle of his arms. Cat stiffened. Was he hiding his eyes from her? She inhaled a deep breath and the comforting scent of him weakened her stupid feminine resolve. She leaned into him, surrendering to the welcome feel of his masculine strength around her and the broad flat width of his chest against her cheek.

Her breath whispered across his T-shirt. "This is going to get worse before it gets better, you know."

"What is?" he asked, softly. "Looking for Sarah's killer or us?"

Cat pulled up straight. His eyes shone in the half-light and her heart pulled to his. "Both. It's both going to get worse."

He brushed some fallen hair from her face. "I can handle it if you can."

Before Cat could respond, he dropped lips that tasted of sweetened strength and burgeoning belief to hers. Moaning, she kissed him back and wondered what the hell to do next. How was she supposed to keep accusing him? Wondering? Suspecting? His lips moved against hers, the pressure increasing and she didn't fight him. She wanted this. Wanted to believe him an innocent and good man.

It hurt like hell that she couldn't.

She eased back. "Jay, not here. Not now. We have work to do."

He raised his hands in surrender. "You're right. I'm sorry."

She nodded and turned away before she pulled him back to her. "Okay, well, first I want us to comb this entire area. I don't doubt the police have done a thorough job, but until I know we've checked every square foot of this marked space and beyond, I won't be happy."

He drew in a heavy breath behind her. "Then let's get started."

NIGHT HAD FALLEN AS Cat strode through the patio doors of Jay's cabin and onto the vast wooden veranda stretching its width. She walked to the surrounding balustrade and crossed her arms tightly around her torso. The forest in the distance drew her gaze and her mind's eye once again filled with images of Sarah's smiling, happy face. Then those images merged with the photos pinned crudely on the incident board at the police station.

Instinct reared hot and heavy in her stomach as the suspicion she'd had earlier gathered strength. Sarah knew her killer. Cat was sure of it. The problem was, in a place like Templeton Cove, where everyone seemed to know everyone, how did she start to narrow down possible suspects and eliminate Jay?

She tipped her head back and squeezed her eyes shut. Growls of anger and whimpers of fear reverberated in her head. Time and again, since they'd scoured the crime scene, Cat could almost hear the murmur of Sarah's final conversation. Although by no means psychic, more often than not Cat sensed a victim, felt their final moments ring with fear and loathing in her brain.

This time she sensed a man more than a woman with her friend. Sarah knew him either intimately or maybe he was someone she'd known since childhood. She felt their connection, felt her friend's desperation to be heard. Unable to hear what they said or even the timbre of their voices, Cat forced her brain to the sounds and emotions coming from Sarah and her faceless companion. Nothing but a barrage of white noise and the thundering of Cat's blood came through.

She opened her eyes and shivered. Purposefully turning her head from the forest, Cat concentrated her gaze on the blinking lights and neon signs of the Templeton Cove town center in the distance. It looked beautiful. The picture-perfect holiday destination for fun and frolics, good times and laughter, yet even the soft warm breeze drifting over her skin did nothing to appease the tension aching at the base of her neck—or lessen the knowledge that a seaside town could prove just as dangerous as an urban town like Reading.

She gripped the balustrade. Thoughts of Jay asking her to stay, asking her to find out if anything still lingered between them mixed with everything else on her mind. She couldn't deny that something still burned hotter than fire between them. It had shot through her heart like an arrow the moment she'd realized it was him on the train. He was her friend, the person who lifted her, believed in her. Every summer she willed her father to press harder on the car accelerator so she could get closer to Jay's smile, his spirit, him.

When she left that final summer before her father died, neither she nor Jay followed up with the other. Neither made sure they didn't lose what they had. What did that say about their relationship? Did it mean any love they had wasn't real? Or that they were both stupid enough to let a one-time love slip through their fingers? Cat swallowed. They'd been stupid. Both of them. Now their lives were tainted with addiction. Jay's in the past. Hers in the present. The stain ran deep.

Her gaze returned to the forest. Looking back provided little more than a rose-tinted memory of Templeton and a rose-tinted memory of Jay. They were all grown up now and if she proved his innocence in Sarah's murder and they tried to start anew, this time it wouldn't be a one-time thing. She'd want it for life or he'd break her heart. It wasn't her fear he wouldn't want the same, it was the knowledge he would that frightened her.

Sarah would never enjoy another summer in Templeton—so why should she? Was her dearest friend any guiltier of keeping secrets and telling lies than she and Jay were? No. So Cat would return home and help her mum. Once she was in recovery, maybe things would change.

She swiped at her cheek and shot a glance in the direction of the patio doors. Jay had left the kitchen. Damn it. He could be watching her from an upstairs window for all she knew. Could have seen her wiping her face and known she cried. She turned back to the vista ahead and straightened her shoulders. He couldn't see her weakness. He would want to swoop in and fix her, wipe her tears and kiss her lips.

She wasn't handling her life well, buckling beneath the weight of her inability, and Jay was an available, desired release. She had to resist him no matter what. Yet she came to the Cove to solve a murder as well as spending time being the old Cat. The Cat with a mother who cared for her, who didn't drink…who knew when her daughter was sad and lonely. She was away from home and responsibility and, God help her, she'd relished the raw need in Jay's eyes in the forest. Enjoyed the way he looked at her like she was a real woman. Not a savior or prop but a real bona fide woman whom he wanted to take to bed and taste every part of.

Didn't she have the right to feel human, loved and desired? Even for a while?

The ringing of her cell phone startled her and Cat pulled it from her back pocket without looking at the display. Her hand shook. She'd fight her feelings for Jay. There was no alternative.

"Hello?"

"Good evening, little sis. How's it going?"

Cat shot back to reality like a bullet from a gun. All thoughts of Jay obliterated. "Chris."

"The one and only."

Cat glared. Had she ever sounded so damn chipper when looking after their mum?

"Well, don't you just sound fine and dandy," she said dryly.

He laughed. "So? Is that bad?"

"Yes, it's bad. What have you done with Mum? Taken her to the Severn bridge and tossed her over?"

"Well, isn't that nice. Don't you trust me?"

She ignored his question. "Why are you so happy? What's going on? Do I need to come home?"

"Will you stop? Mum's fine…well, coherent anyway."

Cat closed her eyes as her pulsed throbbed at her temple. "Great. I suppose you're getting a feel for how hard it is now, right?"

"Uh-huh."

Cat blew out a breath as his silent apology whispered down the line. "I've been doing my best to keep her sober for the last six years since you moved out. It's not easy, is it?"

"No, but I'm here now."

She stared toward the forest. "It hurts to hear you smiling through this, Chris. It makes me feel…useless."

"You're not useless. You're amazing. These past three days have been hard, Cat, and I've only just got here. I think you're amazing and you've done your best…which doesn't make what I'm going to say next any easier."

Cat turned her back to Jay's land and stared at the house instead. She pursed her lips together, scared to say more, scared her brother would sense just how lost and helpless she felt. Or how, deep down, she burned with envy for his happiness, his future and his whole damn life.

"Are you there?" Chris's exhalation rasped against her ear.

"Yes."

"Mum is in the grips of something neither you nor I can help her with. When I checked in with you from time to time, you never said things were this bad. Why? Did you think you could fix this alone?"

Cat clenched her jaw. "Of course I didn't. She begged me. Begged me not to tell anyone, including you. She drinks, then she sobers up, then she drinks some more. It's a damn roller coaster and when you look after an alcoholic you love, you'll do anything to protect whatever scrap of dignity they have left. It's not black-and-white."

"I know that. At least, now I do."

"You've come in at the tail end." She shook her head. "When you look at Mum now, you're seeing the now-or-never moment. Alcoholism happens so slowly, you barely notice it until one day you come home from work to find your mother asleep in her own vomit."

Silence. Cat screwed her eyes shut and willed her racing heart to slow. Everything she'd held in check poured out. All the hurt, the pain, the disappointment, the helplessness rolled around and around and flew from her mouth in a ball of desperation. She bit back a sob.

"I want a life. I want to find someone like you have. Want to plan my own wedding one day."

"And it makes me happy to hear you say that, because that's what I want for you, too. There's no right or wrong way for either of us to handle this. Mum needs to be in rehab."

Cat pressed her fingers to her closed lids. "I don't think I can abandon her. Not after all these years of trying to get her sober."

"You think you're abandoning her? Come on, Cat. You're a cop. You know there are situations best left to the professionals. That damn pride of yours is getting in the way of what's right for Mum."

She opened her eyes and drew in a shaky breath. Jay was walking around the open-plan kitchen, clearing up their dinner of takeout Chinese. She probably had fifteen minutes, tops, before he came outside.

"Look, I can't get into this right now. I'm not down here on holiday. I'm trying to find out who killed one of my best friends. Sarah was—"

"Sarah. Damn it, where's the letter?"

Cat frowned. "What letter? What are you talking about?"

"Hold on."

Crunching and shuffling of what sounded like papers being tossed aside filtered through the line.

"Chris, what are you doing?"

"Got it."

"Got what?"

"The letter I assume is from Sarah."

"What?" Trepidation dropped like a stone into Cat's

stomach. She turned her back to the house and gripped the balustrade. "You've got a letter from Sarah? But—"

"It's postmarked four days before you left, and as you've been speaking to Jay on the phone for longer than that, I knew it wasn't from him. I'm assuming Sarah wrote it before she died."

"That means someone had it for a week before mailing it. Open it right now and read it to me."

CHAPTER TEN

CHRIS CLEARED HIS THROAT theatrically, and Cat rolled her eyes. Her nerves were stretching to breaking and her pulse hammered with trepidation. Sarah had written her.

"Dear Cat," Chris read. *"This is Sarah. It's been far too long since we've spoken and now this silence is something I can't believe either of us allowed to happen. You are my best friend. Always have been. But so many things have happened over the past seven years I can't begin to explain everything in a letter.*

"I need to see you, Cat. Desperately. I'm in trouble. Big trouble.

"I know it's wrong of me to expect you to help me after all these years of no contact, but please, please come to the Cove. Things are escalating at a rate I can no longer control and I'm scared. Scared that by the time you read this letter, I'll be dead."

Chris stopped and sucked in a breath. "Oh, my God. She knew, Cat. She knew someone was after her."

Cat squeezed her eyes shut and pressed her hand to her stomach. "Keep reading, Chris. Don't stop until the end." She glanced toward the cabin. Jay met her gaze and she waved. He waved back and then continued cleaning up.

Chris cleared his throat once more. "Okay, where was I? Ah, right. Okay. *Once I have finished writing this letter, I will make a final bid to change things. To stop you*

*being involved. But right now, I don't know who else he'll
listen to. You are my last hope.*

*"I am praying that between us, we can convince him
he has to give himself up and stop the madness.*

"Drugs are an evil, evil thing, Cat. They ruin lives.

*"For now, I'm just begging you to come. I've taken
fifty thousand pounds of his money as ransom. He has
to listen to me. He has to. He has to stop what he's doing.
With his money gone, I hope he understands my desperation. I've hidden it on Cowden Beach. When you get here
I will tell you where and my lover's name. It's too dangerous to tell you now.*

*"I love him so much, I'd leave the Cove tomorrow for
him, Cat. I want us to get married, have a family.*

*"But if I'm dead when you get here, it's imperative you
find the money. I've left his name with it as evidence. He
told me he would kill me. He has to face a trial if he takes
my life. I love him, but my parents deserve to know I still
believed in justice despite the stupid decisions I've made
in the name of love. If I'm dead, it's my lover who killed
me. I love you, always, Sarah."*

The seconds beat hard in Cat's head as silence hummed
down the line. After a long moment, she heard Chris draw
in a heavy breath. She opened her eyes as thoughts and
scenarios ran riot in her head. Sarah must've been so
scared. Confused. Ashamed. Alone. Not knowing which
way to turn. Who was this man? This lover? She'd known
he would kill her. She had actually known her life was
in danger.

"Cat, are you still there?" Chris asked.

"I'm here."

"What are you going to do?"

What was *she going to do?* "I don't know. I need to
think. Look after Mum, okay? I'll call you."

"Cat…"

"I'll call you." She snapped her phone shut and stared out into the night.

Sarah had written Cat the same day she'd asked Jay to meet her…the same day she'd died. Regret sped Cat's heartbeat, and helplessness crawled over her shoulders. It was likely that Sarah would've phoned her, too, if she'd had an up-to-date number to call. An old-fashioned letter had been her terrified friend's only option because of the years that spanned silently and unnecessarily between them.

Somehow they had allowed contact to waver. If they hadn't… Cat shook her head. She couldn't go there.

Jay. Jay was an addict. Sarah mentioned drugs. Wanting to marry this man. Was it Jay? Was Jay her lover? Revulsion knotted her stomach and Cat sucked in a breath against the pain that slashed her heart. No. Tears burned her eyes. She couldn't think that. She wouldn't allow herself to think that until she was forced to.

Her heart beat painfully as she stared blindly ahead. Jay…

Cat shook her head. *Focus. Focus on the facts.* What had caused the delay in mailing the letter? Why had it not reached the mailbox until over a week later?

Cat closed her eyes. God, this was hopeless.

Was Sarah's lover a close friend or colleague? Jay? Or someone neither of them knew? Sarah had wanted this mystery person to leave Templeton Cove with her, but was it for his safety rather than love? Cat gripped the phone tighter.

Their friend had called out for her and Jay, and they'd failed to get there in time. The cop in Cat told her that was no coincidence. Was her killer possessive enough—

or guilty enough—that keeping Sarah's best friends at a distance had been his most important mission?

Cat stared out into the darkness. If the killer found out about the letter, he could have intercepted it. A paper trail could be followed. Did he send it anyway, making a huge and vital mistake? What happened that day, a week later?

Questions whirled in a kaleidoscope inside her head and a slow ache pulsed at her temple. She raised her eyes to the millions of stars above and counted her breathing. In for three, out for five, in for three, out for five. She stared at the breathtaking phenomenon of the Templeton Cove sky at night. A blanket of black velvet punctured with stars and a crescent moon, bright and dazzling white, a magical scythe close enough to touch.

She lifted her hand as though intending to pluck it right out of the sky.

"You'll never catch one."

Jay's voice seeped into the silence, deep and smooth.

"Hey, you, what took you—" Her heart lodged in her throat, cutting off her words and a wave of violent nausea lurched in her stomach. He stood in silhouette, holding two bottles of wine by their necks in one hand and the stems of two glasses in the other. Two bottles of wine. Her gaze went from his face, to the wine and back again.

Someone with Jay's addictive background shouldn't be drinking. The fact he had two bottles was a pretty clear indication he didn't have any intention of stopping at one.

"What are you doing?" Her mind raced as goose bumps erupted on her arms. Why hadn't she considered that Jay might not take drugs anymore but could easily be using something else as a crutch? The counselor had warned her about the same outcome if her mum ever became ready for treatment.

He stopped. "What's wrong? Why are you looking at me like that?"

Raging disappointment gathered momentum and burned like acid in her stomach. "Like what?"

"Like I'm about to attack you or something." He stepped into the amber light cast by the glow of the lamps dotted around the veranda. His teasing smile dissolved. "My God, are you crying? What happened? I saw you on the phone—"

"Why have you got wine? Was the water you served for the last two nights a way to lull me into a false sense of security? Now I've been with you awhile, now you've kissed me in the damn forest, you think it's okay to get hammered?"

"What?"

She dipped her head toward his hands. "The bottles, Jay. The *two* bottles."

"These?" He held them up. "It's these making you look at me as though I'm Freddy Krueger?"

"Yes. It's exactly that."

His shoulders slumped and his brow creased. "Cat, you're going to have to help me out here." He stepped closer and she stepped back. His eyebrows lifted. "What have I done? I thought we could have a glass or two under the stars, that's all."

She swallowed against the lump in her throat and wiped her fingers beneath eyes that wouldn't stop running. Raw, biting hurt hummed over the surface of her skin as she stared at him. What was she supposed to say? How was it fair she'd left behind one addictive personality only to travel hundreds of miles to be faced with the same thing in Jay?

Her initial anger seeped from her bones, leaving her defeated and weak, emotions she felt all too often around her mum. "Should you really be drinking?" She quietly slipped back into the familiar, if unwelcome, role of addict support.

His frown deepened. "Should I be drinking?" His jaw tightened. "I don't drink. The real stuff is for you and the fake stuff is for me."

Cat started. "One of those is non-alcoholic?"

"Uh-huh."

Her breath left her lungs in a rush and she covered her face with her hands. "God, I'm sorry. I'm such an idiot. I thought…"

He stepped close and pulled her hands away. "You are an idiot, but you're my idiot, so it's okay. I've been sober a long time and I'm never going back down that road, so you can relax."

"I'm sorry. I shouldn't have jumped to conclusions like that."

He smiled. "Don't be. I love that you care enough to want to slice my balls off if I ever touch anything again."

Relief swelled her heart with love and respect for him. She looked into his gorgeous brown eyes and his sincerity stared back at her in all its cocoa-colored glory.

"Still, I had no right—"

"Enough with the apologies, Sergeant Forrester. I imagine clearing up Friday night drunkards makes most cops a little edgy around alcohol. You're entitled to a little wariness."

She dropped her gaze to the planks of wood at her feet. "Exactly."

Seven years ago she couldn't hide anything from him and feared the same would be true again. Jay knew her like she knew herself and in a life partner that was a good thing…but in a friend you'd soon say goodbye to, it wasn't.

Getting anything but the truth past him made her feel like a rabbit trying to get past a bloodhound.

"Hmm."

She looked up. The concentration in his gaze as he studied her stripped Cat bare and heat warmed her face. "What?"

"It's more than the wine, isn't it?" He leaned his body toward the small bistro table beside them. The bottles and glasses clinked against its wrought-iron surface as he set them down.

His gaze returned to hers. "Well?"

Panic thumped in her ears. She couldn't tell him about her mum. She couldn't let him know what she was dealing with at home. Shame twisted like a tornado inside her after all the admiration he'd bestowed on her. Guilt that sometimes, like right then, she wanted to run home, far away from him, and deal with her mess without having to look at him and see the desire for her to want him in his eyes. She needed to sort out her personal problems herself. Help her mum recover herself.

They weren't together. They were separate. One a cop, the other a suspect.

No more Cat and Jay. No more Jay and Cat.

"Cat?" His gaze bore into hers.

"It's just… I can't." She blew out a breath. "Can we talk about Sarah? That's the most important thing right now."

He stared for a moment longer before walking to the table and sitting. When he reached for the wine, Cat joined him at the table. "Non-alcoholic for me, too."

His gaze lingered on hers, intense but kind. "Hey, you can drink around me, you know. I don't mind."

She struggled to keep her gaze steady with his. "I know that. I just don't like alcohol. I'd prefer the non-alcoholic stuff."

He shrugged. "Sure."

He filled their glasses and they drank, their gazes locked above the rim. He winked, sending Cat's stomach into a violent frenzy of lust and longing. Their kiss at the forest had been sensational, her body willing to take the moment so much further. It had been scary and right all at the same time. She'd had lovers, occasional as they were, but nobody came close to causing the barrage of physical sensations inside her Jay had—and did.

Her gaze wandered over his handsome features, the smooth curve of his jaw, down over the strong masculine neck to the solid ridge of his shoulders. The sight of him pushed an unexpected lump into her throat.

"You've done well for yourself," she said quietly. "I'm proud of you."

He smiled and took her hand. When he lifted it to his lips, Cat watched him press a lingering kiss to her knuckles. "Thanks."

They fell into silence and he looked out over the veranda. His face relaxed in thought. She took a sip of her wine with her free hand, wanting him to keep hold of the other. If he held her, she couldn't run away. They might well have a significant lead to Sarah's killer with her letter, it might be the thing to clear Jay from her professional wariness and into the realm of innocence she hankered for.

All too soon she'd return to Reading where her mum needed her and when she left, she didn't want it to be with him in handcuffs.

As time passed, who was to say her heart wouldn't become his again? Her passion for him was growing at a rate so fast it made her head spin and her common sense seep from her pores on a sea of hopelessness. He turned and lowered his glass to the table.

"So, do you want to tell me who was on the phone?" The concern in his voice brushed over her skin like silk. "Is everything all right?"

Putting her glass on the table, Cat shook her head, refocused. "No. No, it's not."

He frowned. "What's wrong?"

"I was talking to Chris."

"And?"

Cautiously, she ran her gaze over his face, prepared for a reaction she hoped she didn't see. "He had some news for me. News that puts Sarah's death in a clearer light in some ways, a dimmer light in others."

He leaned forward. "What do you mean?"

"Sarah wrote me a letter the day she was killed. It wasn't postmarked until a week after she died." She stared. "Do you know anything about that?"

"What?"

She held his gaze. "Do you know anything about a letter?"

His hand slipped from hers and he pushed to his feet. He stared down at her, his gaze intense in the semidarkness. "I don't believe it."

"What?"

"You really suspect me, don't you? You really think I could kill Sarah."

"Jay—"

He raised his hand. "Don't, Cat. Just don't."

Anger and defensiveness burst behind her rib cage. "You lied to me, Jay. What else am I supposed to think? We have been together all afternoon and you've made no attempt to tell me what happened with Sarah at the bakery. Were you hoping I'd forget about it?"

He glared. "Of course not."

"So what is it you expect me to believe? You were the

last person she contacted. I need something from you to prove it's impossible you could have killed her. I need you to prove it to me so I can draw a line through you as a suspect. You cannot expect me, a cop, to believe you just because you ask me to."

"I'm not asking *the cop* to believe me, Cat. I'm asking *you*."

She shook her head. "No, you don't get to do that."

"Do what?"

"Play the emotional card. You give me facts. You start being honest with me. I want to know what happened. I want to look at you and know you're telling me the truth. How am I supposed to do that when you haven't told me what happened that day?"

Their breathing sounded loud in the quietness of the night. The sky felt closer and the forest darker. How would they ever get past the brutal murder of their best friend? Cat clenched her jaw and waited. He would answer her question or face the real brunt of her wrath because right then she had no other way to look than at the person she still loved despite seven years of pretending she didn't.

He raised his hands in surrender. "I stupidly thought the explanations could wait until after we'd found the real killer. I stupidly thought you'd know I would never hurt Sarah and that Bennett was a moron for wasting time on the wrong damn person. Clearly I was wrong."

She glared. "Yes, you were. So let's get it out there. Why didn't you tell Bennett about Sarah calling you? And why didn't you meet her as she asked you?"

The seconds beat like minutes, the tension heavy and tense between them.

Jay exhaled and his shoulders slumped. He pulled out his chair and sat. "I didn't tell Bennett about the call because our exchange when he questioned me wasn't the most productive conversation between an inspector and a civilian, that's why." He picked up his drink. "The guy is an arrogant prick."

"All cops are to a suspect when they want answers. Wait until you see me questioning someone I don't like the look of."

The glass halted at his lips, his gaze darting over her face. "Is that what he said? He didn't like the look of me?"

"Not in so many words, but I can tell he's got you down as a spoiled rich kid. How much trouble did you give him when you were using? You might want to cut him a little slack if that's the only impression he has of you."

He drained his glass. "I didn't give him any trouble."

Cat lifted her eyebrows. "Are you sure about that?"

He scowled. "Yes, I'm sure. Anyway, I had nothing to tell him. He gave me a look like he didn't believe me and he left even though I gave him my alibi."

"And what if Bennett still suspects you and brings it up in my face again?"

"He can't suspect me. He hasn't been back here. I'm clear."

Cat swallowed knowing he was far from being in the clear as far as Bennett was concerned. Jay was the only suspect the police had—and that made him more vulnerable than he could ever understand.

"Where were you, Jay? More important, who were you with?"

His jaw tightened. "Working."

Unease prickled the hairs at the back of her neck. "At eight o'clock at night?"

"Yes."

She closed her eyes and counted slowly to five to get her racing emotions under control. In her heart she felt Jay's innocence but it wasn't enough. She had to know for sure. He met her gaze and Cat's heart ached to see the despair, guilt and loss there. "Jay?"

"Sarah was at the bakery when I was supposed to meet her. I was late because I was working. I'm always working. That night I was with four visiting executives. I gave Bennett their names and assumed he'd follow up with them for their statements. Why wouldn't he? He cannot ignore four people." His gaze dropped to her lips, sad and full of regret. "It's what Marian meant when she said she believed I could change when others don't. I craved work like I craved drugs. I let Sarah down because of work and I'm going to know that for the rest of my bloody life. I didn't tell Bennett about the phone call because I felt like crap, Cat. Even with the alibi, I was possibly the last person she spoke to, and I'm a drug addict. I ran scared. I'm an idiot, but, my God, it's why I rang you. I needed you because you're a cop and I knew...or at least thought I did, that you'd know I'd never hurt her. Ever."

He pushed to his feet so abruptly his chair clattered to the floor behind him. With a final look at her, Jay turned and stormed into the house. Cat stared after him. This was a murder investigation and he'd lied to her. She shouldn't trust him. So why did she want to go into the house, put her arms around him and promise him she'd fix this? She'd fix everything.

She leaned her elbows on the table and dropped her head into her hands.

What was she supposed to do next? She longed to wave a magic wand and make everything okay again. God, she'd do anything to bring Sarah back to them alive and well. But she couldn't do that any more than she could take Jay's words or anger as proof he was innocent of any wrongdoing. She was a cop. She needed proof, no matter what her heart wanted to believe.

She lifted her head and stared at the patio doors through which Jay had disappeared. She was also the daughter of an alcoholic, an addict. That had taught her more about disappointment, broken promises and lies than even her years in the police force could. Inhaling a long breath, she stood and slowly walked toward the cabin. One way or another, Jay had to understand her head and her heart. Only then could they move forward for Sarah—and each other. Together or apart, Cat would not allow her feelings for Jay to sway her decision making, personally or professionally.

Addicts lied, addicts swore they'd changed but so rarely did. If Jay wanted her trust, he would have to prove himself to her in more ways than he could ever understand.

CHAPTER ELEVEN

WHEN CAT WALKED INSIDE, Jay was sitting on the couch with his head in his hands. Pulling back her shoulders, she slowly approached and sat beside him. The ticking of the wall clock sounded loud in the pregnant silence. His cologne teased her nostrils and she inhaled.

"I want to believe you didn't kill her, Jay. I want that more than anything."

His hands slipped from his face and he turned to look at her. His forearms stayed on his thighs, his shoulders slumped with exhaustion. "But?"

"But in the end what I want counts for nothing without proof. I'm sorry."

He stared and then closed his eyes. "You're doing your job. You know what I am now. An addict. Someone who was so messed up at one point he frightened the hell out of his best friend. I don't blame you for wanting proof."

Her heart aching, Cat slid her hand into one of his. "Then we'll find it, okay? If you're innocent, the proof will materialize. It has to."

He opened his eyes and she stared deeply into them. "It will be all right, Jay. We'll find the killer and you will be free from all that guilt you're carrying around."

His gaze dropped to her lips and he leaned closer. Even knowing what he was going to do, Cat didn't move back. His mouth covered hers and she lost her head when his tongue touched hers. The passion and frustration, for each other and Sarah, surged into the moment and they went with it, heedless of its ramifications or what happened next. His hand came up and slid under her hair to grip her neck. Cat welcomed the domination as he tugged her against him, her breasts crushing against his chest. Jay. Her Jay.

The kiss deepened, their hands moved and explored, his thumb brushed her nipple… Cat pulled back, her breath short. They stared, both searching for something from each other. When nothing but the plea to trust him materialized in the deep brown depths of his eyes, Cat looked away.

"We find Sarah's killer and then we deal with this."

"This? Meaning us?"

She met his eyes. "Yes."

He smiled softly. "Sounds like a plan."

She tentatively met his smile. "Good. But right now, we need to find out why Bennett hasn't eliminated you from his enquiries." She swallowed the frustration stuck like a rock in her throat. "We need to find that out so we can lay your part, and your mistakes, to rest once and for all."

He dropped back against the settee, his gaze fixed on the fireplace in front of them. "I like the sound of that."

A modicum of tension left Cat's shoulders as she watched his profile from beneath lowered lashes.

He blew out a breath. "You know, my parents aren't proud of what I've done since I've been out of rehab. They're scared."

Cat frowned. "Scared?"

He nodded. "They think work is consuming me but know it's better than cocaine so they leave me alone. It's hard facing them every time I go home for a strained family dinner and watch them tiptoe around the drugs… and now work."

"They're working on forgiving you. You should do the same. We all have to think that way or else we'll be taken under."

"But how do I deal with the fear on their faces that I might start using again? You have no idea what it's like to feel so untrustworthy. I thought seeing the distrust in their eyes was unbearable, but in yours it's ten times worse."

Cat looked to the floor, shame burning deep inside as her mum's face filled her mind's eye. Jay's words proved he was well on the way to recovery. He recognized and acknowledged people's fears for him, his family's deep emotional worry. Her mum couldn't care less about seeing shame or fear or anything else in her daughter's eyes and that was the heartbreaking thing about Cat's inability to cure her.

She turned to look at him, took his hand and squeezed. "You've got so much to be proud of. Because you care, you're getting better. Your not being there didn't kill Sarah. The bastard who put his hands around her throat did that."

"Cat—"

She shook her head. "I mean it. And Sarah has to be held accountable for some of this, too."

He stared at her as though she'd lost her mind. "How can you say that?"

Tears stung her eyes at the unnecessary loss of such a wonderful woman. "Why didn't she go to the police? They could have helped her. Why did she need us?" Cat cursed the crack in her voice. "Only Sarah knows why. Why didn't she ring you again after you didn't show at the bakery? We know she was killed around the time she was due to meet you, but how soon after?" She stared at him, willed him to vanquish some of the guilt that shone clear in his eyes. "We'll never know why she thought she was doing the right thing by walking into that forest. So, no more blaming ourselves, okay?"

He shook his head. "I don't know if that will ever happen, but I'll try. In the meantime, what are we going to do about Bennett?"

She inhaled a shaky breath. "You leave Bennett to me."

A small smile lifted the corner of his mouth. "Uh-oh."

Feeling some of the tension dissipate between them, Cat smiled. "Let's focus on Sarah's letter first and I'll deal with Bennett after that. Sarah said she needed my help. She asked me here even before you did. She knew her life was in danger and we were the only people she could trust with whatever was going on. I'm more convinced than ever her killer is local." She paused. "We need to find her lover."

"Wouldn't Bennett be looking into that?"

"He didn't mention a lover to me but you're right, that doesn't necessarily mean they don't know about one." She raised her eyebrows. "Bennett wasn't exactly generous with information. He knows I'm going to be poking around but I'm not convinced he's entirely happy about it."

Jay lifted his shoulders. "As far as he's concerned, I couldn't give a damn. Sarah's letter is a step forward. If she knew her killer, that eliminates the hundreds of possible strangers we would have had to consider before."

Cat stared down at their joined hands and took a deep breath as she prepared to throw yet another problem into the investigation. "Things are going to get a lot worse before they get better."

He turned, his brow creased. "Why?"

Cat grimaced. "She stole over fifty grand of her killer's money."

"What?" Jay's eyes grew wide. "Fifty grand?"

She nodded. "It doesn't take a genius to work out the

killer's motive. The complexity of her murder has grown worse with her letter, not better. I can't help thinking Bennett suspected exactly that when he decided to let me in. He needs all the help he can get."

Jay slipped his hand from hers and pushed it through his hair. "Jesus. What was she thinking?"

Cat looked at him. "She wasn't. She was terrified. Doing whatever she could to make this person see sense. You know Sarah, she probably thought she was helping him rather than inviting his anger. Or in this case, rage."

"Did she tell you where it is?"

"All she says is that she hid it on Cowden Beach. She didn't give me her lover's name, either. Said she couldn't take the risk of writing it down but she'd tell me as soon as I got here. The point is, she wrote me the letter on the day she died but it wasn't posted until after she was killed."

"Meaning someone must have read it."

"Exactly. Whoever that someone is has probably been waiting for me to arrive and now knows I'm here."

His jaw tightened. "Then you're in as much danger as Sarah."

Cat shrugged. "Maybe. The difference is I can shoot a gun and have a black belt in Tai Kwon Do." She winked.

"This isn't funny. I'm not letting you go—" He looked to the ceiling, shook his head and then met her eyes. "This isn't funny."

Cat's heart lurched. What had he been about to say? She couldn't see past the mania burning in his eyes, the raw anger and frustration seeping from his pores, threatening to pour out of him like liquid anarchy.

"Listen to me." She grasped his hand. "I've gained access to the incident room once and I'll do it again by using this letter. It'll be another way to get to show Bennett I'm playing hardball. Maybe he'll give me more of what they know."

"If the person who mailed the letter was in any way involved with Sarah's murder, wouldn't they have burned it? Surely they'd want that letter gone, not for it to reach you."

"Not necessarily. Maybe whoever mailed it knew Sarah had told someone else about it and didn't want the cops asking questions about a letter that was sent but never arrived."

He pulled his hand from hers and stood to pace back and forth in front of the fireplace. Cat dropped back against the couch and crossed her arms to counteract the cold feeling seeping across her shoulders. Jay wore the expression of a man trying hard to maintain control.

She'd bet a hundred pounds his mind was as wrapped up in her as it was in Sarah and the letter. He looked mad. Protective.

Cat watched him. He had to get ahold of his emotional reaction to her being under the same dangerous threat as Sarah. The anger visibly coursed through him. He loved Sarah…and he loved her and God only knew what nastiness they were yet to uncover. Cat was braced for it, trained for it, but the way Jay's face shone with undisguised fury beneath the subdued lamplight spoke volumes.

His eyes were two pools of blackened rage. His frustration evident in the sharp line of his jaw and the vein pumping like a broken arrow down the center of his forehead.

He gaze locked on hers as he came to a standstill. "So what next? We try to find the money?"

Cat ignored his question. "Are you okay?"

"What?"

She pushed to her feet and fisted her hands on her hips, mirroring his stance. "Are you okay? Because you don't look it and I've watched too many potential witnesses, civilians and victim's family members be so torn apart by rage and guilt they lost sight of everything else."

His jaw tightened. "I'm fine."

"Because if you're not, your concentration is blurred and you'll be no help to me or Sarah. You have to keep calm, Jay. You could be the person who needs to focus the most, who unconsciously knows the most. You could be the key to this and if you're mad you could miss a vital and intricate piece of the puzzle."

He continued to glare, his mouth pulled into a tight line. The fraught silence stretched like a rubber band around them, threatening to snap and leave a great red welt of their failure in its path.

He tipped his head back to look at the ceiling. "You're in serious danger here, Cat."

Cat's heart swelled with love for him. "I know, but we won't let that stop us finding who did this."

His gaze locked on hers. "The guy has your number. He could be watching the cabin right now for all we know. We're pinning your hopes on nothing." He shook his head. "How the hell are we supposed to find money hidden on a couple of miles of sand? It will take hours of manpower to search an area as big as Cowden Beach. Sarah might as well have tossed it in the damn sea."

Irritation simmered inside her and Cat struggled to keep it in check. Attacking him, shaking him wouldn't help either of them. "It will be in one of the places we used to go as kids. I'm sure of it. If she wanted our help, was scared for her life, it makes sense she'd want us to find it before anyone else."

He crossed his arms. "We don't know that."

"But it's somewhere to start. If we can get ahead of Bennett and his team, I will be even happier. I want us to be the ones who find her killer. Don't get me wrong. If Bennett finds him, great, but wouldn't it be peace for us knowing we did that for her? That we brought her killer to justice even if we couldn't save her life?"

"Of course it would, but by the time we scour every inch of the places we used to go, you'll be called back to Reading and then what?" He pushed his hand into his hair and held it there. "I can't do this on my own, Cat. We have to solve this while you're here or I'll go insane, I swear."

"We'll find it." Cat took his hand, willed him to believe. "We will. We just need help. Help from people you and I can both trust..."

An idea so preposterous it could only be right, filtered into her mind. *Could they?*

Cat smiled. "I've got an idea."

Jay shook his head. "Uh-oh, you've got that look on your face."

"There are two particular people we both know who love nothing more than sticking their noses in everyone's business and will practically combust thinking they have superior knowledge over Bennett."

He stared at her for a moment before comprehension lit in his eyes and a smile curved his lips. "Please tell me you're not thinking of letting Marian and George in on this?"

She grinned. "Why not? They are an elderly couple with the gumption of two people half their age. Who's going to suspect them of being up to anything at the beach? They'll fly under the radar, Jay."

He grimaced. "I don't know. This could be dangerous."

"I know. I know." Cat whirled away from him and paced the room. "But it would work. I'm sure of it. Marian strikes me as the kind of woman who doesn't quit. As for George?" She turned. "He'll do anything for either of us. I know this is dangerous, Jay, but it's for Sarah."

"And if anything happens? It goes wrong?"

"It won't. We can't think that way. If I thought that way, I wouldn't do my job and I wouldn't expect my team to risk their lives every day. No one will take any notice of them. This is not the best option, but damn it, it's the only one we have to gain us more time. If Marian and George are looking for the money it frees us up to find out who Sarah was seeing and what hold he had over her to make her get involved in something so dangerous."

"And what about you?"

She frowned. "What about me?"

"If Bennett—hell, if your boss finds out you put not one, but two civilians in such a precarious position you'll be kicked out of the force."

Cat stared, adrenaline pumping through her veins. "That's a risk I'm willing to take for my best friend. We have to do it if we stand any chance of catching her killer sooner rather than later. It's only a matter of time before he leaves the Cove with or without that money. It's been almost three weeks since Sarah died. The money could already have been found, but it's unlikely. It will be somewhere another adult wouldn't think of looking. We can get Marian and George to search all the places we can think of."

He came toward her and took her hand, leading her back to couch. He pulled her down beside him. "Okay, we'll ask them. They might shoot us down in flames, but knowing them as we do, that's highly unlikely. It makes me sick to my stomach to think Sarah might've actually loved this guy."

Tears burned behind Cat's eyes. "I know. Love shouldn't get you killed."

He turned and stared into her eyes. "Why not? I'd die for you."

The room fell into silence and Cat attempted to pull her hand from his but his fingers clamped on tighter.

"Jay—"

"Don't panic." He smiled softly. "Take it as a given and move on."

She tugged on her hand and he let her go. What was she supposed to say to that? She couldn't deny he would risk his life for her. In her heart she knew his words were true. He'd said he'd do anything for her seven years ago and he said it now.

She met his eyes and promptly drowned in the sincerity, the care, the love shining back at her but fought to the surface to survive.

"I have to go back to Reading, Jay."

"And whatever is going on back home is stopping you from fighting for this new chance for us to work, right?"

Heat pinched her cheeks. "No, of course not."

"Then what is it, Cat? Is it me? My addiction? Because if it is, I understand—"

"We've *both* changed so much, that's all." Her gaze wandered over his face, taking in every line, every blemish, every perfection. She wanted him; her entire body screamed for him. "We're living entirely different lives than we were before."

"You didn't answer my question."

She cupped a hand to his stubbled jaw. If only her mum… She forced her hand back onto the couch.

"It's not you." She pressed her fingers into the soft cushions to keep them out of trouble. Thoughts of the life waiting for her when she got home pressed down on her chest. "Thinking about starting a relationship now… What if I hurt you?"

"You wouldn't—"

She shook her head, firmly shutting the door creaking on its hinges in her heart. "I can't do this. I can't take that risk."

Cat turned and stared ahead at the huge stone fireplace. Sadness enveloped her. They would never work. It would be too much for both of them. She shifted the subject as far away from the personal as possible.

"Sarah's letter might not have given me the name of who she was helping, but we'll know when we find the money. She left the name of her killer with the money."

"What? Why would she do that?"

She turned. "Think about it. Whoever found the money would know who killed her and have a serious decision to make. Would you want to hold on to fifty grand when it was with a letter signed by a woman naming the man who likely killed her? A woman whose face has been all over local television for the past three weeks?

"She worked this out, Jay. If we find it, we have the name. If somebody else finds it, then they have a name and fifty grand cash to hand into the police. If the killer finds it—"

"He could take the money and the accusation and run."

"Exactly. So, out of those three options, we hope to God it's not the last one and the money is still somewhere waiting to be found."

"We'll find it. I promise."

She smiled at the renewed optimism shining bright in his eyes. He was so handsome, so strong. Conquering his addiction was like a wrongful aphrodisiac to her. It made him fifty times as attractive to her messed-up mind, body and soul. God, she wanted him. Wanted him more than he realized. Just having him near her brought feelings she had buried under a sea of pain, hurt and frustration.

She closed her eyes and battled the need for him as it poured hot and reckless into her blood.

"Sarah says in the letter she took the money from the person as ransom. She'd only tell him where it is if he stopped what he was doing." She opened her eyes. "Someone must have seen her with him and Marian and George are as good a starting place as any."

His eyes darkened with regret. "I can't think of anyone. I saw her cross the street if she saw me coming toward her. I saw her leaving the bakery without speaking to me. I saw her, but she didn't want to see me, so I haven't a clue who he could be."

"Was she always alone?"

"Yes."

"You're sure? Maybe she was with the same person so often it hasn't registered. Maybe you know the person and think it couldn't possibly be them."

He turned away and emitted a low, guttural moan of frustration before shaking his head and staring at the ceiling. Cat stared at his profile. As a young woman, she'd thought him her idol, and now, older, wiser and a cop, he was her constant. The man she still loved.

He blew out an exhausted breath and turned to look at her. "Just kiss me."

Her breath caught. "What?"

He inched closer. "I said, kiss me."

Her center ached and her nipples tingled. "Jay." A pathetic whisper of a laugh escaped. "Don't be ridiculous. Didn't you hear what I just said? We can't do this. The kiss in the forest—"

His lips crushed hers before she could speak another word. Delicious shockwaves of pain and pleasure rocketed through her. He pulled her forward in a tight grip, pulling her on top of him as he fell backward onto the couch.

Guilt scratched at the periphery of her conscience, but she ignored it, pushed it away. Her breasts crushed against his hardened chest with erotic disregard, and she scored her fingers into his hair, bringing him closer.

As she melted against him, her internal protestation against them being together stormed inside her mind. She couldn't let this happen. Couldn't risk her heart and his this way. Yet, where her intentions were strong, her body and heart were weak. Just one time. Just one moment of being someone else. The desperate need to be the woman she was before her father died broke wide open.

His tongue found hers and she met its ardent warmth with animalistic hunger. Memories and familiarity flooded her brain and emotions. A primal moan escaped him and vibrated against her chest and into her mouth. They took what they needed without finesse or tenderness. Sarah was dead. They clung to each other as physical heat and need overtook their senses. Her body ached for him; her heart wept for him.

Cat was forced to pull away for breath. Her blood rushed into her mind, putting in a heady, exhilarating state of want. She met his eyes.

"We can't do this."

"We can. And we are. Let's go to bed."

CHAPTER TWELVE

WITH HER FINGERS CAUGHT in his, Cat let Jay lead her into his bedroom. They moved straight to the bed. The jade-green drapes lay wide open; a single bolt of moonlight split the dark silken duvet in two. She eased her hand from his and crawled onto the bed, her heart slamming hard against her rib cage, her stomach knotted with want and crazy abandon.

He stood immobile by the side of the bed and stared down at her. Despite his face being in shadow, his admiration swept over her and Cat felt beautiful.

His shaky exhalation broke the silence. "I feel as though we've wasted a lifetime."

Smiling, she held out her hand. "Then get up on this bed before my common sense comes back."

He slid his hands onto the bed and his body followed. Lying down beside her, he cupped his hand to her jaw and Cat watched him watch her. His thumb moved higher to graze softly against her bottom lip and she resisted the urge to trap it between her teeth.

"I'm going to make love to you, Cat Forrester. I should never have let you go."

His lips came down on hers, claiming her, and Cat surrendered to the emotions, need coursing through her blood and heating every hungry, desirous inch of her body. Her breasts ached for his touch, for the release only Jay could give her.

She returned his kiss, gently teasing him with the soft provocation of her tongue against his, pulling back to tease his lower lip, then plunging back inside, her tongue an appetizer to everything her body wanted from him.

He groaned and pulled her over on top of him, his hands tugging her blouse from her skirt so his fingers could slide over her back. Her skirt was a crumpled mess high on her hips as her naked legs welcomed the harsh scrape of denim. The cool air sliced across her skin, ironically fanning the flames burning beneath her semi-exposed panties. All that separated them was a scrap of cotton and the thick denim of his jeans. Cat pressed her groin to his.

She opened her eyes and watched his closed lids flicker and jolt, as he moved his hands from her back to grip her buttocks and draw her closer. The distinct coolness licked at her core, readying her. She increased the pressure of her mouth, taking more of him, fueling his arousal and hers. He needed to know how she wanted this. Needed to know this was as much for her as it was for him, despite everything she said minutes before. She hadn't lied to him. They couldn't last, but they could have this. A moment she'd hold in her heart and never regret.

Her mum, her real world, felt far away. Hidden in another place where Jay need never discover it. There would be pain, there would be hurt, but for the joy singing in her heart and forever in her memory right then, it would be worth it. Jay cared for her. Always had.

Cat didn't want the gentle, caring lover who worried about hurting her, worried about being her first. That was before. She'd been with other men since and today she was a grown woman. Exhaling as his teeth nipped at her neck, she relished the erotic pain mixed with pleasure as it washed over her senses.

"I want to touch you," she whispered. "All of you."

Drawing away from him, she inched back until she sat upright against his groin. Feminine power roared through her blood as the delicious feel of his erection through his jeans touched her naked thigh. With her gaze locked on his, Cat slowly unbuttoned her blouse. His eyes widened and his jaw grew tight as she tossed it to the side and reached around to unhitch her bra.

She flung it to the side, her nipples tightening under his gaze. "Your turn."

He sat up and their faces were barely inches apart. Lust swirled in his eyes as hunger raged and desire burned. He clasped one naked breast in his hand, massaged it possessively, swallowing Cat's shocked gasp with his mouth. Her arousal skyrocketed and she fumbled for the hem of his T-shirt before roughly yanking it over his head. Their lips separated for seconds before reclaiming as they fell back onto the bed.

Her breasts and torso nestled against the soft brush of hair running across the middle of his chest and down his washboard stomach. Her heart swelled and her mind emptied when he moaned her name.

He tilted her to the side so she lay on her back and Cat fell into his gaze, unaware of anything but him. The sexy lift at the corner of his mouth sent her insides into a girlish loop-the-loop as their connection slammed into place and locked. She fought the fear of it, the resistance; they were joined in finding their friend's killer, and they were joined in their anger and passion. They were joined.

However temporary, it didn't make what was happening less tantric. His fingers smoothed over her thigh and she clamped her teeth together. His progress was tortuously slow, her body trembling with anticipation.

Silent understanding passed between them and Cat

disregarded the emotional tidal wave rising inside her, threatening to destroy every intimate barrier she'd so meticulously erected since her mum's downfall. This was Jay. Her Jay. He wouldn't hurt her, wouldn't ask for more than she could give. She was safe. She swallowed. Safe as a wooden house in the line of a smoldering fire.

Her breath caught when his fingers roughly tugged her cotton panties aside and he plunged his fingers deep. Tenderness was absent, possession was rife and Cat's eyelids grew heavy as he rediscovered her by moving within her, his thumb simultaneously smoothing over her silky wet nub.

"Oh, God, Jay."

He covered her mouth; his tongue sought hers. Cat clasped her hand to the back of his head, demanding he kiss her longer, deeper. He teased her with diligent precision. In and out, around and around. He massaged her to a near frenzy until Cat's toes curled and her heart raced.

Cat exhaled. "Take them off. I want you."

He moved from the bed and stood. His eyes feasted on her as he yanked his belt from its buckle and snapped open the buttons on his jeans. He tugged the denim and underwear over his hips and muscular thighs in one slick motion. Cat's gaze shamelessly zoomed in on his arousal.

Some things certainly didn't wither over time and her center pulsed its appreciation. "Have you got a…"

He leaned toward his bedside cabinet and produced the wrapped piece of permission. Tossing the packet on the cabinet surface, Jay climbed onto the bed and slid close to her.

Cat ran her splayed hand over the broad expanse of his chest, up and over the smooth plane of his shoulder and down over a biceps wider than the span of her hand. She shifted and he fell back when her hand curled around his shaft. She moved up and down the length of him, her thumb circling and spreading the bead of moisture around its tip.

He muttered a curse and a wicked smile curved her lips as her body trembled with need and impatience. Impatience she'd curb until they were both ready, until she prepared him as he had her. She picked up the pace and relished his guttural moans, rode the satisfaction when he flung his arm above him to grip the iron headboard.

Faster and faster she rubbed him, bringing him closer to the brink and then releasing him to cup his tight balls in her hand. His hand dropped and he grappled for the condom. Releasing him, she took the packet from his hand and ripped it open, feeling the power of his gaze on her. She rolled the protection over him, taking her time, smoothing her hand over him again and again until he pushed her back against the bed.

He held her hands above her head and she surrendered. Their eyes locked as he kneed her legs open and moved between her thighs. His gaze burned into hers as he probed the tip of his erection against her, teasing, tempting, and then with a possessive thrust, he entered her.

Their gasps of relief punctured the air and his weight dropped onto her. He slid his hands down the sides of her body, from the curve of her breasts to her waist, until they slipped under her buttocks and hitched her closer.

Cat shuddered beneath him as they moved, harder and harder, then tantalizingly slow, then hard…

The waves built, lapping at the outskirts of her release. She reached for him and curled her fingers around the muscular strength of his shoulders, her nails digging into the hardened flesh. As he took her his eyes filled with longing, possession…and love.

Every withheld emotion, any hope she dared to think or

believe, every desire she wanted and refused to act upon came to the surface. Her body became his, her heart tipped closer and then they were there. He tensed beneath her fingertips as her orgasm came closer. Cat couldn't keep her eyes open any longer. Her orgasm crashed through her and she cried out as her body convulsed and tightened around him.

"Jay."

A groan ripped from him, turning into a yell, her name reverberating around the moonlit room making her feel like the most treasured woman in the world.

"This isn't it, Cat. This isn't the only time." His weight dropped against her.

Cat held him as though the rest of her life depended on it even as whispered warnings crept into her mind. They had made love without her knowing for sure he was innocent. She'd made love to a man she wanted to trust and love with everything she had. She had made love, and she would not cry.

THE BRIGHT MIDMORNING sun filled Jay's bedroom and Cat smiled. If she'd been shy about her creeping, almost-age-thirty weight gain before, she had no right to feel that way again. To say she was wanton and adventurous and downright insatiable was an understatement. Jay groaned beside her and her smile stretched.

Turning her head on the pillow, laughter bubbled in her throat and her heart swelled dangerously in her chest. Jay lay facedown in the feather pillow, one arm thrown across her torso, the other hanging limp over the edge of the bed. She shoved him.

"Are you breathing?"

Silence.

Another shove. "Hey, Casanova, can you hear me?"

He turned so one brown eye met hers. "I think I've had a heart attack."

She grinned. "What's the matter? Not enough stamina for a real woman after all the lightweights you've been sleeping with over the last seven years?"

"You're not a woman."

She laughed. "Excuse me?"

"Tossing a man of my size around the bed like he weighs next to nothing isn't normal."

She sat up and grabbed her pillow and swiftly brought it down on his head. "I did not toss you around the bed."

He was up and had her pinned beneath him before she had time to lift the pillow a second time. His teeth came down on the curve of her neck and he savagely nibbled as her screams echoed around the room. Happiness tickled her insides as she pummeled at his back.

"Say you'll stay here forever and I'll let you go."

Cat froze. No. Not yet. Her happiness dissolved. "Jay, let me up."

He pulled back, concern creasing his handsome brow and clouding his eyes. "I know it's not what you want to hear, but I have to say it. I want you to stay."

His gaze wandered over her face and suddenly his super-king-size bed felt like a single divan. She wriggled to get out from underneath him, thankful when he rolled to the side releasing her.

"We can't be together. I told you that last night. Nothing's changed."

"Why?"

"There's stuff I can't talk about. Please accept that." Cat scooted off the bed, taking the cover with her and wrapping it around her body. "I'm taking a shower. We've got work to do."

He stared. "Will you just talk to me?"

Distress shivered through her dousing the passion of the night before like the coldest water being thrown over the most sensual and gloriously romantic fire. She tilted her chin against the pain.

"Look, it's a new day. Sarah comes first, okay?"

"You don't want to talk. I get it. But you may as well know right now that I don't believe for one second that whatever it is making you tense up like a coiled spring is work related."

Annoyance prickled at her nerve endings and she scowled. "Will you stop this? It's not fair. We can't make my being here about us. It's about Sarah."

The ringing of her cell phone sliced through the atmosphere. Cat marched across the room and snatched it from Jay's bureau. "Cat Forrester."

"Did you have sex with him? Was it good?"

Revulsion curled into a knot deep inside Cat's stomach. She met Jay's questioning gaze. "The caller," she mouthed, tightening her grip on the phone. "Well, good morning to you, too."

His low burst of laughter was muffled beneath whatever disguise he used to alter his voice. "Not much ruffles those fiery feathers of yours, does it, Sergeant?"

"Did you ring for a chitchat or is there something you want to tell me?" *Come on, you son of a bitch. Give me what you've got.*

Jay pushed off the bed and stood behind her. Unconcerned about his nakedness, he slid his arms firmly around her and Cat trembled. Whoever killed Sarah was watching them.

"What do you want? I haven't got all day to stand around talking to some damn coward who likes to hide behind a telephone instead of facing me like a real man."

She squeezed her eyes shut. "If you've got something to say to me, just say it."

Even muffled, the coldness of his laugh seeped down the line and into her blood.

"Oh, I've got plenty to say to you, Sergeant. Plenty. But first, I want to play with the Cat a bit longer, stroke her fur like your millionaire playboy just did."

Her eyes snapped open as bile rose bitter in her throat. Jay's arms came tighter around her and she knew his face would be set in rage. She loved him for letting her do her job, for curbing his masculine instincts until she gave him the right and proper place to unleash them.

"Go to hell."

Another low burst of laughter. "How was your visit to the forest yesterday? Swept the place clean, haven't they? Nothing left of me for the poor sergeant who came all the way from Reading to find."

Cat tightened her grip on the phone. "I'll see you behind bars for this. I swear to God."

Another laugh. "Will you? You are so far away from finding the killer, it's a joke. You're blind, Detective. Maybe even blind drunk like your lush of a mother. What do you think?"

Cat sucked in a breath.

"See you around, Sergeant."

The line went dead. Cat's hand shook as she quickly pressed the call list. Nothing. Unknown number. She dropped her head back against Jay's chest.

"He's watching us. He knows…" She swallowed the revelation. He knew about her mum.

Jay turned her in his arms and stared. "He knows what?"

"He knows what we're doing and when we're doing it."

A muscle leaped in his jaw. "Ring Bennett. Ring Bennett now before I do something stupid."

"I can do better than that."

He frowned. "Like what?"

"Like see Bennett face-to-face. Chris scanned Sarah's letter and emailed it to me. I checked while you were asleep and it's on my BlackBerry." She moved out of his embrace as her fear evolved into determined anger. "Whoever that was has just made the biggest mistake calling me again. He's going to pay big time."

"Send the letter to my email and I'll print it off."

She nodded. "Then I'll take it to the station and speak to Bennett. Tell him about the letter and find out what the hell he's doing about the bastard who's daring to mess with me."

He blew out a shaky breath. "Fine. But I'm not leaving your side, so we're both going to see him."

"But you can't—"

"No arguments." He walked toward his dresser.

She had to keep him away from the station. If Bennett found out Jay knew as much about the case as she did, he'd have her ass back on a train to Reading before she could spit out another word…and she wanted to question Bennett. Find out once and for all why Jay hadn't been eliminated from the police's suspect list. What did he know about Jay or his alibi that she didn't?

"I want you to speak to Marian and George, remember? We can't waste any time."

"Already done. We're meeting them at the bakery later."

"What?"

"You're not the only one who can creep around when someone's asleep." He winked as he pulled fresh underwear out of a drawer.

"Great." Damn it. She continued toward the ensuite bathroom. "When we find out who did this…"

"I'll make sure no one disturbs you when you're in a police cell bashing his brains out."

She widened her eyes in mock innocence. "I'd never do any such thing."

Jay laughed and came forward to press a kiss to the tip of her nose. "Sure you wouldn't. We'll see Bennett and then when we've done as much as we can today, you and I will talk about how you're going to get a transfer from Reading."

Dread struck like a knife in her chest. "I told you. Work—"

He raised his hand. "I don't believe you, but if you insist it's work keeping you there, there's no problem."

She swallowed. "How do you figure that?"

He smiled. "Because after you solve this case for Bennett, he'll offer you a job here, anyway." He narrowed his eyes. "Unless, as I suspect, it's not work stopping you from moving to the Cove in the first place."

She gripped the duvet tighter at her breasts. "It's work."

"Fine. Then we'll talk later."

Her mouth opened but when no words came, so Cat shot him a glare, turned around and marched into the bathroom. She slammed the door and threw the lock into place.

With her heart racing and her hands trembling, she leaned against the door and cursed. She'd made a big slip. Jay would now pick at the tiny thread, pull and pull until the entire, disgusting truth of her home life came unraveled, leaving nothing behind but shame.

She didn't want to regret last night…or this morning, but the fingers of doubt crept up her spine, threatening to make her turn away from him. He'd asked her to stay, said this wasn't it for them—made love to her as though she was his world.

Tears fell onto her cheeks and Cat pushed away from the door. She started the shower. With each passing day, the memories of the Cove and the potential to make more, poured into her blood, filling her up as they had every summer she came there.

What if her feelings for Jay grew stronger every day it took to find Sarah's killer? What if, when she had her killer behind bars, she couldn't go home without irreparably breaking her heart...and Jay's?

"Cat?" Jay's knock at the door made her jump. "Can I come in?"

"I'm in the shower." She quickly dropped the duvet she'd forgotten she still clutched like a child's comfort blanket. "I can't hear you."

"Then how come you just answered me?"

She grimaced and stuck her head under the shower. Now she couldn't hear a thing.

CHAPTER THIRTEEN

HALF AN HOUR LATER, Jay poured a second cup of coffee and took it out onto the veranda. The sun's rays burned warm on his bare skin. Having put the phone call from the sicko from hell on the back burner for now, he puffed out his chest in satisfaction. Despite having to face Bennett again shortly, the previous night lingered in his memory. The night ended in the perfect way, making love to the girl whose green eyes, dark red hair and perfectly toned and smooth-skinned body had haunted his dreams for seven long years.

Cat was as flawless now as then. Their night of love-making had left him exhausted and pleasantly aching, but the need to touch her again had woken him at first light. He willed his penis to grow up. The last thing he wanted was to frighten her away with this overpowering need to make up for lost time.

Taking a hefty mouthful of black coffee, the memory of the fear in her eyes when she looked at the wine bottles disintegrated his smile. His initial instinct was to attack, but her shock was so profound it had sucked all the temper from his gut and replaced it with an overwhelming sense of protection.

Her eyes had grown wide as her body trembled. Then she blinked and her cop training slammed into place like a closing door. Her discomfort about him drinking set off warning bells all around him. Passion and blatant, undisguised fury burned in her eyes. He was sure it was aimed entirely at him. She loved him. No one cared that much if they didn't. Cat Forrester was the woman for him. Come hell or high water, he would have her.

Turning, he stared at the house. She was taking forever in the shower. He shouldn't have pushed her about staying with him in the Cove, but what Cat failed to realize was that, try as she might to hide them, her feelings for him were clearly written in her eyes. She was scared. So was he. She didn't want their friendship ruined. Neither did he. Most of all, Jay wanted peace in his life…and feared Cat was his only hope of ever achieving that seemingly impossible future.

He gazed out toward the sliver of ocean to the left of him, avoiding looking right toward a daylight panoramic view of the forest. Sarah's smiling face filled his mind's eye. He was an addict. He would always be addict. Sarah's cry for help toward both him and Cat meant she lived in some sort of self-inflicted hellhole, too. Only, by the time she'd called them, the ground was already receding from the edge of the abyss, sending Sarah hurtling to the bottom in the most violent way possible.

Jay clenched his jaw. Love would be the only thing Sarah would risk her life for—love for the kids she taught, or her killer. Jay's mind whirled but produced nothing but a messy carnage of unanswered questions.

"Goddamn it."

Tossing the dregs of his coffee over the balustrade, he turned and marched back inside the house. A slow burning headache pulsed at his temples as he looked toward the pinewood staircase at the edge of the room. Cat made love to him with raw ferocity. The bedroom had been filled with the scent of fresh air and the sea coming from the open windows. The sound of the waves crashing against the rocks down on the shore had been overtaken by their animalistic grunts, moans and pleas. It had been a bigger reality than Jay's wildest fantasy.

Then the phone call changed everything. He curled his hands into fists and stared blindly ahead. The caller was playing with them. With Cat. The knowledge stuck like a boulder in his gut. This person…this vermin had killed one of his best friends, but there was no way in hell he'd come within six feet of another. He loved Cat with his every fiber. He would kill for her.

Blinking, Jay slowly exhaled. He needed to play it cool. Reign in his temper and prove his counselor wrong. He didn't want Cat just because of their past. He needed to silence the unease battering around in his chest like a damn Ping-Pong ball and find the man who was a threat to their rekindled love affair. And it was a love affair. Whether Cat wanted to accept that or not.

Jay placed his mug on the table and glanced at his watch. Eleven o'clock. They were wasting precious time. He headed for the stairs.

When he pushed open the guest-bedroom door, he stopped. Cat wore a sleek black pencil skirt and white cotton blouse. Simple, professional. Except for the four-inch stilettos on her feet, which were as sexy as hell.

"Wow."

She jumped and turned. "Ah, there you are."

He smiled. "There I am? I've been downstairs waiting for you. Your coffee is stone cold."

Jay moved forward, cupped his hands to her jaw and kissed her. When they parted, she softly eased his hands from her face and brushed past him. His jaw tightened. She couldn't look at him. She walked to the bed and picked up her BlackBerry, lipstick and keys and tossed them in a black handbag. She hitched it onto her shoulder.

"Right. Bennett first, then we can check in with Marian and George."

"Yes, sir." He saluted and gestured toward the door.

As she sashayed past him, Jay bit back a growl as his irritation wavered. Her perfect ass and her shapely legs were a bad man's dream.

He followed her out of the room and down the stairs.

Ten minutes later, they pulled out of his driveway and he glanced at her as she stared out of the side window. She was still as stubborn as a mule when she didn't want to do something, but he'd wager his cabin that whatever held her in Reading—and from him—had something to do with a loved one and zero to do with her work. Cat's loyalty reigned supreme and her father's passing would have kicked her obligation to her mother into overdrive.

His gut told him this had something to do with Julia… or maybe Chris.

The stream of cars in front of him slowed at a red light and he touched her leg. She whirled around, her eyes a storm of wariness and surprise. Their jade-green newness darkened to almost emerald and a flush of color stained her neck. Jay's gut clenched with guilt. Why did he suddenly feel like a damn stalker?

"Are you okay?"

"Sorry, I was thinking about Sarah." She looked down at her hands clenched tightly in her lap. "I want to solve this case quickly. Her parents need to bury her and the man who did this, who's calling me? I want to see him pay for what he's done."

He tentatively covered her hands with one of his and squeezed, relieved when she didn't pull away. "We're on it, okay?"

She looked at him. "If you mean that, can you do me a favor?"

"Anything."

"Promise me you'll drop the subject of me coming back to the Cove…permanently. It's a pipedream and one I don't want to contemplate because it's never going to happen."

The traffic started to move and Jay pulled his hand from hers and onto the steering wheel. He eased the car forward. "I know you feel as though I'm putting pressure on you—"

"I don't feel it. You are."

He stared ahead, frustration edging in. "Fine, maybe I shouldn't have said anything, but you sleeping in my arms last night felt so right. Cat, it felt amazing. I don't want us to miss a second chance when the first went without us trying." He drew in a breath through flared nostrils. "Doesn't this feel right to you? Us, together again? I need you and Sarah needs you. I know you have a fabulous career and a family who are hugely proud of you, but the two friends who lived here, the ones you loved spending time with each summer, have properly messed up their lives. Unfortunately, we both need you to make it better again."

"No pressure, huh?"

"You've got a good life in Reading, I get that. But that doesn't mean—"

"You have no idea what you're talking about."

He glanced at her and her eyes filled with tears. "God, Cat. Don't cry. That's the last thing I want. I'll back off. You don't want this."

Jay turned to the windshield. He didn't want to make her cry. The sadness in her voice grated his heart but the need for her to come clean about what was going on at home was stronger. Guilt for demanding more from her than she was willing to give scorched and seared his conscience, making him want to obliterate whoever or whatever caused her so much pain. He willed her to crack—knowing she never would.

Tension hummed around them. She was hiding something from him, something important. He frowned. How could anything be as bad as the things he told her about his life? She knew he'd taken drugs, humiliated Sarah at her workplace and let her down in the final moments of her life. What could be so bad Cat couldn't share it with him?

"We can get through whatever it is."

He hadn't meant to say his thoughts out loud and from the corner of his eye, he saw her inch away from him as though he might grab her.

"There is no 'we.' As soon as Sarah's killer is found, I'm heading home on the next train out of here. Last night doesn't change that. Today is a new day."

Goddamn it.

There was a long moment of silence and then she huffed out a breath. "Clearly, having sex meant more to you than the great opportunity for a bit of release it meant for me."

He flinched. *Ouch.* It was a good effort, but the first swipe of her knife didn't even break the skin. He turned and fixed her with his stare. She tilted her chin, but from the telltale shift of her neck, she clearly struggled to maintain eye contact.

He smiled. "The red-hot moaning told me you were as hungry for me as I was for you. So you can cut the crap." He turned back to the road.

"That is a disgusting way to describe what happened between us."

He shrugged. "Sex is sex, right? Isn't that what you're trying to get me to believe?"

Silence.

"We've still got it, and I, for one, fully intend to embrace it."

"What do you mean 'it'? We were together once. That hardly makes us past lovers. We might have had a tumble in the bedclothes last night, but we're friends. Nothing more."

His confidence wavered closer to the edge of irritation. "Are you serious?" The word *friends* crashed into his heart, knocking the wind from his lungs. "Friends?"

"Yes, friends."

Jay shook his head and curled his fingers tighter around the steering wheel. "We were never 'just friends.' I've got no intention of being 'just friends' now."

What the hell was going on in her mind? Her heart? He hadn't for one moment considered she wouldn't think of their lovemaking as anything less than the start of something great. As he did. His ego absorbed the blow of her rejection as he glanced at her perfect legs beneath the hem of her skirt. His gaze shot to her face. It looked set in stone. To hell with this.

"I'm not letting you go a second time. No way, no how."

She met his eyes and her expression changed to shocked anger mixed with mute disbelief. He hadn't seen either look on her face before and male pride surged through him, knowing he'd managed to shake her cool nonchalance. Her eyes blazed like emeralds under a scorching hot sun.

He concentrated once more on the road and waited for the explosion.

"Is that so? Well, I have news for you. I'm not anyone's woman to boss around. If I say we're just friends, we're just friends."

He bit back the urge to smile, thinking it might get him a right hook in the face. "Fine. We'll talk about this later."

"No, Jay. We won't. I am sick to death of people drowning themselves in whatever substance they think suits the occasion and then wallowing in self-centered pity." Her voice cracked. "I don't need your crap, okay? Just let me do my job and then I can go home."

Substance? Self-centered pity? Nausea rose bitter in his throat. No one had spoken to him like that in three years. Not since his father grabbed him by the scruff of the neck and hauled his ass into rehab. She was ashamed of him. Ashamed of his past. All her words saying how proud she was of what he had done since had been bullshit.

Anger and blistering shame ripped through his body and his knuckles ached from his unrelenting grip on the steering wheel. He'd never be free from what he'd done. Never. He was an idiot. An idiot who'd thought he could redeem himself after the hurt he'd caused by facing one person at a time. Cat hadn't seen him then, he hadn't hurt her while high, yet still the narcotics permeated his future and killed it dead with its poison.

He looked at her. Shit. He'd brought tears to her eyes. Again.

CHAPTER FOURTEEN

Cat stared out the car window and swallowed the lump of fear and anger stuck in her throat like a limpet to a rock. She had hurt him, saying anything to throw him off the scent of how she really felt. He didn't deserve it but she was running out of ways to stop her feelings from gathering momentum and making her believe her mum's problem could be handled. That she could be happy again.

She hadn't come to the Cove for this—a relationship couldn't be on her agenda when her mum needed her the way she did. She'd come for Sarah, and Jay needed to accept that and so did she. So, who was it running hand in hand up the stairs with him last night and leaping onto his bed, embracing the moment as if it was her last night on earth?

The remainder of the ten-minute journey to the station passed in pregnant silence until Jay pulled the car into the parking lot and found an empty space. He cut the engine.

"You're right. We're here for Sarah. Let's focus on that for the time being."

Cat closed her heart as a heavy sense of loss weighed it down. "The time being is not enough."

"It is. For now."

She met his eyes. "You're not listening to me."

"Because you're not making any sense. Why is it so bad to enjoy our time together while you're here?"

"You want more than that."

"I love you."

Cat stared. Pain caught and pulled at her heart; the reciprocating words danced on her tongue. Pursing her lips together, she trapped them inside and unsnapped her seat belt. She dragged her gaze from his beseeching brown eyes and pulled her handbag into her lap as guilt lurched inside her.

"I can't do this, Jay. I'll end up hurting you."

"I'll take the risk."

She shook her head and blinked back tears. "You're lonely."

"Aren't you?" he asked softly.

She was. So much. "That doesn't make this right. My life's in Reading, yours in the Cove. I can't leave Reading and you can't leave here."

"Who says? If coming to Reading is what it takes, I'll come."

Panic ripped through her. "No."

"No?"

"No." *Say something. Do something. He has to stay away. For him, for me...for Mum.* "Just because you can't find a new woman in Templeton to seduce, it doesn't mean you get to pursue the one you had seven years ago."

"You think that's why I'm asking you to stay? Because I can't be bothered to find anyone else? It's you. It's always been you."

She stared at him, her body leaning closer...

Sitting bolt upright, Cat fumbled for the door handle. She couldn't let this happen. She wanted him like she had before. Only this time, that want might turn to need.

She yanked on the handle and leaped from the car. The cool air was welcome against the steaming heat of her face. She flinched when his door slammed shut. What was she thinking, sleeping with him last night? She hadn't thought. Her body had screamed for him as though she was dying and he was her only hope of survival.

Not a single second of common sense had filtered through her brain before or during—but after? After, everything came crashing in. He was a suspect. Worse, she loved him, and feelings that strong were hard to fight. When he had walked into the guest bedroom with a smile wider than the Sahara on his face this morning, her bad decision slammed into her stomach like a boxer's punch.

"Go back to the cabin, Jay. I don't want you here."

"Cat, wait."

She glared. "You're a suspect. Don't you get that? Go home."

She marched away from the car and stormed toward the station, leaving him to do whatever the hell he liked. The last thing she'd come to the Cove for was more emotional stress. She had it in sackfuls at home already. She swiped at the tears that dared to fall. Damn him for making her think of the life she might have lived if her dad hadn't died and her mum hadn't chosen to slowly kill herself with the same thing that killed her husband.

"Cat—" Jay's hand gripped her elbow like a vise, strong, insistent and entirely capable.

She closed her eyes as the fear she didn't have the inner strength to fight him settled over her shoulders. "Jay, don't. It's not fair."

"Will you just look at me?" His tone was soft yet urgent. "The last thing I want to do is upset you. All I want is for some good times to come out of your being here."

She turned around. "So do I, but this doesn't feel like a good time."

"If Sarah hadn't been killed, if I hadn't been deemed a suspect, maybe I would never have called you. But I needed your help. So did she. Our friend is dead. Trying to lay her to rest is the hardest, cruelest thing I hope either of us ever experiences, but it's united us in a way nothing else could. Why can't you see that?"

Cat opened her mouth to protest but he pressed his hand to his chest, imploring her.

"If you don't want me, I'll back off. But just promise me you're turning away because you want to and not because of something else."

His pain and sincerity came off in waves. Another piece of Cat's heart splintered for Sarah, the girl who'd made her laugh until she thought her stomach would split wide open. "I miss her so much."

His gaze ran over her face, lingered at her lips. She hadn't answered his question. She knew it and so did he. After a moment, he took her hand and pulled her into his arms. "Me, too. I know she's watching our every move, willing us on, not just in the investigation but in us, too."

Cat closed her eyes and slumped against him. "Then why won't you just enjoy the time we have instead of pushing me for more?"

He eased her back. "Because I want more and so do you. I see it in your eyes and I felt it in every part of you last night. Whatever problems you're dealing with at home, I can help. I won't turn away."

She stared. He was still a suspect; did he not see that? Did he not understand what they had done? What *she* had done? Cat's heart picked up speed. If Bennett or Harris were to find out...

He smiled and brushed the hair from her eyes. "Good, no answer. That means there's hope you understand I'm talking sense. When you left that last summer seven years ago, I didn't think I'd never have another lasting relationship or not think of you when I kissed another woman, but that's exactly what happened. So if you can't give me more, I'll learn to live with it, but while you're here, we're going to make some memories. Good ones."

She shook her head even though her heart longed for his. "It's a bad idea."

"Whatever happens, we'll deal with it then." He took her hand, raised it to his lips and pressed a kiss to her knuckles.

The silence pressed down on her chest as their eyes locked and his hungry, sexy gaze bore into hers, trapping her like prey. The scent of his aftershave and that tanginess that was strictly Jay whispered between them. His lips brushed hers and Cat leaned into him wanting more, her eyes closed…

"No." She snapped her eyes open and pushed her hand against his chest. "Go home. We're not doing this here. I'll come back to the cabin after I've spoken to Bennett."

He raised his hands. "Fine. Fine. You deal with Bennett. Show him the letter. Do what you have to for Sarah. After that we'll go and see Marian and George. I'll be here in an hour to pick you up."

"No. If Bennett sees you here—"

"I'll park along the road and you come find me. Then, when we've done everything we can for Sarah today, you and I are going to talk about us."

Frustration burned and yearning for his kiss grew. "Fine."

He pressed a kiss to her forehead. "See you soon."

Cat stared after him as Jay headed back to his car and slid into the seat. The engine roared to life and he left the parking lot, leaving her feeling more alone than she'd felt since she arrived in Templeton. Drawing in a breath, she turned and headed toward the open double doors of the station. She needed to focus. She pulled the copy of Sarah's letter from her bag and tilted her chin. Police work. That she could control. That she knew how to handle.

"Well, good morning, Sergeant."

Cat halted at the sound of Inspector Bennett's voice a few feet away. She plastered on a smile. Crap. Had he seen Jay? "Good morning, sir."

"I assume you're here to see me?"

She straightened her spine and dismissed the lingering tension left by her argument with Jay. "Yes, sir. I've brought something to show you. Something I hope will further the investigation." She held up the letter. "This came to my home address in Reading."

He glanced at the letter. "What is it?"

"A letter from Sarah."

He lifted an eyebrow. "She wrote to you?"

"Yes, sir. The day she died."

Color seeped up from the collar of his pristine white shirt to his already ruddy cheeks. Cat cleared her throat.

"Sarah asked me to come here before Jay did. She knew she was in serious danger and implicates her killer as being her lover. The thing that makes Sarah's letter so vital is the way she talks about him. He's local, sir, which means there's a big possibility he's still in the Cove, rather than halfway around the world."

A muscle jerked and jumped in Bennett's jaw. "And you've held on to this letter since you saw me three days ago?"

Cat met his cool gaze. Whether he was angry at her for withholding the letter or the fact that not only Jay but now Sarah wanted her there, she couldn't be sure.

"Not at all, sir. She wrote it the day she died but it wasn't posted until five days ago, which means someone else put it in the mailbox to me, not Sarah. Whoever that someone is would have expected me, or at least waited

to see if I arrived. Clearly, they had no choice but to mail
it and ultimately facilitate my coming here, or else risk
being traced as a possible suspect. I think someone else
as well as the killer knew about this letter and feared a
paper trail leading us to his front door."

"Hmm." He took the letter from her hand and his brow
furrowed as he read the spidery script. "When did you
get this?"

"This morning. My brother read it to me over the phone
last night and then emailed me a copy."

He closed his eyes. "Jesus, Sergeant. Your brother has
read this?"

"He rang me from Reading telling me a letter arrived
and possessed the intelligence to realize if the letter wasn't
from Jay, it could be from Sarah."

He sighed. "All right, all right. It's good he did." His
gaze turned to the letter once more. "Well, we certainly
haven't identified any boyfriends or close friends who
could possibly be a person she would 'leave the Cove tomorrow for.'"

"Sir, I understand your feelings about Jay Garrett being
involved, but whether we like it or not he's involved by
Sarah's invitation. He has an alibi for the time of her death
and I believe he can help. Why else would she want the
two of us here if the path to her killer wasn't in some way
connected to us? She wanted our help. That must mean
something to her and the killer."

Bennett snapped his gaze to hers, his face a closed
mask. Unreadable even to her, a trained detective. A civilian under arrest stood no chance if he chose to turn up the
heat. No doubt they would be quivering in a molded plastic chair, but Cat dealt with scarier threats at home every
day and Jay standing up to demons that belonged in
hell. Bennett would be a walk in the park…she hoped.

"Yes, Jay Garratt and his alibi," Bennett murmured.

Cat frowned as Bennett's face twisted with derision. "Sir?"

"We'll get back to that in a second, Sergeant. First I want to talk about what Miss Cole says in this letter implicating a lover. She had sunk to such a low point in her life that she was involved in drugs. Since when have you ever known a woman like that to have a regular boyfriend?"

Where was he going with this? "Well, I—"

"There is no lover. If she was having sex, the man either paid her or owned her."

Annoyance stung Cat's cheeks. "I disagree. Sarah was sober enough to write me. If she says she had a lover, I believe her. One way or another, we need to pursue this. I'll ask around, see what I can find out and let you know if and when I discover anything."

"She admits to taking money." He rubbed his hand along his jaw. "Even says it's somewhere on Cowden Beach." His eyes met hers and Cat resisted the urge to shiver. They were ice-cold. "Do you think she's serious when she says the name of the person she thinks capable of killing her is with the money? That seems a very dangerous and stupid thing to do. Sarah Cole never struck me as either."

Cat stared. "Why would she say it if it wasn't true?"

He shook his head. "It makes no sense, so I'm still going to work on my theory Miss Cole was a runner for someone. The problem is, despite bringing in every user and dealer we know of in the Cove, none of them are squealing. Believe it or not, whatever their social differences, they liked her. It seems the whole damn town did, yet no one is bringing us any evidence to help find the son of a bitch who killed her." His jaw tightened and he nodded toward the station. "I'm going inside to get a team down to the beach as soon as possible. I will speak to you again later."

He moved to walk away and Cat took a step forward. "Sir?"

He turned. "What?"

"What about Jay?"

His mouth curved into a wolverine smile. "Ah, yes, Mr. Garrett and his rock-solid alibi."

Cat swallowed as trepidation tiptoed over the surface of her skin but she kept her lips tightly closed.

"Garrett is an ex-addict who was hauled in and out of the station several times before his father swooped in, cleaned him up and then passed him a thriving business out of the kindness of his heart." He narrowed his gaze. "The *gentleman* you have decided to bring in on an official investigation now lives in a five-bedroom luxury cabin at the top of a hill that happens to have a full, unbroken view of the forest where Miss Cole was found strangled."

"You still believe Jay had something to do with Sarah's murder? Even when he has not one but *four* people who've given statements where he was that night?"

Disbelief passed over his eyes. "You really have been sucked into believing whatever that man says, haven't you? Have you two got something going on that I need to know about? Something that will have you back on a train to Reading quicker than you can draw your next breath?"

Cat's heart kicked inside her chest and she tilted her chin. "Of course not. We're friends."

"Is that so? Well, your *friend* needs to keep his nose clean and his mouth shut because only two of those four investors were willing to sign statements saying Mr. Garrett never left the restaurant at all during the time they ate and again when they went for drinks at the Jukebox.

Apparently, Mr. Garrett left time and again to answer his cell and two of them aren't willing to testify that he didn't disappear for longer than half an hour at a time."

Cat cursed the hitching in her nerves. "Half an hour isn't enough time to get to Clover Point and kill someone. Surely—"

"Both men have said independently that he could've been gone longer. In your experience, Sergeant, how long does it take to throttle someone after a fifteen-minute drive?"

She shook her head. "But that's speculation. If two of them said he was there…"

"Two out of four is enough for me to keep Jay Garrett under the microscope." He took a step closer and stared into her eyes. "I also find it interesting that he asked you to come to Templeton. Why not leave the investigation to us when he knew damn well we were following every avenue…including the one leading to him?"

I slept with a suspect. I slept with a suspect.

Cat's mind whirled as hurt and shame at her stupidity took turns at the front of her mind. "It's because you suspected him that he rang me. He has no idea any of the men he was with didn't give him a solid alibi. He hasn't spent a moment worrying about it when he's been with me. Don't you think a man who was suspected of killing his best friend would be jumpy about that unless he knew he was innocent and had an alibi to prove it?"

Bennett stared for a moment longer before raising his hands. "Fine. Maybe he didn't do it, but until I know for sure, Jay Garrett is a suspect. Just because he was once friends with Miss Cole it doesn't eliminate him from our inquiries. Understand?"

Cat swallowed against the bitter taste in her mouth. She could not afford to further provoke Bennett if she were to stand any chance of having access to his progress. "Yes, sir."

"Good. Then let's move on. I'll get a team down to the beach and let you know if we find anything...or not, if I so choose."

Annoyance swept over her. He may be right to still suspect Jay but be damned if he wouldn't acknowledge Jay's achievements. "Can I just say one more thing? Jay has been clean and sober for nearly three years and didn't hassle Sarah to reinstate their friendship in that time. Their estrangement was what Sarah wanted, and despite Jay wanting to make amends, he respected her wish to remain apart."

Bennett raised his eyebrows. "Which doesn't help his cause. How do we know Miss Cole's refusal to reconcile drove him to do something you seem to think impossible?"

Cat stared in disbelief. "Even when he was high, he wasn't violent. Most of the people in Templeton have known Jay his entire life. I can't believe anyone would think him capable of that."

"Except me, of course. Is that what you're thinking? Let me tell you something, Forrester. I might not have lived in the Cove as long as some of my colleagues, but to me that's an advantage. I look at every resident here with new eyes. No rose-tinted memories to fade my better judgment. I ordered the search of Garrett's home because it was necessary, and you can continue to look at me like that for however long you like. It won't bring Miss Cole back."

Cat struggled with the accusation, of other people thinking Jay capable of such a heinous crime against a woman he held in high respect. Her entire body hummed with frustration and fear that what Bennett said had merit and her professional judgment had been blurred by her love for Jay.

"The fact Mr. Garrett knew Miss Cole personally only adds strength to why he shouldn't be involved. I want him kept out of this. Do I make myself clear?"

"Absolutely." She wanted Sarah's killer found and behind bars. If that meant sacrificing her friendship…and possible relationship with Jay…then so be it. He'd called her here for Sarah and that remained Cat's priority.

"Good." He blew out a heavy breath. "And as far as that phone call you received, it led nowhere. The number was untraceable. So—"

"Two calls."

"What?"

Cat met his unwavering gaze. "He rang again this morning. He's watching me. Could tell me where I'd been and when I'd been there. I need to stay a part of this, sir. He's enjoying the contact with me. He's going to slip up. I'm sure of it."

His gaze settled on her with the intensity of someone trying to look into her soul. "Then that's more reason than ever for you to get the hell back to Reading and concentrate on your jurisdiction instead of mine. I don't want a murdered cop on my hands on top of everything else. Go home, Forrester. You're not wanted here."

You are not throwing me off of this. "What about the school, sir?"

He frowned. "What about the school?"

"Have you spoken to the teachers there, the pupils?"

"Of course we bloody well have. What do you take me for?"

Cat didn't trust herself to answer that. "What did they say?"

"You really don't listen, do you?"

"Sir, please, I can't walk away from this. I can't leave Sarah…or ignore Jay's plea for help. It's just not who I am…as a cop or a human being. Please. Let me go to the school, talk to some people there."

"And what do you think you're going to uncover at the school that my officers haven't already?"

Cat lifted her shoulders. "I have no idea, but I tend to have a good affinity with kids. And they notice things we don't. It's worth another try."

He studied her. "If you go to the school, I'm coming with you. Trust has to be earned, Sergeant, and right now you don't have mine."

Cat inwardly cursed. It wasn't what she wanted, but it was clearly the best he was going to offer her. She nodded. "Deal."

"Fine. Then we'll meet outside the primary school tomorrow at ten o'clock. I've got a debriefing first thing. Don't be late."

"Yes, sir."

CHAPTER FIFTEEN

CAT STRODE FROM THE parking lot struggling with a mix of excitement and trepidation. On one hand, she had managed to maneuver another way in to ask questions and get Bennett to trust her judgment—on the other, she understood more than ever just how precarious a position Jay was in as far as Bennett was concerned.

Only two out of the four men who were with him that night were willing to sign their names confirming Jay would not have had time to disappear for a long period of time and come back without them noticing.

In Cat's mind, Bennett's thinking was shaky at best. Even if he truly believed Jay would have had time to kill Sarah and return to the nightclub, surely Jay's demeanor and general concentration would have roused suspicion. Bennett hadn't offered any more of what the men had said. The men who held Jay's future in their hands.

She understood Bennett was giving her the bare minimum, and she respected that. She wouldn't have been any different if she had been heading up the investigation. It didn't make her uneasiness any easier to bear, however.

So, what next? She glanced at her watch. She had half an hour before Jay arrived to pick her up and take her to the bakery to see Marian and George. Her chest tightened. She loved George like a father. And now she had to ask him the biggest favor she'd ever asked of any civilian—a favor that would certainly put him in harm's way.

She moved along the sidewalk, her usually confident gait weakening with each step. She could see no other option but to send George and Marian to the beach if there was any hope of not drawing any attention to whoever was making the phone calls to her.

Was he watching her now? Was he the killer or just some sicko who had somehow found out about her working on the case and knew she'd come to Templeton from out of town? Anger raised the hair on her nape. Did he know about Sarah's letter?

Cat sat on a wall to wait for Jay. A headache snaked its way across her brow and she lifted her fingers to her temples. She tried to massage the pain away, knowing an aspirin would be needed along with a cool glass of water once they got to the bakery. She tried to focus her mind on happier times in a bid to ease the tension, and thoughts of her and Jay's lovemaking filtered in. Her body traitorously heated from the memory. It never should have happened. She never should have surrendered to a single moment of selfish need.

Jay loved her and she loved him. That was not the issue. It was the fact that only her heart pleaded his innocence. She had no evidence to eliminate him. True, the facts and evidence didn't condemn him, but they didn't extricate him, either.

Damn it, Jay. Why did she have to be found on Clover Point? Why did you have to do what you did at the school that day? Why couldn't you have just told Bennett about Sarah calling you?

Jay's car came around the corner and Cat stood as her palms turned clammy. What was she supposed to say to him? She worried her bottom lip as he drew to a stop by the curb. Did she tell him about the weakness of his alibi?

That two of the four men he relied on hadn't delivered? Or did she keep that information to herself?

He lowered the window. "How was it?"

"Fine." Cat walked around the hood to get in the passenger side. She opened the door and slid into the seat, purposely concentrating her gaze on the seat belt as she buckled herself in.

"Cat?"

She turned. His brow was etched with concern, his gorgeous cocoa eyes on hers. "What happened?"

Indecision raged a war inside her. He was a civilian. A suspect. "I can't talk about it. Let's just get to the bakery."

He took her hand. "I'm going nowhere until you tell me what happened with Bennett."

She hadn't expected any different. Jay didn't get to where he was by giving up easily or taking no for an answer. Her shoulders slumped and she looked at their joined hands. "Bennett still suspects you."

"What?" His eyes widened. "Why isn't my alibi enough? Why is he so determined I had something to do with this?"

Cat looked at him. His cheeks were red and his mouth tight. Frustration hovered around his every muscle. She sighed. "We have to accept Bennett has a job to do and without evidence to eliminate you, he's doing it well. It's me who's acting unprofessionally, not him. I'm letting my feelings get in the way of what's right for Sarah. And that's wrong. Really wrong."

"You're right to listen to those feelings. Cat, I swear to you. I had nothing to do with Sarah's death. Nothing. Jesus, if I'd been there to meet her…"

"I know." She stared at his bowed head and resisted the yearning to kiss him. "For now we have to concentrate on what we can do and not what we can't."

He looked up. "The money?"

She nodded, her gaze falling to his lips. "What happened between us last night can't happen again, Jay. *We* can't happen. Let's just focus on finding the money and then maybe, just maybe, we can clear your name and find the man who took our best friend's life. I don't want our relationship becoming a problem that leads to Sarah's killer getting away with what he's done. Do you understand?"

For a long moment he stared into her eyes, and Cat fought the urge to look away. She had to face him. Had to show him she was serious…and not let him see through her eyes that her heart broke for everything the two of them couldn't have.

He shook his head. "No. I don't understand that at all." Abruptly, he turned and gunned the engine. "So how do we play this, *Sergeant?*"

Cat turned. The emphasis on *sergeant* was heavy with sarcasm. She'd pushed him away for the final time, and once they found the man who killed Sarah, they would go back to years of silence, most likely never speaking to each other again. The final shred of Cat's heart splintered and broke. Her eyes stung with tears and she blinked them away.

"Ideally, I want Marian and George at the beach before Bennett's team."

"Uh-huh."

"Jay, look at me."

He turned, his eyes dark with anger.

Cat swallowed and tilted her chin. "I need your help. The chances Marian will go to the beach on my say-so is very unlikely. George, not so much." She gave a quick smile. "But this is the quickest way we can start looking for that missing money and avoid drawing the attention of whoever's watching us. Are you happy to talk to her? Convince her to help?"

A little of the anger left his eyes and he turned away. "Yes. I don't like it, but we need to do this. Their help will make all the difference and keep the watcher with us. I get it." He blew out a breath. "George usually pops in for a cup of tea and a bun about now. We might be lucky and catch them together."

His cell phone rang from its hands-free holder and they both turned to the display. It showed "Tessa." Cat's gut lurched at the sight of a woman's name calling Jay. She turned to the side window, detesting the immediate pang in her chest that felt far too much like jealousy. What was the matter with her? He was a free agent. And, after all, she didn't want to stay here....

"Hi, Tess."

"Hi, Jay, where are you?" Tess's voice came through on the loudspeaker.

"Why? What's up?"

"Do you think you could make a quick detour to the pier? There's a problem down there between the manager and your accountant."

"What sort of a problem?"

"From what I can gather between the swearing and general testosterone overload, you signed off some of the profits to the new build on Sandringham and the manager is claiming it was never a done deal."

"He knows it was. Ring him back—"

"I've tried talking to him. He's not listening."

Cat started when Jay touched her leg. She turned. His eyes asked the question of what he should do.

"Go," Cat whispered. "You can come by and pick me up when you've finished."

"Jay?" Tess pressed. "Can I tell the accountant you're on your way?"

"Sure. I'll be there in fifteen minutes."

Tess's sigh of relief sounded over the receiver and Cat smiled when Jay disconnected the call. "I assume that's your personal assistant?"

"Yep, and the woman who keeps me sane."

"Hope you pay her well." Some of the unmerited jealousy seeped from inside the rolling ball of heat behind her rib cage. "A woman to put up with you must be worth her weight in gold."

"She is, but the one who marries me is going to be worth even more."

Cat's heart kicked and she forced a laugh. "God help her."

"God help you, you mean."

She tried to look away but he held her with his eyes. They brooked no argument, and undeniable joy churned inside of her, heating her blood with temporary relief from reality, a dream she was in Templeton dating Jay, rediscovering him and contemplating a future with him. If only he knew how much she wanted to dip her toe in that sea of possibility and dive in, the way every other person did when they pursued the rocky road of finding someone to share their life with. Chris and Melinda shot unbidden into her mind.

She released her held breath and reached inside her bag for her phone. "I should ring Chris."

"Why?"

"I told him I would let him know if the letter helped move things forward." She smoothed her hands over her skirt.

There was a long silence and Cat's heart beat out the passing seconds. He clearly considered saying more. She practically heard the cogs of his brain turning and weighing things. She glanced at his hands as they tapped the steering wheel and then down to his thighs. One leg lifted up and down as he bounced it.

"Jay, what's wrong?"

"We're busy. I don't want Chris spoiling your concentration."

"Why would he?" She frowned. What did Jay know about Chris? The possibility that the two of them might keep in occasional contact hadn't crossed Cat's mind until then.

She and her brother were hardly close. They'd very rarely spoken until Jay's phone call asking her to come to the Cove. While she'd spent the past seven years worrying and cleaning up after Mum, had Chris been talking to Jay? Did he know about Jay's drug problem?

Did Jay already know about their mother and hadn't told her?

Panic and humiliation stole the air from her lungs. What if Jay had been waiting for *her* to raise the subject of her alcoholic mother? He brought the car to a halt outside Marian's and cut the engine.

"Jay? Why would Chris spoil my concentration? Have you spoken to him?"

He lifted her fisted hand from her lap and twined his fingers through hers. "No, but judging by the look on your face, I need to. I could tell you were upset when you talked to Chris on the phone the other night, and I can tell you're dreading ringing him again."

She forced a smile and resisted the urge to pull her hand from his. She sensed he needed the contact and she would not hurt him any more than she already had. "We're fine."

"Don't lie to me."

Heat seared her cheeks. She wasn't lying…but she

wasn't telling him the truth, either. If she had her way, she never would. The closeness of him and the smell of leather and diesel closed in on her.

"I'm not lying to you. We're fine, just brother and sister stuff. He works. I work. We don't see a lot of each other these days."

"If he's upsetting you, I want to know about it. I might not have spoken to Chris for years, but I'm pretty sure it would come as no surprise to him that you're still my number one girl."

Years. He hadn't spoken to Chris any more than he had to her. Relief relaxed her shoulders. "There's nothing wrong."

He stared. "Are you sure?"

His phone shrilled through the tension and they shot their gazes to the display. Tessa.

"I'll go. Meet me here when you've finished." Feeling like a complete and utter fraud for deceiving him, Cat leaped from the car, slammed the door and rushed inside the bakery.

JAY STORMED FROM THE pier and into his car as if a million werewolves were in pursuit. What a waste of time. The funfair and arcade located at the end of Templeton Cove pier was yet another arm of the Garrett family business that Jay was renovating, improving and making a good investment for his siblings and any future Garrett children.

He slid into the driver's seat and started the engine. Children. His children, if he had his way. They would be a perfect blend of Cat and him. He was determined not to let her go this time. But he didn't want to harangue her into staying, either. He wanted her to stay of her own free will. Which meant he needed to pull back and let her take the reins; otherwise, she'd dig her heels in. She had more tenacity in her little finger than most people did in their entire bodies.

He pulled away from the curb and his thoughts filled with her flame-red hair and the smell of her perfume that seemed to linger beneath his nostrils throughout the last hour he was stuck in the middle of a showdown between his pier manager and accountant. The subtle, sexy blend of something flowery and feminine mixed with something sexually raw teased him, goaded him and totally infuriated him as he played mediator between two grown men.

Shaking his head, Jay joined the holiday traffic streaming along the road. It was the first time he'd thought about business since Cat arrived and where it once would have been normal to get things done one way or another, his need to succeed in the business world was diminishing. Instead, the need to fill his life with Cat burgeoned—as did his need to right his wrongs. If he could have Cat and make up for the mistakes he'd made and the people he'd hurt, his life would mean something again.

His smile faltered. The mammoth task of starting to make up things to people felt amazingly more achievable than keeping Cat in the Cove. If she really didn't want him, he would let her go.

Then why don't you? How many more times does she have to say she needs to go back?

Jay frowned as he stared ahead. He sensed that her reasons for returning to Reading had very little to do with her personal happiness and until he knew for sure, he couldn't give up. He hadn't followed her seven years ago but instead embroiled himself in his own dreams—he wouldn't blame her if she thought he might do the same again.

Today, his need for her shone supreme and with it the knowledge they had serious work to do with regard to Sarah's murder and their personal lives, if they stood any chance of a future together. Jay truly believed the pair of them together was what they both wanted. Desire flared in her gaze whenever they were alone. Her body trembled under his fingers when they'd made love…and then were doused when her thoughts turned to home.

Suddenly the desperation to get to Cat increased with every stop and start of the car in the snail-like traffic. If need be, he would relocate to Reading. She needed to understand that. Jay frowned. It would mean leaving behind the carnage of four years of drug-addicted chaos. Would people see his leaving as running away? His entire life before Cat came back had been about atoning for the pain he'd caused his family, his friends and associates of his father's. If he left, would everyone think he didn't care?

Jay tightened his grip on the steering wheel. Nothing could be further from the truth. He'd find a way to apologize for the things he'd done, wherever he was. Moving to Reading didn't mean he was running away, but rather finding the freedom and peace of mind he needed to show his regret as a new and improved man. He would do whatever it took to be with Cat this time.

When he reached Marian's bakery, Jay parked and haphazardly pointed the key fob over his shoulder to lock it. The bell above the door announced his arrival and when he stepped over the threshold he came to an abrupt standstill.

Cat grinned from ear to ear as she served the customer in front of her. She looked stunning. Breathtaking. Her deep-red hair was caught up in a white hat, her nose lightly powdered with flour, making her enticingly full lips look redder and more provocative than ever. When the customer walked away, Cat's gaze locked with his, her green eyes widening and cheeks flushing before she looked down at her hands.

Jay's heart kicked. She was even more beautiful when she was embarrassed.

He cleared his throat and walked closer. "Is this what I think it is?"

She met his eyes and her smile stretched into a grin. "Good morning, sir. Coffee? Full breakfast?"

He laughed and his gaze dropped to the lips that had trailed over his chest, shoulders and neck the night before. "What are you doing?"

She executed a mock curtsy, holding out the hem of the white apron she wore. "I'm working."

Jay stared as his mind wandered to the soft-porn place of wanting her to bring the apron home so she could wear that, and only that, later on. He swallowed, glancing behind her where Marian was busy issuing orders to her staff.

"I can't believe she has you working behind the counter," he whispered. "You do realize you've signed up for the summer season, whether you like it or not?"

Before she could respond, Marian turned around and marched toward them, the two oversize oven mitts she wore looking far too much like boxing gloves.

"Oh, here he comes to wreck the day."

He looked to Cat for support, but she just shrugged. He dragged his gaze from hers and faced the woman who always gave him a harder time than his mother.

"Well, thanks for the cheery welcome."

"It isn't a welcome. It's a warning." Marian snatched off the gloves and fisted her hands on her hips. "Cat arrived here over an hour ago tossing me questions like I had all day to sit around answering them. No doubt you were off gallivanting around doing something or nothing and left this poor girl to tackle Sarah's murder by herself."

He turned to Cat.

She smiled. "I've already asked Marian if she thinks she and George are up for a challenge."

Marian's small brown eyes shone with excitement. "If there's something George and I can do to help, we will."

"George will be here in anytime now." Cat wiped her hands on a towel. "Then we'll sit down and work out what we're going to do."

"And in the meantime you thought you'd help out?" He quirked an eyebrow.

"Exactly. You're not the only one who can learn the bakery business from the bottom up, hotshot."

Marian laughed. "Oh, it sure is good to meet someone who can match that mouth of yours, Jay Garrett. If you two end up in bed…well, people better run for cover."

"Ain't that the truth." His gaze locked with Cat's.

Marian cleared her throat. "Why don't the pair of you sit over there and I'll bring you some coffee while we wait for George?"

Jay watched Marian expertly wrap two loaves in paper for the next customer. "I'll tell you something about this girl, Jay. She's been here conducting her investigation and all the while serving my customers like she's worked here for years. That's not something to sniff at."

"I'm sure it isn't." He faced Cat once more. "You must be wanting a break. I'll be over there."

He walked to the four or five tables set out in the far corner where people could watch the world go by while enjoying a cup of coffee and a slice of one of Marian's sinful cakes. As Jay waited for Cat to join him, he willed his heart rate to slow. His rush to get back to the bakery hadn't been just about telling Cat he was willing to leave the Cove, but also fear for her safety.

Yes, she was capable of knocking a guy down, but what if he took her by surprise? What if the killer watched her right now? He noted the numerous familiar faces sipping cups of tea and buttering scones. One or two raised their hands in greeting and he flashed them a returning smile and wave. Danger lurked like an invisible phantom. The sooner they solved this murder, the easier he would breathe.

Whether Bennett was first to catch the son of a bitch or they were, it didn't matter. Jay just wanted him behind bars. Once they had spoken to Marian and George, he would have no choice but to leave Cat alone again while he went to his old drug haunts. He didn't want her anywhere near the places he once considered home and it was time he started doing some investigating of his own. He clenched his fists under the table. Especially if Bennett still suspected him of wrongdoing. He watched Cat exchange a few words with another customer while untying her apron.

He needed to cover the drug area of the investigation pretty damn quick before it occurred to Cat to go there alone when his back was turned. He stared at her. She'd managed to blend seamlessly into yet another role in the name of duty and he could easily imagine her walking straight into one of those filthy neglected places without so much as a blip in her stride.

Yet despite his fear for her, pride burst like a balloon behind his rib cage and a smile tugged at his lips. The sight of her behind the counter when he walked into the shop gave him more relief than he thought humanly possible. The woman was a dynamo. His dynamo—and he wanted her to stay alive.

Cat took the coffees Marian held out to her. When she reached the table, she held out one of the cups to him.

"Here. Black, no sugar. Blame Marian if it's wrong. Although, she did look incredibly disappointed I didn't know how you took your coffee. Clearly she thinks I should know such things about you despite being here less than a week."

He took the coffee and blew across the top. "Hmm, you don't know that, but you do know I have a birthmark on my butt."

Her burst of hushed laughter jerked his groin and she glared. "Stop it. Right now."

Jay grinned as she slid into the seat opposite him, clearly struggling to control her smile.

"We're here to get things rolling." She looked at him pointedly. "Once we have Marian and George busy, we'll go to every place you think we'll find a lead on any possible drug connection Sarah might have had. But I am still holding out hope that Bennett is wrong about that and Sarah got the money from somewhere else." She took a sip of her coffee.

Jay met her eyes and any optimism he had that Cat might not want to go with him died. "I'd prefer to go alone."

Her gaze turned steely. "I'm coming with you."

"Cat—"

"Don't get all macho and protective on me. There is nothing at these places that can surprise or shock me. I'm a cop. I've seen it all before."

"It's not your inability to deal with what you might see that bothers me."

"Then what?"

He took another drink to ease the dryness in his throat. Their eyes locked over the rim of his cup. "It doesn't feel good to know you'll see how low I sank, see the lifestyle I let myself get dragged into."

She reached across the table and took his hand. "You've told me everything and I've dealt with what happened, okay? It's time you did, too. The only reason I want to go with you is because I can use everything we hear or see in court if I have to testify." The skin of her neck shifted and a soft apology flashed in her cool green gaze. "Unfortunately, my testimony will hold a lot more substance in front of a judge than yours."

"Because I'm an ex-junkie." Anger seeped into his blood along with a hefty injection of shame and regret. "My God, will I ever be allowed to forget how much I screwed up?"

She squeezed his hand. "Yes, and I think going back to these places will help you see you're a success story, one of the few that survived, rather than be a harsh reminder of what you once were. This will be good for Sarah…and you."

He turned toward the window. How could she look at him with such admiration when she'd known him before the drugs? Knew how his life was there for the taking, but how even when every opportunity was available to him he flung it all back in his parents' faces? The night they spent on the beach, he promised her the world and then stayed away despite knowing her life must be falling apart when her father died. What could he say to make it better? What could he do to let her see he would never let her down again?

Watching the sun glint off the gray pavement, turning it silver, Jay curled his fingers tighter around hers. "It's hot out there."

"What?"

"The heat will send the junkies running for cover rather than heading for the beach like anyone sane and sober. It should be pretty easy to find Jordon."

"Who?"

He faced her. "Kyle Jordon. The main man in Templeton when dealing with narcotics. If Sarah was involved in that scene in the slightest way, he'll know."

"So he's dangerous." It wasn't a question. "Could it be him?"

"That killed Sarah?" Jay lifted his shoulders and inhaled a shaky breath. "It's possible."

She drank her coffee, her eyes not telling him anything of how that thought affected her. "Well, we'll find out either way, won't we?"

The regret of their lost years culminated and fell heavy into Jay's heart. "I'm sorry I didn't check up on you, Cat."

She smiled softly. "Don't apologize. Never apologize. We're human. We've both made mistakes."

There it was again. That sadness in her voice. "What mistakes have you made? What is it you think you've done wrong?"

Her gaze darted over his face and she slowly slipped her hand from his and clamped it with her other around her coffee cup. She stared into the milky-brown depths. "I'm making mistakes every day and have no idea how to stop."

"What are you talking about?"

She looked up. "Can I ask you something?"

Jay's heart twisted and he braced himself for whatever further admission he would have to make. Whatever she asked, he wouldn't lie to her. "Shoot."

"When you were in rehab, did you ever feel abandoned?"

"Abandoned?" *Where had that come from?* "No. Never. I felt violently angry at the start, when I wanted a fix, then scared when the hell of withdrawal racked my body with pain like I've never known, but never abandoned."

She stared deep into his eyes. "Honestly?"

"Honestly." The pain in her eyes was more than Jay

could take and he stood, gesturing for her to slide along the seat. "Move over."

"What?" Panic burst into her gaze. "What are you doing?"

"Move."

He pulled back his shoulders. She might have had him totally under her control in bed last night, so weak with lust for her if she'd told him to get on all fours and bark at the moon, he would have. But that was then, this was now.

She hesitated another moment before sliding along. Jay sat beside her and put his arm around her shoulders, pulled her close. She trembled and he held her tighter. The scent of her perfume, musky and enticing, wafted under his nostrils and he fought the urge to press his face into her hair.

"Why did you ask that? What's going on?"

She hesitated and then her body slumped under his arm as though the fight slipped from inside her. "I don't think I can do it anymore. I'm so tired." Her voice cracked.

Whatever it was she didn't want to do, she didn't have to. He'd fix it for her. Whatever it was, he'd fix it. "Can't do what? Work for the police? Sarah?"

She shook her head and her hair fell like a ruby red curtain over her face, hiding her from him. "Mum. I don't think I can help Mum anymore."

"Julia?" He knew it. Every instinct in his body had screamed her sadness was rooted in her mother. "What is it, Cat?"

"Whoa, now what's going on here, then?" George's voice boomed to the side of him.

Jay flinched and Cat leaped away from him as though he'd bitten her.

"George." She laughed, her voice forced and tight. "You're here."

"Yes, I am. And look at you all snuggled up to Jay like you've never been away."

CHAPTER SIXTEEN

CAT'S HEART THUNDERED. What had she been thinking? Now Jay would be like a horse with the bit between his teeth. He wouldn't let this go easily. Goddamn it. How could she weaken like that? She blinked, George's smile faltered.

"Are you okay, lovely?"

She plastered on a smile. "Of course…all the better for seeing you."

George looked from her to Jay and back again, his eyes narrowed. "Are you sure? Because just a second ago you two looked very cozy—"

Cat patted her hand on the table, steadfastly avoiding turning around to look at Jay. She could practically feel his gaze boring a hole in the side of her head. "Come and sit down. We've got something important to talk about."

George slid into the seat opposite her. "Yes, indeed. Marian tells me you need our help."

Guilt pressed down on her chest and Cat's smile wavered. "I do. I have a huge favor to ask. But if you're not comfortable with it, you say no and we'll not talk about it again. Okay?"

He frowned. "Is it serious? Is this to do with Sarah?"

Cat swallowed. "Let's wait for Marian, okay? Then I'll explain everything."

She hated doing this to him but she had to focus on the outcome. She was willing to risk disciplinary action being taken against her if her boss ever found out she used civilians to help in a murder investigation. But that was the very worst that would happen. She'd make sure of it. Marian and George would be fine.

Nerves stole the saliva from her mouth. Everything would be fine.

Jay cleared his throat beside her. "So, George? Dad's back from vacation and keeping you busy?"

George turned. "As always, Jay. As always."

The two of them struck up a conversation and Cat exhaled. She was too personally involved with everyone this investigation touched—but that didn't mean she would, or could, turn away. She'd had enough of running and hiding. She trusted Jay and needed his help. He'd been honest with her about his addiction, and the more Cat was with him, the more she felt she owed him her honesty, too.

His past and her future were too closely entwined for them to be together but it didn't mean she had to reject him entirely. He didn't deserve that when he'd come so far despite everything he'd done to himself and others.

She didn't want to run from life anymore. If Jay could do it, so could she. But for now, they were on a mission to find the money Sarah had hidden. Whether or not Jay could help with her mum she'd soon find out. Maybe she shouldn't have opened the subject it had taken a week to even contemplate sharing with him, but she had.

Even when Jay's alibi was not as rock solid as he presumed, and that he hadn't been there for Sarah. Cat swallowed. She must be mad. Or in love. She'd fallen in love with him all over again. Stupid, stupid woman.

Blinking against the burning in her eyes, she looked across the bakery. Marian was at the coffee machine. She looked up and gestured to Cat by raising her finger that she would be just a minute. Cat forced a smile and mouthed "okay."

She looked down at her clasped hands and worried how best to explain to Marian and George what she and Jay had learned about the danger Sarah had been in. Everything suddenly felt like such a mess. Was she feeling so out of control because she and Jay had slept together? That she had forgotten her fears and worries and released her frustration with the man she loved for one blissful night?

Cat risked a glance at him and pain struck her heart afresh. Bennett had made her doubt everything Jay had told her. She couldn't ignore the fact that he'd lied to her about meeting Sarah that day. Yet deep inside, she knew Jay would never be capable of locking his hands around Sarah's throat.

She shoved her doubts into submission. This trip, even with its sickening cause, was allowing her the perspective and space she needed to figure out how to help her mum and herself from falling into the abyss of hopelessness that grew wider every day. These thoughts about Jay were born from her perpetual doubt about everything. Nothing more.

She blinked when she saw Marian approaching the table and forced a wide smile. "Ah, here she comes."

Marian stopped at the table and placed two steaming cups in front of George and a tray of rock buns in the center. "Help yourselves. Freshly made this morning."

Cat glanced at Jay and their eyes locked. His gaze was soft with concern.

Please, Jay. Leave it. Not now. Later.

Panic simmered through her blood as Cat silently pleaded with him. After a long moment he nodded and she exhaled a shaky breath before turning to face Marian and George.

"Right, then. Shall we get started?"

Emotions tumbled around in her heart. Fear she was doing the right thing by Sarah, Jay, Marian and George tormented her mind and messed with her usually solid and professional judgment. Cat tilted her chin. For better or worse, there were choices to be made and for now, the late afternoon and ensuing hours belonged to Sarah.

She met Marian and George's wary gazes. "You're probably wondering what I meant by needing your help. Well, that help is tied up in the investigation into Sarah's death and it involves a visit to the beach."

Marian's eyebrows lifted. "The beach? What's the beach got to do with anything? The poor girl was found murdered on Jay's land, not the beach."

Jay stiffened. Marian might as well have poked him in the eye with a needle of accusation.

"First of all, the forest isn't Jay's land." Cat's tone was firm. "Secondly, the beach plays a massive part in finding Sarah's killer because I'm confident he won't leave the Cove without something that's hidden there." She looked from Marian to George and back again. "How well did you know Sarah?"

Marian blew out a breath and her eyes turned glassy. "Not well enough, it turns out." She swiped her hand under her eyes. "I didn't know she was in trouble. I thought she was her usual happy self and that hurts me down to my very soul. I thought I knew her. I really did."

George took her hand in his. "No one could've known what was going on, love. No one. Sarah was a good girl who the devil went after. It's no one's fault we didn't see him. In disguise, he was. Isn't that right, Catherine?"

Cat smiled. "Absolutely. No one could've known, but what we know now starts us moving toward a conclusion that I hope will give Sarah's parents a modicum of peace.

We now know Sarah hid some money on the beach. Her killer's money." She drew in a breath and exhaled. "I want you to find it."

George and Marian stared at her with identical expressions of stunned bewilderment. Silence. Cat waited. She had seen this a million times before and knew their brains would kick in sooner or later, but then Jay waved his hand in front of their faces.

"Hey, are you okay? Did you hear what Cat said?"

Biting back an entirely inappropriate smile, Cat pulled his hand to the table and shot him a glare.

She reached into her handbag and pulled out a piece of paper. "Here's a list of places Jay and I think Sarah could have hidden the money. Places the police are unlikely to consider but Sarah knew well."

George's paralysis was the first to break. "She hid money on the beach? Her killer's money? My God."

"Exactly. Until I'm convinced it's no longer there, I'm sure he's still in town. Here." She offered him the list.

His eyes darted over her compiled locations. "How are we supposed to know—"

"Just follow the directions." Cat looked at Marian. "It's imperative neither of you draw attention to yourselves or act in any way other than normal."

Marian turned to George. Their faces were etched with worry and confusion. She reached across the table and gestured for each of their hands. Silently and slowly, Marian put her hand in one of Cat's and then George followed. Cat clasped their fingers and prayed that she could gain their confidence to do this.

"What I'm asking you to do is huge…and I'm sorry that I even have to consider it. I…we, Jay and I, are possibly being followed. Whether by the killer or someone else, I don't know. He has rung me twice and given intimate details he could have only known if he was watching me on both occasions."

George's jaw tightened and his eyes narrowed. "Did he threaten you? Have you told this Bennett character about this?"

Cat nodded. "Yes to both questions. So, you see, if he's following me, there's every possibility he will follow me to the beach."

Marian looked toward the bakery window. "How do you know he's not watching us right now?"

Unease rippled across the back of Cat's neck. She had considered it, but it was a risk she'd had to take. He wanted her or Jay, or maybe both. They were the link to Sarah. They were the ones she'd contacted before her killer struck. Intellectually, Cat knew he would have no interest in what Marian and George were doing. Emotionally, the knowledge of sending them to the beach still sent a horrible chill down her spine. She had no option but to trust in her own intuition that this was the best way forward.

"The truth is, I don't, Marian. But he wants Jay or me. Not you." She tightened her fingers around Marian's and George's and looked at them in turn. "You don't have to do this. I'm asking you, but by no means forcing you. It is risky, but I think the risk is low enough that you will be safe for the short time I need you to go there. The killer will be watching me and Jay if he's watching at all." She glanced at Jay. "We have a house visit to make and then we'll come to the beach. It will be dusk soon and the light will be no good for a proper search. I just hoped we could get a head start before Bennett's team arrives."

Marian frowned. "Don't trust him, either, eh?"

Cat stared. "I trust him."

"No, you don't. It's written all over your face. Why don't you trust the inspector?"

Heat seared Cat's face. *Because he thinks Jay did this.* "It's not that I don't trust Bennett to do his job. But I want to be the one to nail Sarah's killer. It sounds stupid and misplaced. But Jay and I…" She turned to Jay. "We've got some making up to do as far as Sarah's concerned."

A sad silence enveloped the table and Cat shut her eyes. Sarah's smiling face appeared behind her closed lids and Cat squeezed back the tears.

"Okay. We'll do it."

Cat snapped her eyes open. "You will?"

"Yep." Marian grinned from ear to ear.

George grinned. "Abso-bloody-lutely."

Fully alert once more, Marian gestured toward the paper. "George, give me that."

Cat let out her breath on a rush of relief and when Jay stole his arm around her shoulder, she turned and smiled. He winked, sending her stomach into a mess of knots and tangles. She turned to Marian and George. Marian's keen gaze ran over the list.

"I know a lot of these places, which means other people will, too." She shook her head. "The chances of the money being there are slim, but if it is, we'll find it, won't we, George?"

He pulled back his shoulders and jutted his chin. "Yes, ma'am, we will."

"Good, then we'll leave you to it." With a final encouraging smile, Cat slid from the booth and stood to the side, hitching her bag onto her shoulder. "Fifty thousand pounds is a lot of money, and with your help, we'll soon know the name of Sarah's killer and be able to arrest him before Bennett tries to send me back to Reading."

Jay stood beside her. "Ring either of us as soon as you know…or find anything. Wherever Cat is, I'll be, okay?"

George gave a curt nod. "Will do."

Cat walked to the door and then stopped. She turned back. Marian and George were sidled close together, their heads bowed over the list with Marian's face sternly issuing instructions. George lifted his hand into a salute every time she took a breath.

Tipping her head back, she met Jay's eyes. "They're on it."

He smiled. "Good. Now I hope we can finish the conversation we started."

Cat swallowed but didn't look away. No more looking away. "Okay."

He arched an eyebrow, surprise showing in his steady brown gaze. "Okay?"

Hope and optimism surged into Cat's heart as she realized she wanted to share the burden with him. Wanted him to know her true life and not the one she constantly portrayed to the entire world. She nodded. "Okay."

His wide, satisfied smile set her heart thumping as Jay took her hand and led her to the car. Their eyes met over the roof before they opened the doors and got in. Cat pulled on her seat belt, her hand trembling as he started the engine and pulled away.

"Do you want to go back to the cabin?"

She shook her head. "No, we'll talk on the way to the drug haunt. If I don't do this en route, I'll feel like we're wasting precious time for Sarah. And what I have to tell you is hard enough to share as it is."

He gave a slight nod and turned back to the windshield. When his hand slid over hers and held tight, she didn't pull away but squeezed her eyes shut instead.

"Mum's…" The words caught and lodged in Cat's throat like tiny bullets of guilt. The perpetual feeling of responsibility rained down on her. Betrayal of her mum was the last thing she wanted, but over the years, Cat had weakened and Jay was her strength. Always had been. *Tell him. Say the damn words.* "She's an alcoholic and I don't think I can help her anymore."

Silence passed with each beat of her racing heart. She turned. His gaze was focused straight ahead, his jaw tight. "How long?"

"How long has she been drinking? Seven years."

"Since your dad?"

"Since Dad."

"Right."

Silence. Cat pursed her lips together. Nothing else needed to be said. He knew addiction. He knew the grip of its long-stretching fingers, knew its gradual and destructive path. He had lived in the midst of its all-consuming hunger for both for the victim and anyone they held dear. The emotional strain of what he'd done and what he wanted to make better showed in every line on his face, every beat of his heart.

He coughed. "You want an end to it? Is that what you're saying?"

Shame consumed her day after day even though Cat knew it was irrational and unsubstantiated. She'd told on her mum. Told on her to a boy who only knew her as one of the most glamorous mums in the world.

Tears burned her eyes. "Yes."

"Does Julia?"

"I don't know."

"Then there's nothing you can do right now."

"Sometimes she does, but then hours later she's drunk and any hope I had is lying at the bottom of an empty bottle."

"She has to want this for herself, Cat."

"I know, and I want you to help me show her."

His gaze drifted over her face. He nodded. "Okay."

Blowing out her held breath, Cat returned his smile and tightened her fingers around his.

CHAPTER SEVENTEEN

JAY STOOD ON THE PAVEMENT and stared up at the three-bedroom end terrace house as though it were Dracula's castle. Evening was falling and the facade of the once-white painted house looked grayer and uglier than he'd dared to remember. Filthy nicotine-stained net curtains hung haphazardly at the windows, the small front garden was strewn with wind-whipped sheets of newspaper, tin cans and beer bottles. A tiny window hung open downstairs and the smell of cannabis drifted along the evening breeze, tainting the prewar housing estate with its invisible evil.

Cat inhaled a shaky breath beside him but Jay didn't turn. He didn't want to see the look in her eyes.

"You ready?"

Jay exhaled. "As I'll ever be."

"Jay, look at me."

He turned and met her beautiful green eyes. She looked somehow lighter, happier, more determined.

She made to touch him and then dropped her hand to her side as though remembering where they were. The skin at her neck shifted. "We're in this together, okay? You know my stuff. I know yours. When we go inside there, I won't be looking at anything and imagining how you were. I'll be inside that dump as a cop and a cop only, okay?"

Tension rippled along his shoulders, making his neck ache and his hands curl into fists at his sides. "Okay."

She turned back to the house. "It's imperative nobody gets the slightest idea there might be something personal between us. If they do, they have the perfect weakness to attack."

He followed her gaze as fury for the past and present burned inside his veins. "I'm not going to let anyone in there touch either of us. They'll have to kill me first."

"That's exactly what worries me."

Jay drew in a long breath and exhaled. Whatever happened behind the chipped and peeling front door, he was supposed to pretend Cat was nothing more than a cop investigating a murder. Not the love of his life, not the woman he wanted to spend the rest of his life with.

The heat of her stare burned at his temple. "I'm carrying Mace and that's the first thing I use if anything gets nasty, okay? If you don't let me take the first step, you could find yourself in front of a judge. Jay?"

He couldn't drag his gaze from the house.

"Jay, answer me or we get back in the car and leave. If you can't promise me you'll let me lead this, I can't promise I won't come back here on my own."

His suppressed anger heightened. She had him by the balls and damn well knew it.

"Fine. I promise."

She blew out a breath. "Right. Then let's do this."

They moved forward and when they reached the door, Jay rapped his knuckles on it in a succinct and rapid motion. The mail slot at waist level flipped outward and Jay leaned down, his hands splayed on his knees.

"Hey, it's me."

"Bloody hell. Jay?"

"Open the door, Captain. Got someone with me."

The mail slot opened higher, trembled and clanked shut again. Jay sent up a silent prayer for God's help as the sound of three locks being shunted back echoed against the door. He turned and met Cat's eyes. She stared back at him, her green gaze softening for an imperceptible second as though reassuring him before they turned ice-cold once more.

Nothing would happen to her. Nothing.

The door slowly opened and the smell wafting from the small open window blasted Jay's face in a cloud of unwelcome remembrance. Resisting the urge to reach back and take Cat's hand, he stepped over the threshold. She followed him inside. Seconds later the door slammed shut behind them. Jay fought the memories that rushed into his brain and sped his heart. This was for Sarah. For Cat. For him.

Captain, an emancipated man/boy of nineteen, worked as the door lookout in exchange for his drug of choice. The boy's life was as wasted as anyone's ever could be. Jay's hands curled into fists. One by one, he wanted to save them all. The decision to do something, anything poured into his blood on a wave of angry revulsion. He had run from his demons for too long, and now he wanted nothing more than to strike them down and bury them alive.

Once Sarah's killer was found, he would come back here. He'd come back and get this place shut down.

Once he threw the bolts back into place, Captain turned his weary-eyed stare on Cat. His eyes traveled over her from hair to shoes and back again. Although Cat was dressed in jeans and a vest top, Captain leered at her as though she were naked and bitter anger shot into Jay's throat.

"Oi, Captain, look at me. Not her."

The boy turned. "Who's your friend?" He swiped his scabbed forearm over his mouth. "She want turning?"

Jay's anger burned hotter and he stepped toward Captain, barely controlling the need to clench the boy's chin in his fingers. Aware of Cat's gaze on him, Jay fought the memory the smell coming from Captain evoked, the sad truth there had been a time when Jay lingered in the same rancid cloud of self-hate.

A storm of emotion churned inside him as Jay glared into the boy's eyes. "This is Detective Sergeant—"

"You brought a cop here?" Panic showed in Captain's gaze as it shot to Cat over Jay's shoulder. "Have you got a death wish?"

Jay grabbed his arm and dragged the boy through the hallway and into the back room where he knew the most people would be. He didn't need to turn around to know Cat was right behind him. He'd never been more aware of another person in his life. Impatience and desperation to get her out of there burned like lit paraffin through his blood. He should be alone with these people, not exposing her to a life that filled him with self-hatred and shame. Everything wafted over him and seeped into his pores, he would do something to change this if it took his last breath. No more.

He lingered in the doorway, squinting his eyes, willing them to adjust before someone who might be lucid jumped him. After a moment, he pushed Captain forward and stepped toward the black sheet hanging at the window. He yanked it down and twilight spilled across the room in a hazy white spear.

Jay froze as memories immobilized him. Three men and two women in different states of undress lay in varying levels of consciousness against each other. One or two of them lifted their hands above their eyes, shielding them against the unexpected brightness.

Captain stared. "What's this about? What's a cop doing here?"

"Jay."

Cat's voice was abrupt behind him. Jay whirled around. His heart leaped into his throat. Renowned dealer and all-round underground boss, Kyle Jordon, stood a head-height above her...smiling like all his damn Christmases had come at once.

Jay's eyes locked with his as blood roared in his ears. "Kyle."

The older man's smile grew to a grin. "Jay, my man. Look at you. Never thought I'd see the day you'd step back in here." He ran his gaze over Cat's hair. "And with a damn sexy cop, no less."

Stepping closer, Jay met Kyle's eyes as adrenaline ripped through his veins and with it, the growing knowledge he'd knock Kyle out if he so much as laid a single finger on Cat. This was his fault. His fault this beautiful woman was in such a godforsaken hole. His eyes shifted to hers and she stared back confidently, her hand already poised on the Mace she concealed at her waist.

"Can you spare us a few minutes for a chat?" Jay shifted his gaze to Kyle.

Kyle grinned and gestured toward the doorway, indicating they leave the partially comatose party and head into the equally filthy and squalid kitchen.

Cat cleared her throat and stepped away from him. "Why don't you lead the way? I'd hate to get lost in here."

He smiled. "Now, we wouldn't want that...although, I wouldn't mind a quick game of hide-and-seek with you, pretty lady."

Jay clenched his fists as Cat kept her gaze level with

Kyle's, her entire demeanor screaming control. She smiled. "A pretty lady who could quite easily lift her knee and ram it in your gonads before you had time to draw a breath."

He laughed. "Yum. She's as fiery as hell, too."

Cat brushed past him. "I'll tell you what. I'll find my own way because if I have to stand here smelling your breath much longer, I'll throw up."

Biting back a smile as pride filled his chest, Jay watched Kyle eye Cat's retreating backside and slowly walked toward him. At six foot two, Kyle wasn't small, and when Jay stood in front of him, their gazes were level.

"She's here investigating a murder, not your drug pushing. So back off and just answer her questions, okay?"

Kyle arched an eyebrow. "Are you telling me what to do in my house?"

Jay leaned closer to him and huffed out a quiet laugh. "Your house? You're about as likely to spend a night in this place as you are of sharing another ounce of breathing space with Sergeant Forrester."

The older man laughed, his wide grin revealing teeth that must have cost him a good chunk of his illegal fortune. "Well, well, well. I think somebody's got a soft spot for the sergeant. Interesting."

"Just answer our questions and we'll leave." Jay hated that his feelings for Cat were so damn transparent he might as well have had an "I love Cat" placard hanging around his neck. "Neither of us wants any trouble, so let's get this done and then we'll be on our way...unless I decide to make it my personal mission to save the people screwing up their lives like I could have mine."

"Aww, you want to help them?" Kyle's smile dissolved and his eyes flashed dangerously.

Anger burned in Jay's gut, making his heart race and

his head pound. "Nothing you do scares me, Kyle. I'm sober and I'm ready for you."

"Have you two finished?"

Cat's voice barely penetrated the veil of suppressed rage beating around Jay's body. She stepped in between them and splayed a hand on each of their chests. His gaze remained locked on Kyle's as Jay trembled with fury.

"I want the pair of you to move into the kitchen right now before I call for backup," Cat said quietly. "None of us wants that. Not me, not Jay and especially not you, Kyle. Now, will the pair of you drop the testosterone face-off and get into the room that I assume once resembled a kitchen?"

Cat walked out. Kyle was the first to break eye contact and follow her.

Knowing he was in serious danger of blowing sky-high any chance of either of them obtaining vital information, Jay focused on controlling the guilt, shame and sadness coursing through him. He drew in a long breath through flared nostrils and followed the man he once thought was his savior. The knowledge stuck like a rock in his throat.

CAT'S HEART BEAT LIKE a drum and her hands were clammy. She leaned against the counter, then thought again and stepped away, hoping nothing unrecognizable was stuck to her backside. The place reeked of stale food, drugs and sweat. She swallowed, not wanting to inhale. The low hum of Jay's and Kyle's voices stopped and she crossed her arms to stare hard at the doorway as she waited for them to appear.

Kyle came first. His scowl turned to a grin.

"Why didn't you sit down?" he asked. "There ain't nothing on those seats that wouldn't come out in a sixty-degree wash." He laughed at his own wit.

Cat sniffed. "Sixty degrees? The water will have to be past boiling to tackle the smell on my clothes when I leave here, let alone anything else." She uncrossed her arms and slid her hands into her jeans pockets. "Why don't you sit down so we can have a little chat?"

He walked farther into the room and Jay came in behind him, his expression a telltale picture of how hard being back in the crack house was for him. His brow was deeply furrowed, his jaw tight. Cat sent up a silent prayer to God asking Him to give Jay the strength to get through the next fifteen minutes or however long it took for her to get what she wanted from Kyle. She briefly met his eyes over Kyle's shoulder.

They were stone cold, looking through her rather than at her. He was gone, lost in his own soul-destroying memories. Cat's nerves hitched a little higher. Jay needed to hold on to whatever sorrow whirled around inside him. Anything less could ruin the only chance they had of gaining cooperation from a massive player in the drug scene. Cat had a feeling no one would talk to them if Kyle said so, and if anyone did, he would order their legs gone and possibly their lives.

"You going to stand there staring at my boy Jay all day, Sergeant, or is there something you wanted to ask me?"

Cat turned. Kyle pulled a cigarette box from his inside pocket and shot one into his mouth. "Got things to do, places to be." The cigarette bounced on each word as he pulled a silver lighter from his pocket. He stared at Cat above the flame, the smoke rising between them.

She took a step closer and Kyle grinned like a maniac. "Is there something funny, Kyle?"

He laughed. "If you and my man aren't bouncing the bed springs, my radar is way off."

Heat pinched Cat's cheeks. "Why don't you shut up and sit down?"

He held his hands up in mock surrender but made no move toward the chair behind him. "Didn't mean nothing by it. I think it's sweet a junkie can end up shagging a cop of your caliber."

Every part of her trembled with suppressed annoyance that he'd picked up on something between her and Jay. Cat forced a soft smile. "What would you know about a woman's caliber? Judging by the haunted look on the women's faces in that other room, you don't differentiate between man, woman and child when you're dealing. As long as you get your money, huh, Kyle?"

His ruddy cheeks darkened and his sanctimonious smile dissolved. "Do what I have to do to survive."

"Survive? You think pushing drugs is the only way to make a living?" Feeling some of her upper hand returning, Cat cast a surreptitious look at Jay. He now stood at the counter, his hands curled into fists beneath his crossed arms. She needed to take control of the situation before she lost personal authority or Jay erupted without thought or feeling.

She stepped toward Kyle, hating the fact she had to tip her head back to meet his gaze. "I want to know how well you knew Sarah Cole. So why don't you take a seat?"

He leered. "The dead girl? The dead girl found on Jay's property?" He smiled at Jay behind her.

"That's the one. She was my best friend so I'm hungry for blood. Hopefully not yours but we'll see, won't we."

He ran his gaze languidly over her face and neck before lingering at her breasts. Her stomach lurched as lust burned like wildfire in his eyes but she held fast. The sticky sound of Jay's feet moving across the filthy linoleum hitched Cat's nerves higher as he came to stand behind her. She silently willed him to stay put, to keep control and not pummel Kyle to the floor the way he deserved.

The seconds passed like minutes until Kyle snorted back phlegm like the animal he was and shot Jay a sneer over her head before turning away and sitting astride a battered white chair. "Sarah Cole was your friend. Well, well, well." He leaned his beefy forearms across the back of the chair. "So I'm guessing you and Jay go way back, too."

"Something like that." Jay stood so close behind her the whisper of his harried breathing brushed back and forth over Cat's crown.

She stepped to the side. Jay didn't move.

The sound of muted laughter, glass clinking and matches being struck filtered through the open door, reminding Cat of exactly where they were and how dangerous a situation this could become. They needed to get out of there before someone decided to play stoned hero, or before more "clients" arrived looking for their next fix. The odds were already stacked against them.

Cat brushed past Jay's frozen form and quietly shut the door before walking back to stand in front of Kyle.

"So…" Cat stared. "Did you know her?"

His smiled dissolved and his brown eyes hardened. "No."

"You're lying."

A flicker swept over his face. Anger? Guilt? Nerves? Cat narrowed her eyes and waited.

"Why would I lie?" Kyle grinned. "What is she to me? Nothing. I'm finding it interesting the cops have brought you in from God knows where, though. Where are you from anyway, pretty cop lady?"

"It doesn't matter where she's from." Jay took a step

closer. "We want to know why there are rumors Sarah was involved with drug money. If she was, you'd be the person who'd know about it. Now…how well did you know Sarah?"

The tension in the room increased. She should be asking Kyle the questions, not Jay. The emotional strain of being back at the house where he spent God only knew how many hours showed on Jay's face, in the curl of his fingers. Cat's heart went out to him, her respect for him higher than ever. He sensed as well as she did that Kyle was the man who could provide at least another stepping stone in the right direction.

Kyle looked at them, his eyes steely and determined, his shoulders bunched to just below his earlobes. "I didn't know her, but I knew *of* her."

Cat frowned. "Meaning?"

"Meaning she didn't come to my house for dinner, but she taught my grandson at Templeton Primary."

Jay took a step toward Jordon and Cat immediately stood in front of him, grasped his trembling wrist in her hand. No heroics. No trouble. If Inspector Bennett found out they were there, he would no doubt have her suspended and Jay charged with police interference. She'd agreed to share any information and the inspector would view a visit to the town's drug lord as information, so they needed to keep this meeting nice and amicable—on all sides.

Kyle grinned. "That's it, Sergeant. Keep Jay under control. He's like a viper when he gets going."

Ignoring the jibe, Cat glared. "So, you didn't know Sarah, which makes me think she wasn't selling drugs or handling drug money. Agreed?"

He drew on his cigarette, inhaling the poison deep into his lungs before exhaling. The smoke rose in a cloud between them. "What happened between you and her, Jay? Not the cop here, the teacher."

"That's none of your damn business." Jay's voice was like a growl above Cat's ear.

"I heard this Sarah bird was the one who got your ass thrown into rehab." He took another pull on the cigarette before grounding it out on the surface of the filthy Formica-covered table beside him. "Hope you didn't come back to kill her for her trouble."

"I owe Sarah my frigging life, you moron."

He grinned and shrugged. "Just asking."

Cat tightened her fingers around Jay's wrist, silently pleading with him to let her take the lead. Silently telling him she understood how hard this was for him to go through—and silently telling him Sarah was with them, cheering them on and there was no fear of her messing this up. Cat stared deep into Kyle's eyes, renewed determination spreading through her.

"Where do you think all these rumors came from, Kyle? The ones about Sarah's drug involvement, that it was her who got Jay into rehab and then, of course, that she stole a hefty amount of money, drug money, from her killer?"

Something flickered in his gaze before he blinked and it was gone. "Has the money been found?"

Cat stared. *Got you.* "Why? Is it yours?"

He laughed, but when he pushed his hand through his hair, it trembled. "'Course it ain't mine. Do you think anyone in their right mind would steal from me?"

Cat shrugged and released Jay's wrist as his trembling abated. She meandered away from Kyle and around the small kitchen. She felt his eyes penetrating her turned back and knew the mention of stolen money hit the intended target. Money was all Kyle cared about. Money and power. Murder and morality were low on his scale of personal concerns.

"Maybe not directly, but how about indirectly? Have any of your runners lost money they owed you over the past couple of months?"

"None because if they did, they'd be dead."

She spun around and charged toward him, planting her hands on the back of the chair so quickly, Kyle leaned back lest she smack her head into his. Jay gripped her elbow. Whether to stop her or help her, she couldn't be sure.

"Sarah's dead. Was it you? Did you take your fat drug-coated hands and stick them around her throat and squeeze until blood seeped from her nose? Did you?"

"No," he roared, standing and shoving the chair forward. Cat toppled backward into Jay's waiting arms and Kyle dug his hands into his hair. "I do not go around killing innocent women. That girl was my grandson's teacher. I didn't touch her and she never ran for me, got it?"

"Then where did she get the money?" Jay yelled.

Kyle stared at him, his chest rising and falling. "How the bloody hell should I know?"

Cat stepped from Jay's arms toward Kyle. "If you really don't know, I'll put my ass on the line you suspect something that could help us. Now, why don't you do the right thing for once in your life and help the cops put a good woman to rest?"

The seconds passed with each beat of her racing heart but Cat didn't take her eyes from Kyle's or move when Jay turned away from her and leaned his hands against the wall, his head bowed. The situation grew more risky with each minute they were there but Cat refused to leave with nothing. What else could she throw at him? What else could she offer Kyle as an incentive? She opened her mouth to feed him whatever crap she could think of when he spoke.

"Cops." He snorted.

Cat fought her frown. "What about us? We interfere with your business from time to time?"

His smile made her shiver. "The cops are just fine and dandy to me."

Her eyes narrowed. "Is that so?"

He continued to smile, but she said nothing, knowing he would break before she did.

"Do you know for a fact she had some money?" Kyle asked.

She lifted her shoulders. "It's speculation at this point, but I think it's warranted. Why?"

He tipped his head back and stared at the damp-stained ceiling. "Did the cops tell you that or someone else?"

What was going on here? He looked smug. Ahead of the game. Cat glanced at Jay who lifted his head and met her eyes. He shrugged, indicating he didn't know where Kyle was going with this, either. Adrenaline seeped into Cat's veins as she sensed something coming. A breakthrough. A deal. Something.

"Does it matter how we know?"

Kyle dropped his chin and his gaze shot to Jay. "Who told you there was money taken? I need to know."

"No one told me. They told the sergeant. Why do you think they would have told me?"

"Because the likelihood is it's someone who knows your weakness. They know you're an addict." He shook his head. "Don't look at me like that. You'll always be a slave to it."

Cat crossed her arms. "Who's 'they'? You keep saying 'they know.'"

His eyes locked on hers. "*They* are the people circulating these rumors. Rumors that bring cops like you knocking on my damn door, nosing into stuff that has nothing to do with you."

"My friend's death has everything to do with me and I'm going to keep coming after you until you tell me what you know. That missing money is yours, isn't it? It's your money and Sarah was either running for you or sleeping with you. Now, which one was it before I let Jay rip one of these chair legs off and bash out every last gram of regret you helped him snort up his nose or inject in his veins?"

Kyle's jaw tightened, his eyes flashed sapphire with rage, but his smile broke and turned wolverine. "I'd like to see him try."

Cat matched his smile. "Don't tempt me, Kyle. If you don't start talking, I swear to God you won't have just little ol' me to worry about but the humiliation of the entire town knowing Jay gave you a kicking. Now talk."

Kyle's gaze shot from her to Jay and then the door. Cat watched him like a predator, waiting for him to bolt. Her left hand hovered above the pepper spray hidden beneath her shirt.

"Do you know what?" He laughed and sat back down. "I ain't got nothing to lose by telling you what I know because if I'm right, you're finished anyway. You ain't never gonna get who killed her locked up and you ain't gonna find that money."

"Tell us." Cat glared. "Tell us what you know."

He met her gaze, his blue eyes burning into hers. "Was it a cop who told you about the money?"

"Why?"

"I ain't asking because I don't know. I'm asking because it matters which cop told you."

Cat watched him. A tiny splinter in the case was about to break. "It wasn't the cops. It was Sarah. Sarah told me."

He stared and slowly his eyes shone with knowing and the corners of his mouth curled in disdain. "Don't insult me, cop lady. I know it wasn't Sarah because she couldn't confide in anyone. Not after she took up with…" He stopped, his smile stretching to a grin. "Whoops, nearly blew the whole thing wide open." He laughed.

Jay passed her in a blur, knocking her to the side in his haste to get to Kyle. Before Cat could reach for her spray as backup, Jay had Kyle's arms wrenched behind his back and the bulk of his body leaning over the rusted, filthy sink.

Kyle cursed and spat, spittle and sweat mingling as he struggled against Jay's fierce, resentment-filled hold. The man was going nowhere.

"Now, what were you saying?" Jay said between clenched teeth. "Sarah couldn't confide in anyone after she took up with…"

Kyle remained silent except for grunting and cursing with the exertion of trying to get Jay off him.

"Just give us the name of who she was seeing, and we'll be on our merry way as though today never happened." Cat glared.

He laughed. "You have no idea what you're dealing with, pretty girl."

Jay wrenched his arm up a notch and Kyle swore in such a way it would've made Al Capone blush. "Then tell us."

"Let's just get one thing straight before I tell you anything, okay?"

Cat shook her head and smiled. "You're in no position to start bargaining. Now just spit out what you know."

"I ain't bargaining, I'm asking."

She and Jay exchanged a look. "Asking what exactly?"

"The reason you came here." Kyle stared into the sink.

"It had nothing to do with me, right? You're here about that teacher, nothing else?"

Jay spun him around and Cat met Kyle's eyes. They shone with something akin to defeat, but not quite. Almost as though he had found his moral compass and felt obligated to tell her something but it twisted his gut at the same time. What was going on here? What was Kyle insinuating? She tilted her chin.

"If you're concerned about our arresting you for what's going on in here, then yes, we're here about Sarah, nothing else."

"Then call off your lapdog and I'll talk."

Cat gave a curt nod and Jay dragged Kyle back to his vacated chair and shoved him onto it. He stood behind Kyle like a sentry, his glare fixed on the back of Kyle's head.

"Well?" Cat pressed. "Who was Sarah seeing? Whose money did she take?"

Kyle smiled, his teeth showing white in the fading light. "You're going to love this."

Cat's stomach rolled uncomfortably and the hairs on her arms raised. "Get on with it."

"I'm only telling you this because that bastard told me the buyer never paid up, not that his bloody girlfriend stole it from him."

"Who is he?"

The smile stretched to a grin. "Well, Inspector Bennett, of course."

Cat sucked in a shocked breath before she could stop it and teetered back on her heels, gripping the back of the chair. "Bennett? Bennett took the money? Killed Sarah?"

"The one and only."

She met Jay's eyes above Kyle's head. They stormed with a rage, bewilderment and hatred that scared the hell out of her. "How can I trust what you're saying? Bennett wouldn't have—"

"Yes, missy, he would. He's taken a cut of my earnings for his silence for a long, long time." He reached into his pocket for a cigarette. "He showed me that damn letter he took from her."

Cat spun away from his gaze, no longer worried about what Jay did or didn't do with her back turned. She fisted her hands into her hair, unable to look at Kyle. "The letter he mailed a week later."

"Yep. Stupid son of a bitch still had the thing. He was all pleased with himself 'cause he took it from her before she could send it." He shook his head. "When I asked him what he was going to do if she told someone about it, or someone watched her write it, he turned whiter than a line of coke. Christ only knows how he got to be an inspector." He laughed.

Cat swallowed the nausea rising in her throat, struggled to focus her mind. "Why the hell would he show you a letter that could get him locked up for murder? You two best friends or something?"

He smiled. "Not best friends, but he's earned a damn sight more money from me in the past five years than from being a cop."

Cat looked to Jay and he squeezed his eyes shut. She turned back to Kyle. "Bennett takes money from you? For doing what?"

"For turning a blind eye. He's got my back covered. What can I say?"

"Yet now you're giving him to us on a plate. Sorry, Kyle, but—"

"He lied to me and he killed a good woman. I may not have the best morals in the world, pretty lady, but no cop deserves to get away with that. Not even my mate Bennett."

Cat looked at the ceiling. "I can't believe this. I was convinced it was someone she loved, someone she was sleeping with."

He grinned. "She did and she was."

"Oh, God." Cat slapped her hand over her mouth and rushed to the sink. She stared down the drain and fought the urge to vomit. She couldn't. Not in front of Kyle. "How could people not notice?"

Jay came beside her, his hand on her back. "Remember your theory that people must have been used to them being together?"

She nodded.

"Sarah worked with the police all the time. With young offenders."

Cat squeezed her eyes shut. A chair scraped behind her. Kyle snorted.

"Yep. Hold on to your hat, Sergeant. You're going to send down the top man in the Templeton police force. Bennett was banging the best damn teacher this town has ever known."

CHAPTER EIGHTEEN

CAT WALKED BACK TO JAY'S CAR with her head held high but
her legs shaking. Bennett? Inspector Bennett whom she
respected? Trusted? She closed her eyes for a second and
swallowed the betrayal burning her throat and stinging
her eyes. His face filled her mind's eye. His cold stare and
holier-than-thou smile swam in her vision. How could he?
How could anyone stand in front of their victim's friends
and family stating he would do all he could to find her
killer? It was sick. Sick and wrong.

Nausea whirled hard and fast in her stomach, and Cat
swallowed against the urge to gag. She'd thought he was
on their side, Sarah's side. Just the day before, Bennett
had stood in front of a horde of television cameras and
appealed for help. That had been the catalyst to letting
her final reservations about Jay's involvement diminish.
It was a public admission they were still searching for a
killer. Cat closed her eyes. Before she could crumple to
the sidewalk, regardless of Kyle Jordon watching her from
the front door of the crack house, Jay caught her elbow.

She trembled at the passenger door as he opened it and
gently eased her inside. Once she was seated, he closed
the door and Cat turned to look out the side window.

Kyle stared straight back at her, his expression unreadable with his arm pitched against the door frame. He
said he was giving them Bennett because he stole Kyle's
money and killed Sarah, but Cat sensed it had nothing to

do with the money and everything to do with Bennett getting away with the murder of a young and vibrant woman with her entire life ahead of her. Kyle had clearly been fond of Sarah, too.

That didn't make him any better a person than Bennett. She turned away, concentrated her gaze ahead. She didn't know which of them was worse. Bennett for his coldhearted, murdering, lying ass or Kyle for thinking Bennett was less than him even though he supplied drugs to men and women often younger than Sarah. They were both killers.

The car purred to life and Jay drove away from the crack house and everything it represented.

He took her limp hand in his. "Are you okay?"

She closed her hand tightly around his. "No."

"I could kill Bennett. Right now. Just curl my hands around his neck like he did Sarah's."

"Me, too."

"He shared information with us. Appealed to the public. Allowed you access to the incident board. Accused me…" He squeezed her fingers. "What do we do next? Do you want to go see him?"

"No."

She turned. His beautiful brown eyes locked with hers, filled with concern…and love. He blinked and turned back to the windshield. The road ahead blurred through her tears.

"I should ring my boss. He should know…" Her voice cracked. "Goddamn it. He's going to kick my ass into next week. How could I be so bloody blind?" She slipped her hand from Jay's and swiped her fingers under her eyes. "Bennett has changed my entire view of mankind. And it was pretty low to begin with."

"Don't lump the rest of the human race into the same

pot as Bennett. What he did…is still doing, is evil. Pure evil. It takes a different kind of person to not only commit murder but to appeal to a small town community for help, to lead a team…"

Cat turned. Jay's jaw clenched and unclenched and his knuckles shone white as he gripped the steering wheel. They had to do something—and do it fast. With both of them feeling not only stupid but used and insulted, the natural knee-jerk reaction would be for them to head back to the station and confront Bennett in front of his entire team. Whip back the blackened curtain he hid behind and let his staff kick the filthy, lying, murdering crap out of him.

She froze. She wasn't thinking straight. "What if Kyle lied?"

"What?"

She turned. "What if this accusation toward Bennett is a smokescreen? What if Kyle killed Sarah? Or one of his runners? Do you believe he's telling the truth?"

He glanced at her. "Don't you?"

Doubt and unwelcome uncertainty whirled in her mind. "I do, but know I shouldn't. Not yet."

"Then we need to prove it one way or another."

Cat squeezed her eyes shut. She had to think, and think fast. "If Bennett killed Sarah, someone else must know. Kyle Jordon doesn't strike me as the type of person who would keep something as damning as that about a cop to himself." She hated having to ask Jay more about the drug community but saw no alternative. "Jay?"

He frowned. "What?"

"Who is Kyle's second in command? Who does he trust? We need another witness."

He huffed out a laugh. "I really am the oracle as far as the Templeton drug scene goes, aren't I?"

She touched his thigh. "We need to do this. For Sarah."

He nodded. "I know who he is. I'll go see him. On one condition. I see him alone. My nerves can't cope with you being around these pieces of scum anymore."

Cat gripped a handle on her brewing frustration. "You can't expect—"

"Alone, Cat."

She slipped her hand from his thigh and slumped back into the seat. Was it wrong that his keeping her away raised the doubts about him in her mind once more? She'd kissed him, slept with him, yet…

Self-loathing whispered over her skin. She had to trust him. She had to.

"Fine. Alone. But you get away from him as soon as you know anything, good or bad. You get yourself back to me in one piece, okay?"

He turned and met her eyes. "Okay."

Nothing but determination and sincerity shone in his eyes and Cat's heart swelled behind her rib cage. This was Jay. Jay would never hurt Sarah. Never. She snatched her gaze to the road.

"We have to do this right. If we rush in riding on a hurricane of emotion and Bennett is guilty, he'll be forewarned and forearmed. He could leave or alter evidence that will clear him. We're dealing with a cop. We can't forget that. He could secure an alibi, bribe a false witness…the list goes on." Cat drew in a long breath. "In the meantime, we'll put the wheels in motion for his arrest, or at least an internal investigation."

"And how are you going to do that?"

She smiled as inspiration struck. "We're going to trap him with the money. I want to make sure it's iron-clad that he did this. Then, and only then, will I ring my boss."

He stared through the windshield, a small smile lifting his lips. "You're the boss."

A strange mixture of pleasure and pain coursed through her as she watched his profile. They were joined in the knowledge and weight of her mum's truth, the same as they were in the burden of his past regret and pain. Neither of them hid anything from the other anymore and what happened next would be without lies or deceit.

Guilt at the lack of contact she'd had with her mum or Chris resurfaced. She'd done the right thing focusing on Sarah and not her mum. She was doing some good being here instead of constantly fighting a losing battle at home. She had made more headway in helping Sarah in the past week than she had helping her mum in seven years.

And it felt good. She was worthy. Her entire life wasn't an alcohol-induced mess. If there was a problem…or more of a problem, Chris would ring her. She had to believe that and do her job.

Jay turned and met her eyes. The love she harbored for seven years bloomed and burst inside her heart. She loved him so much. He raised her hand to his lips and pressed a kiss to her knuckles before putting her hand back into her lap.

"Tell me what to do, Sergeant, and we'll do it together."

Cat smiled. With Jay beside her, she was whole, powerful and happy; without him, she would be helpless and frustrated all over again. She didn't want that. Not anymore. More than that, she wanted to know if their feelings for each other were real or a fantasy.

Was she capable, strong and sexy because of Jay? Or was she pretending *for* Jay? There was only one way to find out. No more running away.

She drew in a shaky breath and pulled her bag from the floor of the car into her lap. "Okay, so the first thing

I need to do is ring Bennett. I'm supposed to be meeting him at the school tomorrow, so first I'll check he's still going and then I'll let slip in something about the money and having a hunch I know where it is."

"He'll see through that."

She frowned. "Are you losing faith in me?"

"No, but I'm not risking losing you. If he suspects for one minute you're hiding something from him or worse, you're onto him, who's to say he won't have his hands around *your* throat next?" He shook his head, his cheeks darkening. "I won't risk anything happening to you."

She stared at him. So this is what it felt like to have someone sober enough to care what she did when she walked out the door each morning. This is what it was to know she had more to live for than work or spending every spare hour trying to stop a loved one from killing herself.

"I love you, Jay."

He turned and his gaze softened. "I love you, too, but don't think for one minute those eyes of yours are going to break me down on my decision."

On impulse, she leaned across and pressed a firm kiss to his jaw. "I wouldn't dare."

He grinned. "Good."

"But I have to do something. I can't just wait—"

"Grab my phone from the glove box and ring Marian. See if they've gotten anywhere in finding the money."

Cat reached forward and took out his BlackBerry, scanning the address file until she found Marian's number. "If they've had no luck at the beach, I'll still meet Bennett at the school tomorrow and find some way not to stab the man in the eye while acting as though nothing is wrong."

He shook his head. "I can't let you be alone with him."

"Jay, I'll be fine. I'm a trained cop. We're going to find

that money, and when we do, we're going to lead Bennett to it like a dog to a bone."

Cat dialed Marian's number. "Hi, Marian. It's Cat. How did it go?"

The older woman sighed. "Nothing. We went to three of the six places you listed before it got too dark to see anything other than our hands in front of our faces. We had to ship out. The police team left half an hour or so before we did, looking glum, so I think we can safely assume they've stopped empty handed for the night too."

Disappointment fell heavy into Cat's stomach. "Okay. Well, you're doing a fantastic job. We wouldn't have made that much headway if you and George hadn't been willing to step in."

"I've got cover for the bakery first thing, so George and I will make our way back down there tomorrow. Don't you worry, if that money's there, we'll find it."

Unease stole into Cat's conscience. She had thought Marian and George at the beach was the best way forward, but risking them being there a second time didn't feel right. Her intuition was telling her to keep them away from the beach. "Get some sleep and let me worry about tomorrow. Jay and I will take the risk and go ourselves in the morning."

"Oh, no, you're not. What about this person watching you? You said—"

Cat closed her eyes. "I know what I said, but the phone calls have stopped. Maybe he's run out of ammunition, moved on to something else more interesting. Who knows what these people want? Sarah's death hasn't been mentioned in the press for a couple of days. Whoever called me most likely wasn't her killer, just someone who gets a kick out of violence in the newspapers. I don't want you in harm's way again, Marian." Cat opened her eyes. "I shouldn't have asked you in the first place."

Silence.

"Marian?"

"Okay, okay. You just be careful. Both of you."

Cat smiled softly. "We will."

"And give Jay a kiss from me."

Cat rolled her eyes. The insinuation that Marian thought Cat would be kissing Jay at some point that night was clear. "Night, Marian."

"Night, lovely."

The line went dead and Cat hung up. She stared at the phone lost in thought.

"Nothing?" Jay's voice filtered her mind.

She turned. "Nothing."

"Right. Well, we'll head back to the cabin. Get a good night's sleep and start again at first light tomorrow."

"Okay."

He squeezed her hand. "It's going to be all right, Cat."

She nodded, unable to find the words to say she agreed. They were still not there. They didn't have the money. They didn't know for sure Bennett killed Sarah. Worst of all, she still didn't know for sure Jay was innocent.

CHAPTER NINETEEN

IT SHOULD HAVE BEEN the start of a perfect day. The vista at the back of Jay's cabin was breathtaking. Cat drew in a long breath. It was one of those idyllic summer mornings when everything was bathed in golden sunlight, the leaves on the trees barely moved, and the sky was a perfect blue without a cloud breaking its beauty. Cat's brow creased. If only it weren't for the vivid reminder of the forest, of the place Sarah took her last breath.

She tightened her grip on the balustrade. It was just past six in the morning, and Jay was inside the house preparing a quick breakfast before they went to the beach. Cat refused to miss a couple of vital hours searching before she met Bennett at the school. Nothing could go wrong. If Bennett killed Sarah, he would pay. An Inspector. A man in authority. A pillar of the Templeton community. It made her sick to her stomach.

She stared at the forest. How were she and Jay supposed to look for the money when the beach undoubtedly already crawled with Bennett's officers?

"Cat."

Jay held his home phone to his chest, his face split with a wide grin. She frowned. "What is it?"

"They found it."

Cat's stomach turned over as disappointment crashed into her diaphragm. "The police? Bennett has the money?"

He shook his head. "Marian. Marian and George have the money."

"Oh, my God. They went down there? Is that her?"

He nodded and held out the phone.

With laughter bubbling in her throat, Cat rushed forward and snatched the phone from him. "Marian? What happened? You have it?"

"Yes, indeedy. The whole lot. We found it in one of the places on your list. It's wrapped in paper with some writing on it but we haven't touched anything. I have no idea what it says."

Cat's breath left her lungs in a whoosh of air. "But it's so early. You shouldn't... Thank you. Thank you so much. This is fantastic. And the police? Are they there?"

"Yep, and so far away from the money, they may as well be in America." She laughed. "George and I just about peed our pants watching them for the last half an hour."

"The last half an hour? But when—"

"Been here since five o'clock. Up with the sun, we were. I couldn't sleep for the frustration we didn't find it last night."

Cat grinned. "Stay right there. Guard it with your life without actually...you know what I mean. We'll be right there."

"We'll be waiting. We found it up on Carter's rock, the smaller of the two at the far end. Make sure you come in around from the west side. The police are running their blind asses off on the east side. You don't want to risk one of them spotting you and telling that snidey Bennett you're here."

Cat laughed. "Got it. West side. See you soon."

She pushed the button and passed the phone to Jay. "They've got it."

"Then let's go."

He smiled and gestured for her to lead the way into the cabin when Cat stopped. "Wait."

Jay turned. "What?"

"I need to ring Bennett first."

He stared. "Why?"

"If Kyle was telling the truth, I want to see Bennett's face. I need to see him when he realizes I have the money. That I suspect him as Sarah's killer."

"We don't know it's him, Cat. Kyle could be lying. Until we know—"

"What if it is? I want to see if he panics, gets angry, rants and raves. If it is him, I want him to know we know. I want him to know we have him and his miserable life is never going to be the same again."

"You're shaking." He stepped forward and pulled her into his arms, held her close.

She stole her arms around his waist and closed her eyes. She would hold the man she loved just for a moment, just for a few seconds before she lit the fuse that would lead to an explosion and what she ultimately hoped was Bennett's demise. Jay was her peace. Bennett her new chaos. Her mum the future problem she would face with the man she loved right beside her.

CAT AND JAY GOT OUT OF the car and walked around the front to stare out across the beach. His fingers wrapped around hers.

"Are you ready for this?"

She turned and smiled. "We've got him. As long as the letter from Sarah doesn't name someone else we haven't a damn clue about, of course."

"It won't." He tugged her hand. "Let's go."

They clambered down the steps leading to the beach.

Still holding hands, they walked along the shore toward the hidden spot where Marian and George waited for them. Wordlessly, they continued forward, silently playing the charade of a couple out enjoying an early-morning walk along the sand, the glistening English Channel beside them. Cat's neck ached with tension, her body wired to high alert. Jay's hand tightly gripped hers telling her what she already knew. This was the point of no return. Sarah's killer was named on that paper.

On and on they walked until the sounds of dogs barking and their owners' whistles and calls grew quiet. Only the soft breaking of the waves and the smell of water and seaweed filled the air. Cat's childhood memories bounced from one rock to another as the sand dwindled and the craggy surroundings grew denser. Even though they were out of sight of the holiday makers and horde of scouring officers at the other end of the beach, they were still in danger of meeting some curious kids out for adventure as Cat, Sarah and Jay had been a decade of summers ago.

They reached the base of the rock formation Marian indicated when she spoke to Cat on the phone, but she and George were nowhere to be seen. Cat raised a hand to her forehead to shield her eyes from the sun and ran her gaze over the cliff face. It was black, gray and brown, and intensely foreboding. Ledges jutted out sporadically. Lethal-looking points of rock stood like sentries here, there and everywhere. If someone took a tumble, it would mean more than a few broken bones.

She shivered, not quite believing how she, Jay and Sarah spent so many hours here and all left alive. Pain struck her heart and her breath caught. Until now. Now Sarah was dead, her life not taken by a slip from a rock but by a man she loved. Cat's hands curled into fists.

They had to get him. If Bennett hadn't killed her, they

would know who had and he would pay for what he had done. Somewhere in those rocks was the key to Sarah's murder, the key to her everlasting peace. Cat wasn't leaving without it.

"Where are they?" she murmured.

"We're in the right place, aren't we?" Jay looked away to another rock formation to their left. "There were so many places we played as kids."

"No, it's this one. I'm sure of it."

"Then we wait. Maybe they've taken the money and letter and—"

Cat groaned. "Don't say that. I specifically told them not to touch it and to wait for us. I want to see it just as it is. Want to make sure this is real and not some sort of set-up." Cat met his eyes. "We don't know her killer hasn't felt the noose tightening. Now that Marian and George have the money, they're in danger. What if—"

"Psst! Catherine, over here." The urgent whisper came from just above her head.

Cat and Jay tipped their heads back.

"Oh, my good God." Cat swallowed the urge to laugh out loud.

George peered over one of the ledges, hunkered down, dressed in black with his face partially camouflaged with something black streaked across his cheekbones. He grinned, his teeth showing obscenely white.

"Quick, up here. We've got it. We've really got it."

He disappeared and Cat turned to Jay, her eyebrow arched in question.

Jay shook his head. "I have no words. Let's go."

Smiling, she let him take her hand and together they climbed the rocks they hadn't visited since they were teenagers. It wasn't hundreds of feet high, but it was high enough. They reached the ledge. George and Marian risked so much by doing this for them, for Sarah. Jay held out his hand to help her over the final hurdle, and together they stood side by side with George.

Cat frowned. "Where's Marian?"

"Here."

Cat turned sharply. Marian emerged from behind another rock Cat hadn't noticed behind them, looking like a rotund version of an Amazon woman. Her face was made up the same as George's, her black leggings and top so tight neither left much to the imagination.

Looking from Marian to George and back again, the humor left Cat at the very real possibility the two of them had risked their lives. If the killer had caught them with the money, what was to say he wouldn't have shot them, beaten them, thrown them down onto the sand, their necks breaking…

Guilt pressed down like a lead weight on her chest. They were in their sixties and she had indirectly asked them to climb these rocks. Fear rose inside her as realization of what she'd done broke.

"Why are you both dressed like that?" she snapped, fear making her words slice the air. "What if Bennett… what if someone saw you? What if you fell?"

Marian's smile dissolved and the excited gleam in her eyes turned to something infinitely scarier. "I beg your pardon?"

Cat shrugged off Jay's hand from her elbow and came forward wrapping her arms around Marian, tears pricking her eyes. "This is serious. You two look so out of place you could easily have drawn unwanted attention. What were you thinking?"

"We were thinking we were helping you."

Cat squeezed her eyes shut. "I'm sorry. I shouldn't have snapped. If anything had happened—"

"Now, you stop that." Marian pulled back and held Cat's hands. "I loved Sarah. I want to be here, and that's the end of it."

"But—"

"But nothing." She smiled. "Now, do you want to see the money or not?"

Cat smiled. "Of course we do."

"Good." Marian turned and ducked down behind the tall rock from which she emerged. Cat glanced at Jay who shook his head as though she had committed a crime. "What?"

"Are you insane taking Marian on like that?" He shook his head but his eyes shone with amusement. His sexy mouth lifted at the corner as he gestured behind him.

Cat looked over his shoulder. George scowled at her. She raised her hands. "George, I'm sorry. When I think of what could've happened..."

George shook his head, silently cutting her off, then muttered something about death wishes and redheaded cops before following his wife inside the enclosed cavern.

Blowing out a defeated breath, Cat exchanged another look with Jay before following on behind. It didn't take long for her eyes to adjust to the semidarkness. Marian stood to the side of her, pointing toward a wide slab of rock down by Cat's feet. Nodding her understanding, Cat dropped to her haunches and pulled a pair of latex gloves from the pocket of her shorts. She snapped them on and met each of her coinvestigators' gazes before heaving the slab aside and reaching into the pothole beneath.

Her hand knocked against the package and she pulled it out with frightening ease. Anyone could have just as easily found this vital piece of evidence. Including Sarah's killer. Slowly, she unraveled the plastic bag around it and placed the bag on the damp ground beside her.

The money was wrapped in a sheet of paper, secured with a rubber band. Cat glanced at the three faces above her, each of them etched with concentration and hope. She drew in a breath and snapped off the rubber band, carefully laying the money down so she could draw off the paper. She turned it over.

Sarah's scrawl was shaky, but her words clear and succinct. Cat cleared her throat and read her dear friend's words aloud.

"I have not been living the life people think I have. I'm a liar. A liar who loved her job and her hometown, but if you're reading this, Cat, it means God has taken me to Him before I can make everything worse.

"This is money I stole from Cameron Bennett, which he stole from Kyle Jordon. Cameron is the inspector of Templeton Cove police and he's my lover. The man is dangerous and shouldn't be the one looking after our wonderful town. As you've found his money, I know he has killed me. Just as he promised he would.

"I love you, Cat. Tell Jay I love him, too. Make my lover pay for his mistakes as I regret making Jay pay for his."

Cat blinked back the tears burning her eyes and stood. The silence was unbearable.

She looked from one face to another as Jay, George and Marian stared at her, expectancy in their gazes where there maybe should have been fear. She couldn't have done it without them, but now it was time to get George and Marian out of there. Bennett's team would soon make their way down to this end of the beach.

She swiped her fingers over her damp eyes. No more tears. "Okay, we have the money and we know Bennett killed her."

"I can't believe it." Marian's voice cracked.

George stole an arm around her shoulders. "You never

liked him, did you? My Marian's got a sixth sense about badness and she always said Bennett was a bad one."

Marian grasped his hand and they exchanged a wobbly smile. Cat watched them. They needed to go. She didn't want their getting hurt on her conscience, along with every other thing building up there.

"Come on. Jay and I will help you back down onto the beach and then I want you to go about your normal day-to-day activities, okay? If I have my way, Bennett's arrest will be all over the local news by dinnertime, so just sit tight."

Marian's eyes lit up. "You're going to take him down?"

Cat laughed and her stomach knotted. "That's exactly what I'm…" she looked at Jay "…we're going to do."

Jay smiled. "Absolutely."

He led the way from the cavern and they slowly made the descent down over the rocks and onto solid ground. After much convincing that she and Jay would come out of this alive, Marian and George walked away, arm in arm, their black clothes still worrying Cat despite knowing there was nothing she could do about them now.

Once they were out of sight, she turned to Jay. "Okay, let's ring Bennett."

"Are you sure you want to do this? Wouldn't it be better to ring your boss and let him arrange for Bennett to be apprehended at the station or something? God knows I'd love to take Bennett down ourselves, but I don't want any loopholes or lack of procedure to result in Bennett slipping through the net."

Cat shook her head. "That's not going to happen, and we're doing this our way. I want to see his face when he realizes he's going to spend a long, long time behind bars, and so do you. Prison isn't a good place for a cop…" She grinned. "Which just breaks my heart."

He smiled and brushed the hair from her eyes. "Then we'd better make sure this goes well because if you come away with so much as a scratch—"

"Oh, she's going to come away with more than a scratch, Garrett."

Cat and Jay spun around.

Bennett stood just feet away from them, a maniacal smile splitting his face. The gun he held pointed straight at Cat's heart.

CHAPTER TWENTY

CAT COUNTED HER BREATHS as Bennett strolled closer. Her body hummed with adrenaline. She wasn't afraid for herself, but for Jay. She couldn't lose him. Not now. Not when her entire life had shifted its pattern and happiness lingered just beyond the horizon. They were unarmed and alone. Her gaze darted to Bennett's gun as he neared.

"Well, here we are." Bennett's eyes shone with malice. "You've led me straight to the booty, Forrester. How do you feel?"

Cat swallowed, gripped Jay's wrist as he moved to step forward. "You're insane if you think you can get away with this. You killed her. You killed Sarah."

He stopped in front of them, his six-foot-two stature and wide shoulders suddenly larger than life. Cat resisted the urge to step back. His eyes were ice-cold. His cheeks flushed and his jaw tight.

"It wasn't me, Forrester." His gaze cut to Jay. "It's Mr. Garrett who killed her. I knew it from the start." His smile widened. "I told my entire team from the very beginning he was our prime suspect. I brought you in because you were his friend. Brought you in so I could keep a closer eye on him. Ask my boss. He knew exactly what I was doing all the way through...and best of all, he supported it."

Jay stiffened. "You bastard. You set me up this entire time?"

Cat grasped his wrist tighter, kept her gaze on Bennett and the gun that didn't even tremble in his hand. He was in control. No emotion swayed his judgment. No regret blurred his conscience. If he released a bullet at this close range...

Was he telling the truth? She looked to Jay. Hated the fear crawling up her spine. The fear that Sarah hadn't written that letter after all. That someone else had. That Jay had. Had Jay been lying all this time? Had she'd been blinded by love? She glanced at Bennett. At the gun now pointed at the man she loved.

Her heart beating hard, she tugged on Jay's wrist. "Jay, look at me, not him." Slowly, he dragged his gaze from Bennett. Cat swallowed past the lump in her throat. "Is he lying?" Her voice didn't waver.

He flinched like she slapped him clean across the face. "What?"

Physical pain seared her heart but Cat tilted her chin. "Did you kill Sarah?"

Hurt and disbelief flashed across his gaze before it changed to anger and revulsion. "If you have to ask me that again—"

He tried to pull his hand from her grip, but Cat held fast. "Answer me. I need to hear you say it. I need to look in your eyes when you do."

His gaze darted over her face, lingered at her mouth before he looked directly into her eyes. "No, I didn't kill Sarah. I loved her. She was my friend. My best friend."

Ignoring Bennett's snort beside them, Cat drew in a long breath and exhaled. "I believe you."

"But you asked me, Cat. You actually asked me again."

Cat turned away from his disappointment in his eyes, the look that told her they would never get past this, that their short-lived happiness had now died with Sarah.

Three times she had asked him to confirm his innocence. Three times. Anger and her breaking heart fueled a fury she'd never felt before.

She trembled as she glared at Bennett. "You seriously think this is going to happen? You're going to frame Jay?"

"It is happening, you stupid girl."

Cat shook her head. "You're insane."

Bennett grinned. "Why? You doubted him."

A low rumble growled in Jay's throat as he stepped forward. "I'll kill you myself, Bennett."

Cat gripped his fingers and held on with all her strength. "Jay, no. He wants this."

He turned his glare on her and Cat's heart completely broke. Their love was over. "What's he going to do? Shoot you? Me?"

"I—"

Bennett laughed and they snapped their heads around to face him.

He grinned. "If that's the way it has to be, I'll kill the both of you. Right here, right now. People know I'm watching you, Forrester. People know I suspect Garrett. Now let's cut the crap. Where's the damn money?"

"It was you behind the phone calls? The torment?" Her body trembled.

Bennett's smile was wolverine-like. "I have people willing to do anything for me, Forrester. Anything."

"You make me sick." Cat drew in a long breath through flared nostrils in an attempt to keep her growing temper in check. She needed to keep calm. She had to make Bennett mad enough to confess. To make him pay.

She leaned to the side and made a theatrical look past him. "No backup cops with you, Bennett? Don't you think it will look a bit suspicious if Jay or I are found with a bullet in us on a beach supposedly crawling with cops?"

His color darkened. "Where's the money?"

Jay's anger vibrated through her arm, his suppressed need to pummel Bennett into the ground parallel to hers. She swallowed and prayed he let her do her job. Let her do what she was trained to do and nail this killer's ass to the wall.

She stared at Bennett. "I thought you'd be more concerned about what we found with the money rather than the money itself."

"Enough with your pissing games, Forrester. Where is it?"

"Aren't you going to ask who *Sarah* names as her killer?" Cat smiled. "Or do you already know? Sarah was an intelligent girl and made sure she could speak to Jay or me from the grave. An intelligent girl who made some naive decisions when she met and fell in love with you. Her killer."

The taut skin of his neck shifted once…twice. "You seriously expect me to believe she says I killed her in some stupid make-believe letter?" He smiled. "I don't think so."

"It's there. I promise you. Best of all, she makes it clear you're capable of killing her. You're now a prime suspect in a murder investigation whether you like it or not. The superintendent's going to be real interested in what you have to say, don't you think?"

The gun shook with a slight tremor and Cat's heart picked up speed. He was getting nervous. Mistakes were made and triggers pulled when nervous people held guns. Jay shifted beside her and Bennett snapped the gun toward him.

"Going somewhere, Garrett?"

"You're not getting away with this."

"Oh, I think I am. The most amazing things happen in this world."

Cat glared. "What's that supposed to mean?"

He grinned and icy dread slipped down Cat's spine. The power was shifting. Bennett had every avenue covered and all she and Jay had was a bundle of money and a letter. Bennett had contacts. Lifelong friends in the force.

Jay released a low growl. "It's over when one of us is dead, Bennett. Whether it's me or you."

Bennett laughed, the gleam in his eyes shining brighter. "Ah, Jay Garrett, the hero. The ex-junkie turned cop fucker."

Jay was out of Cat's grasp before she could react. "Jay, no! Don't."

He charged at Bennett and clamped his arms around his target's waist, bringing him down hard onto the sand. Cat's mind whirled as her body froze. The gun. He had a gun. Bennett's roar reverberated around them and Cat's heart leaped into her throat. She had to do something. Jay and Bennett blurred into one as they struggled for supremacy. Grunts and pants emanated. Curses and whacks of skin on skin thundered out into the quiet that just seconds before was only broken by the crashing of waves and the screeching of seagulls.

Cat rushed forward as Bennett gained control, struggling with the gun so close to Jay's face her blood ran cold. "No!"

She fisted her hand into Bennett's hair and yanked, but the mania rushing through his blood held him fast. "Get off him. I'll kill you, Bennett. I swear to God."

Jay managed to release one hand and threw his fist into the side of Bennett's face. The blow swung Bennett's head to the side as though it were attached to rubber. The gun flew from his hand and skittered across the sand. Cat leaped after it, her heart racing.

She picked it up and turned. Bennett's hands were

around Jay's throat as Jay gripped him by the shoulders. Jay's face was red, his eyes bulging.

Peace and concentration settled over her as Cat planted her legs wide apart. She held the gun aloft. "Release him, Bennett. Right now. It's over. I said…now."

Bennett turned and smiled. "Say goodbye to your boyfriend, Forrester."

She narrowed her eyes and pulled the trigger. The bullet hit his leg as a warning but Bennett merely flinched and continued to grip Jay's throat, choking the life from him, seemingly oblivious. Cat's adrenaline soared. The man was insane. She fired again, this time in his shoulder.

Blood sprayed as Bennett toppled backward, grasping his shoulder. "You bitch. You fucking bitch."

Time stood still. He collapsed and Jay rolled away from him, his face and clothes spattered with blood. Cat's gaze shifted to Bennett's writhing form and she held the gun straight out in front of her. The horror of what he might have succeeded in doing to Jay passed through her mind in sickening slow motion. Bennett could have killed him. Could've taken him as he took Sarah.

Panic threatened to erupt but then Jay's arms were around her and she melted into him, mindless of the mess on his shirt and skin. Just him. Jay was alive and he held her. Sarah's killer lay bleeding in the sand. Without exchanging a word, she and Jay held each other as the thump of running feet came closer and closer. Bennett's team sprinted along the shoreline toward them.

Cat fought the need to touch him as Jay released her and stood rigid by her side. "I'm so sorry."

He closed his eyes. "So you keep saying."

"I shouldn't have—"

"You're a cop, Cat. I shouldn't have expected any more from you. I won't make that mistake again."

Tears blurred her eyes. "I'm sorry."

FROM THEIR VIEW ABOVE the beach, they watched Bennett being taken from the sand on a gurney and lifted into the back of an ambulance as police tape was erected around the area.

She shivered. "I wanted to kill him."

"He killed Sarah. He deserved to die."

"That doesn't mean I'll sleep any better tonight, tomorrow, the next day…"

"No, me, either."

The tone of his voice left no doubt in Cat's mind he wasn't entirely blaming Bennett for that, but her, too. She closed her eyes not knowing what to say or do to atone for the mistake she'd made. "I need to ring my boss in Reading. Harris needs to know what I've been up to."

Jay continued to stare ahead, his jaw set in a hard line. "Could he suspend you?"

"He could. I don't think he will. Harris is the antithesis of Bennett. He's a good cop through to his soul. This is going to anger him so much, I'm hoping he'll forget how Bennett's guilt came to be revealed and how much I went against the rules."

"Right."

The silence stretched and when it was clear Jay wasn't going to say anymore, Cat pulled her phone from her pocket and dialed Inspector Harris's number. He picked up on the third ring.

"Forrester! How's the holiday? Hope you've been eating a load of crap that's gonna put some weight on you, my girl."

"Of course, sir, among other things."

He laughed. "I'm sure I don't need to know about the other things. You're far too young and work far too hard. I don't want to think about what you get up to when you're away from this place."

"You might want to know about this."

There was a long silence and then he cleared his throat. "Why do I get the feeling I need to sit down?"

She closed her eyes. "Are you sitting down?"

A barrage of scuffling, squeaking and paper shuffling came across the line. She had no idea where to start but knew it wouldn't matter because when she finished, there was still a chance Harris would take her badge for not letting him know what was going on sooner.

"Right. I'm sitting. What's this all about?"

Cat started the story from the beginning, from Jay's phone call two weeks before until then. By the time she told him about the money being found with Sarah's letter, Harris had sworn enough times to turn the air blue. Cat closed her eyes as his harried breathing reverberated in her ear.

"Now this Bennett is in hospital? You shot him? Holy Mother of God. You're supposed to be on holiday. What the hell were you thinking? No, don't answer that. Clearly you didn't think."

"Sir—"

"No. No, *sir*. If you had any respect for the word *sir* you would have asked my permission to go there and be made an official part of the investigation. Why the sneaking around? Why the pretense?"

Cat snapped her eyes open and defensiveness prickled along her skin. "Because of this, that's why. Because I didn't know anything for sure and I didn't want it to be official. People are often reluctant to talk to us, sir. You know that. But they might talk to a girl who came to the

Cove year after year and lost her dear friend to a face-less killer."

"You're skating on very thin ice, Forrester."

She turned. Jay watched her, his brow furrowed. She shook her head.

"Sir, I'm sorry, but none of this has been easy. I did what I thought was best considering the police were keeping the drug connection under wraps. Little did I know Bennett was orchestrating the entire thing like a damn puppet master. He wanted Jay framed and he didn't give a crap how he did it."

"That's neither here nor there. If this…Bennett or whatever his name is, wanted your friend dead, he could've killed you, too."

"That was a risk I had to take, sir."

Silence.

"Did you suspect his involvement from the beginning?"

"No." Guilt burned like acid in her stomach as she glanced at Jay. "But very soon after I arrived, I ascertained the killer was local. I knew once I found out who Sarah had a relationship with I would most likely find the killer."

When he didn't say anything, Cat took a deep breath. "When I knew about the money, I thought in all probability the killer was still here."

Cat crossed her fingers and pressed them against her forehead. "So what happens next? Am I under investigation? Suspension?"

"You must have wanted Bennett's balls in a freaking vise."

Cat smiled. "Something like that. He played me. He let me believe he cared about Sarah. That he was doing everything he could to find her killer. Yes, I wanted his balls in a vise and I wanted to be the one turning the handle."

"As much as I understand that, there's one thing that concerns me. One thing you're going to have to prove before this goes public."

"Sir?"

"Why the bloody hell did you believe a drug lord told the damn truth? You've got to give me more than this. I'm not willing to go to Internal Affairs or anywhere until I know we can make what you did comprehensible. If you were wrong—"

"I wasn't wrong, sir. It was him. He wanted me close for a reason. He wanted to see where I was going, who I was with, who I talked to. He was one step ahead the entire time. I saw it in Kyle Jordon's eyes, too. He wanted Bennett caught as much as I did. I trusted my instinct. Usually that's enough for you."

"This is entirely different and you damn well know it."

Angry heat pinched her cheeks and Cat tightened her hand around the phone. "He was guilty, sir. He killed my best friend." *And lost me the love of my life.* "And he's been laughing about it behind my back the entire time I've been here. He knew I was coming and he waited."

Another pause. Cat's stomach knotted with fear Harris would order her back to Reading before she'd had time to explain to Jay why she'd had to ask him again if he'd killed Sarah. Why she had to hear him say it under the worst pressure possible. A pointed gun. Time passed, and with it the chance of her anticipated future with Jay.

Harris cleared his throat. "Right. This is what's going to happen. You get a statement from this Kyle Jordon. A statement we can use in court. If you can't get me that, I cannot see how I can put my career and yours on the line because you had a feeling about him. It's not enough, and if you don't know that, I haven't taught you a damn thing."

Cat released her held breath and met Jay's eyes, a ten-

tative smile pulling at her lips. "Fine. I'll get the statement. Not a problem."

Harris was right. She would have little more than suspicion and Kyle's finger-pointing to back her up when the
enquiry came. And it would come.

"We also have Sarah's letter, sir. She named Bennett
as her killer."

"That's not proof."

"She expected me to find it and named him. If I hadn't
found it, whoever did find it would figure out they found
money connected to a murder and hopefully hand it in.
If Bennett was the one to find it—"

"He was home free."

"Yes, but that was a risk she was willing to take."

Cat squeezed her eyes shut and waited. At last Harris
exhaled heavily.

"Just get this Jordon to give a statement and we'll take
it from there."

"Yes, sir."

"You have until this afternoon to call in with a status."

She looked at Jay and gave a thumbs-up. He turned
away and Cat's heart sank. With Harris's backing, a
weight should've lifted. He was a good inspector and she
hadn't enjoyed conducting the investigation without his
knowledge. Everything should now be slipping into place.
She stared at Jay's turned back and fought the urge to cry.

"Forrester?"

Cat snapped to attention. "Yes, sir?"

"Don't go doing anything else that's going to get you
killed. You hear me?"

"Absolutely."

He grunted and the line went dead.

Cat gripped the phone. "He's on my side, Jay. It's going
to be all right."

He huffed out a laugh. "Funny, I don't think anything will be all right ever again."

Cat opened her mouth and then shut it as Jay walked away and didn't look back.

CAT STARED AT THE CEILING of Jay's guest bedroom, her tears now dry and itchy on her cheeks. Morning had broken, and with it any hope of Jay leaving his room and seeking her out in the night was gone. He didn't want her, didn't trust her and she couldn't blame him. She had no right to ask anything of him. Not even his friendship.

Reaching her arm out of the bed, she slid her Black-Berry from the bedside table and reread the text Inspector Harris had sent her at midnight. Harris had set the ball rolling for the investigation into Bennett's part in Sarah's murder along with other things. She needed to leave the Cove today and report for duty in the morning. That was fine. There was nothing to keep her in Templeton anymore and plenty waiting at home.

Dragging her behind out of bed, Cat whipped her robe from a chair and headed for the door. If she was leaving, she needed to speak to Jay before she left. She would not walk away leaving things as they were. It was now or never. If he rejected her explanation again, then she could go home to Harris…to her mother, knowing she had at least tried to right her awful wrong with Jay.

She slowly walked along the landing and stopped in front of his bedroom door. After silently counting to three, she lifted her fist and rapped her knuckles on the door.

"Come in."

Cat hesitated. Half of her had hoped he would be sleeping. The coward's half. Swallowing hard, she took a deep breath and pushed open the door.

"Jay, we need to talk…oh."

"What?" He glared at her from the bed. He was sitting up, ramrod straight against the pillows. His beautiful chest was bare, his gorgeous floppy brown hair disheveled and his sexy jaw grayed with shadow.

"What are you doing? I thought you'd be sleeping."

"I haven't slept all night. What do you want to talk about? Are you leaving?"

The coldness in his voice shivered down her spine but Cat dragged her feet forward until she stood at the end of his bed and grasped the bedpost with one trembling hand. "Yes."

"Right."

His gaze bored into hers for a long moment until Cat closed her eyes, blocking out the knowing way he studied her, the spark of pain that flared in his gaze. He locked his hands behind his head.

"Go ahead."

Dread dropped into her stomach. "There's going to be an investigation. Plus, my mother needs me. Chris needs me. It's time for me to go."

He continued to watch her, his silence speaking more than words ever could. The tension hummed around them, surrounding her heart and squeezing tight. "Mum's in a really bad way. She needs the kind of help I can't give her anymore. Chris thinks it best we get her into rehab sooner rather than later, but I have no idea how we'll ever get her to admit she's in trouble."

"I'm coming with you."

She flinched. "What?"

"I'm coming with you." He ripped back the bed covers and brushed past her to the bureau.

She stared at his back, her mind whirling. What was he saying? Had he forgiven her for asking about Sarah? Her gaze zoomed in on his naked butt before Cat caught herself and looked to the ceiling, her cheeks on fire. "Jay, this is ridiculous. After what I did…you can't—"

He continued to step into clean boxers, pulled on a pair of black jeans. "I said I wouldn't leave you to deal with Julia alone again, and I won't. I'm coming with you."

"But everything's changed."

He whipped a T-shirt from one of the drawers and turned. "Not everything, Cat. You could throw a vat of hot tar in my face and I'd still care about you. Damn, I'd still love you. What's changed is you don't trust me. That means we're stuck."

"Jay, please." The regret in his eyes burned into her soul, the softness of his voice even more so. "I was scared. I let Bennett scare me."

He pulled the T-shirt over his head and stared at her for a long moment. "I know that…but it still hurt to see the suspicion, the doubt after everything we've been through these past few days. That doesn't mean I won't help Julia."

Pushing her guilt aside, Cat straightened her shoulders when he brushed past her. He leaned down and pulled a pair of sneakers from beneath the bed. She cleared her throat. "I won't let you try to fix this for me, Jay. I need to prove to myself I can do this on my own. Prove that I haven't completely let down the woman I love most in the world when she needed me."

He turned and pinned her to the spot with the blaze of burning frustration in his eyes. "That's crazy. Don't ever think that. This isn't about you letting Julia down. This is about her grief for your father and how it manifested itself." He shook his head. "God, if there's one thing my addiction taught me, it's that it's no one else's job to save an addict, it's theirs."

Cat shook her head. "I won't be free to live my own life until I know I did everything I could to make her life good again. When Chris left, it came down to me and I always felt Dad beside me, begging me to stay. Coming here is the best thing I did…for me, not for her. Now it's time for me to go back. Alone."

He blew out a breath and wiped his hand over his face. "If I let you go, then what?"

Hope rose inside Cat that he understood. Understood her regret of doubting him, that they still had a chance. She stepped closer, stopped just a few feet away from him. Her fingers itched to touch him so she curled them into fists at her sides. Tears pricked her eyes. "Then I'll be back…if you still want me."

For a long moment his gaze locked on hers, his jaw tight but his eyes soft. "I don't know if… I can't let you go, Cat. I love you."

She inhaled. His dark brown eyes shone with desire in the muted light, the strong contours of his face set in concentration, his lips ever so slightly apart. He looked so roguishly handsome, Cat struggled to maintain eye contact.

He leaned forward and the soft welcome warmth of his lips brushed the sensitive flesh beneath her earlobe. Somehow managing not to melt to the floor with her legs wide open, Cat shivered. Any words froze on her tongue. He slipped his hands to her waist and kissed her.

Helplessly, Cat lifted her hands and gripped thick, muscular forearms as Jay groaned into her mouth. Any possibility Cat might resist him puddled like liquid in her stomach. His warm soft tongue sought and took hers as desire twisted and turned inside her. His musky masculine smell, the way he towered over her made Cat believe he could take care of everything.

Her eyes snapped open and she eased him back. He couldn't take care of everything. Only she could. Only she could fix her mum, find Sarah's killer, live her life. She shook her head and looked to the floor.

"Jay, I have to do this for myself."

"Why are you running away again?"

She snapped her head up and her tears blurred his face. "I'm not running. I'm surviving."

"It feels good be back here, doesn't it?"

Cat stared. It felt so good being there with him, being with George and Marian, seeing the beach and the tiny boutique shops. The thought of going home became more and more of a dread every day. She took a step back. "It feels better than good. It feels absolutely right."

"That's what I thought."

Without warning, he lifted her off her feet and laid her on the bed. Cat quivered. Fighting her love for him was futile.

CHAPTER TWENTY-ONE

HE WANTED TO MAKE HER his so much it was more than he could stand every time she insisted on having to deal with Julia alone. With Bennett arrested, Jay's heart had ached all night knowing she would leave in the morning—their words hanging cold and unfeeling between them. He loved her and she was going nowhere without him. He would show her, not tell her how much he loved and wanted her, how much he wanted her in his bed and in his life.

It had always been Cat, and over his dead body would he let her go again.

His heart beat a mad tattoo in his chest as a wave of feral possessiveness stormed through him.

"I love you. When you go back to Reading, I'm coming with you." He stared deep into her eyes, willing her to see how firmly she held his heart in her hands.

Her eyes were wide. "Jay, please. I'm not doing this because I don't want you there. I'm doing this because I have to. Don't make this—"

He swallowed any further protest by crushing his lips to hers and her body stiffened for an imperceptible moment before she melted beneath him. He slowly moved his body over hers. Her arms came up and her fingers splayed over his shoulder blades. She pulled him closer, breathed his name into his mouth and masculine pride rose like a lion's roar inside his body.

His tongue found hers. They fought, they claimed and

Jay's heart burst wide open. There was no going back. Pulling away, he rolled over, taking her with him. She stared down at him, her gaze darting over his face, their vivid green beauty shining with love and laughter.

"Say it," he demanded. "Tell me how you're feeling right now."

The skin at her neck shifted, her cheeks flushed and her wanting gleamed undisguised in her unwavering gaze. "I love you, Jay Garrett. I love you so damn much."

A lone tear escaped over her lower lid and he thumbed it away. "Now we're getting somewhere."

Her gaze changed to something infinitely more dangerous, more demanding, and the air around them charged with electricity. She shimmied back and sat up in his lap, her breasts showing high and pert beneath her nightdress, her nipples spearing the satin. Jay's heart beat wildly, his penis waking beneath her.

She shrugged the matching robe from her shoulders before clasping the hem of the nightdress and pulling it over her head, revealing her perfectly round, deliciously full breasts. Her skin was pure cream, the nipples soft brown and budded with arousal. The pain of wanting her shot straight to his erection, filling every muscle in his body with red-hot fire.

"I swear to God cops never looked like you when I was growing up."

She grinned, her eyes impishly delighted, full of laughter and blatant desire. God, he loved her more than life… loved her more than he should. She scored her index finger along his jaw, down the side of his throat and under the neck of his T-shirt, making every hair on his body rise. Cat was in control and she damn well knew it. Jay was hers for the taking, whether he liked it or not and he did—a lot.

Leaning forward, she kissed him. Jay tried to ignore the sensation of her breasts against his chest, tried to focus his mind wholly on the then and there. They parted and she gently touched his lips. Jay caught her fingers in his hand. Their gazes locked.

He kissed her fingers one after the other and the soft scent of her perfume seeped into his nostrils. Jay committed the smell to memory along with the way she looked at him as though he was the most amazing man in the world. He couldn't hold her as his prisoner. He had to let her go if that's what she wanted but, God, how he wanted her with him forever. Wanted her to be his wife, bear his children.

Cat pulled her hand from his and dropped her gaze to his chest. Torturously, slowly, she ran her fingers down his torso toward the waistband of his jeans. Her forehead was slightly creased in concentration, her body trembling like a flower in the softest breeze. She sharply pulled his shirt from his trousers and ran it up over his body. He lifted his head and she pulled the shirt effortlessly off and tossed it behind her.

Jay's breath caught; his desire flared as if her touch were paraffin thrown on a fire. Her gaze traveled with her hands over his chest hair, over his sensitized nipples, driving him to insanity and back. She slipped off him and her hands moved to his jeans, her red hair falling like a velvet curtain across his stomach. She unbuckled his belt and lowered the zipper. He couldn't see her face but felt her smile as his erection burst free and no doubt tented his boxers like a damn pylon.

He curled his hands into fists to stop from reaching for her, to stop from dissolving the rare and mind-blowing moment of her guard being down, of it just being them. Alone. Together. The outside noise and all their problems forgotten. Leaving his jeans, she shimmied lower and his shoes hit the carpet, the two soft thuds followed by his socks. She tossed him a smile, his breathing the only sound in the silent room. Shifting and lifting his pelvis to aid her seduction, the jeans were soon discarded, his boxers following straight behind them.

"My turn."

Her smile dissolved. "Who said this was a game of equal participation?"

Grinning, Jay growled and sat up straight. She fell backward, giggling, onto the bed, her hair cascading out around her like a sheet of fire. Jay's heart beat fast as animal lust pumped through his veins.

"Turn over," he demanded.

Her eyes widened and then darkened. "What?"

"You heard me. I'm taking these panties off right now."

Smiling, Cat slowly, erotically, turned over and Jay's arousal increased as he slid his hands over the silk of her underwear. They were cut high on her buttocks and he moved his hands over the softness and gently squeezed. She groaned into the duvet and Jay smiled. Payback.

She lifted her pelvis and Jay dragged her panties down over her hips, her legs and feet. He tossed them to the side. She moved to turn and he placed his hand firmly on the base of her spine.

"Did I say you could move?"

"You're a bad, bad boy, Jay Garrett."

Jay smoothed his hands in soft circles over her flawless back, reveled in the feel of her ribs beneath his fingers, the way her body dipped and curved from waist to hip. His breath shuddered. Cat Forrester was all woman. Sexy, successful, her body lean and strong, the internal power she so often forgot she possessed radiated from her every pore, turning heads wherever she walked.

He would make her his if it was the last thing he did.

Images of Sarah threatened at the periphery of his mind and he closed his eyes, pushing them away. Before the drugs, he'd promised Sarah he'd go to Reading and get Cat. Beg her to stay. Now Sarah was dead and there was no way he wasn't delivering on that promise. No way in hell.

Jay dug his thumbs harder into her flesh, massaging them up and over her shoulders. She sighed as he kneaded the strain from her, banishing the pressure of everything she kept from him, both here and at home.

"Jay, you're killing me." The smile in her voice belied her words.

Sarah left his mind as he focused on the most beautiful woman in the world. "Do you want me?"

"I want you."

He stared at the back of her head. "*Really* want me?"

She stiffened beneath his fingers and he silently berated himself for pressuring her. He wanted to hear it before he took her, wanted to know she couldn't deny the power between them any more than he could. After a long moment, her body collapsed into the bed and she slowly rolled over.

Her steady green gaze, slightly glistening with unshed tears, bore into his. "I really want you."

His mouth came down hard on hers. She didn't need to say any more. She wanted him and he'd find a way for them to be together. He would coax her fears out of her and help her fight them. Going back to the crack house had further fueled an unending desire to right so many wrongs. He wouldn't forget the people they had left there and he wouldn't lose the woman he loved.

One of her hands gripped his biceps, the other his shoulder. As his mouth and tongue battled with hers, Jay reached lower and found her hardened nub.

He touched her and Cat clung harder. He smoothed his fingers over and over her most intimate place and she trembled beneath him. He slipped lower into her wetness, hovered and then thrust two fingers deep inside.

"Oh, God."

Her mouth lifted from his and her eyelids fluttered closed as he stimulated and loved her. Jay's erection ached with want. When he sensed her need for him, felt her throb around his fingers, Jay moved away from her and reached over for a condom from his side dresser. He sheathed himself and moved back to her. Silently, he hovered above her, his body poised for the possession he desperately wanted.

Once her eyes locked on his, shining bright with unadulterated trust and love, he thrust deep inside her. She cried out and Jay's heart left his body and merged with hers.

Slowly, he drove his shaft deep into her warmth. Her eyes misted with longing, her lips parting as she called his name on a soft exhalation. Together they rode and took, loved and promised. When she called out his name and her body shuddered and tightened around him, Jay closed his eyes and savored the strength of his orgasm as it ripped through his body. They were joined and nothing would ever separate them again.

THE RINGING OF HER CELL phone shook Cat from her peaceful slumber. "Damn it." She sat bolt upright. What time was it? The sun shone bright and warm through the windows bathing Jay's naked body in golden light. Cat's mind wandered…the phone. *Focus.*

She slipped from the bed, just managing to evade Jay's hand as it whipped out to grab her. She laughed. "I thought you were asleep."

"I am."

Cat shook her head, his eyes were still closed. She walked to the dresser where her phone lay on its surface. She hummed happily to herself, her entire body alert and warm from Jay's incredible lovemaking. She glanced at the display and her smile dissolved. The digital name told her in no uncertain terms that nothing was as it should be at home. She pressed talk and looked at Jay as he flipped over and shimmied up the cushions, watching her. Her gaze locked on his.

"Mum?"

"I've done it, Cat. It's all over, my love. You're free."

Nausea rose bitter in Cat's throat. Her mum's voice was barely above a whisper, her words slurred and incoherent to anyone else but Cat who knew her so well. "Done what, Mum? Where's Chris?"

"Gone. They've all gone. And now I'll finally get to see your dad."

The line went dead and Cat dropped the phone to the floor. "Oh, my God, she's taken something. She's trying to kill herself."

Jay scrambled from the bed and rushed toward her. The entire room spun making her nauseated. His arms came around her but Cat stiffened. She couldn't allow herself to weaken, to give up, to sink to the floor and cry. She shook him off.

"No, no. I've got to go. Now. Where's my bag?"

"Cat, wait. You're shaking. You can't go like this."

"Yes, I can. Just you watch me. Where's my bag?"

She gripped the dresser as she leaned down to retrieve her phone and the carpet rose up to meet her. She teetered backward and Jay's arm came around her once more. "Give me the phone. I'll call Chris."

Cat wavered, suddenly wanting his help more than anything in the world...but then she slammed down her emotions, thoughts and feelings. Her mum tried to kill herself. Tried to end her life because Cat wasn't there. The only person she trusted, her only constant. Holding her hand to her mouth, she shoved the phone into Jay's hand.

"Call him. Do what you want. I have to pack a bag."

CHAPTER TWENTY-TWO

JAY WHIPPED HIS CAR keys from the plate by the door and
followed Cat outside. She stood beside the car, one hand
on her hip, the other across her mouth. The heartbreak
and fear for Julia shone like a beacon in her dark green
gaze. The color that had left her face when she picked up
the phone had yet to return.

He swallowed back his anger and shame. He had undoubtedly put his mother, his father and Sarah through
exactly the same thing. Whatever happened, Jay was getting on that train with her, whether she liked it or not.

Jay pointed the keys at the car, the locks shunted open
and Cat got in, apparently mindless of her single suitcase
sitting beside the car. Jay lifted it into the backseat before
rushing around to the driver's side. He slid into his seat
and shoved the key into the ignition. They roared away
from the cabin, gravel flying up by the side of the car. He
headed down the descending road of Clover Point toward
the town center as fast as he could drive without tipping
them over the edge into the sea.

"Come on. Come on. For Christ's sake, Chris, where
are you?"

Jay turned as Cat shook her phone in the air. "He's still
not answering?"

"No. I can't believe how far away I am from her."

"I called the ambulance, Cat. She's on the way to the

hospital. You know she's stable." He reached across and squeezed her hand. "It's going to be all right."

She snatched her hand from his and glared. "Knowing an ambulance has taken her on her own to the hospital isn't making me feel any better, Jay. I want to be with her. I want Chris with her." She squeezed her eyes shut. "I don't know how I'm going to control myself when I see him. How could he do this?"

Jay turned back to the road. "We don't know what happened yet. You need to take it easy."

"Take it easy? My God, are you defending him?"

"No, I'm saying we have no idea what tactics Julia used to get rid of him. Come on, Cat, if I wanted a fix, I didn't give a shit who I lied to or what I said. Chris is new to this. So is his fiancée. Your mother could easily have set this up."

Jay clenched the steering wheel tighter in an effort to stop from touching her. He'd never seen her so scared or angry—the way she yelled at him to stay away from her when they were at the cabin reverberated in his ears and sliced at his heart. She was terrified. That was what caused the ice-cold anger in her stormy green eyes. She was beyond livid with Chris leaving their mum alone to try to take her life. That was what was behind the venom in her tone. It couldn't be about him. It couldn't be about him annoying the hell out of her on top of everything else she was going through.

Fear and loathing rose up inside him in equal measure. Would his selfishness ever end? Here was the love of his life terrified for her mother and the thought taking over his mind was whether or not Cat would leave and never come back. Why had he not understood her asking him to reaffirm his innocence over Sarah after Bennett gave such an Oscar-winning performance at the beach? Cat was scared, but she was a professional. The question had been about Sarah, not him. He was an asshole.

He slammed his hand against the steering wheel without thinking.

"What the hell was that for?" she snapped.

He turned. "What?"

"You think smashing the steering wheel is helping my nerves right now?"

"No. Sorry."

"Then stop it."

"I stopped."

"Not just with the steering wheel, either. Stop with the scowling and the cursing under your breath. None of it is helping. It's all irritating the crap out of me."

"Has Julia tried anything like this before?" He hoped a change in direction would lessen the tension between them, before she completely flipped out.

"No." She sighed. "Never suicide. Never this. That's why I know it can only be down to me leaving."

Jay shook his head. "You don't know that, so don't think it. Do you know how many times my mother blamed herself for my drug abuse? Too many to count according to my dad. It was half of the reason why it took him so long to look me in the face after I came out of rehab."

"This is different. You were with strangers when you were using. Mum was with me. I was responsible for her. She relied on me being there to pick her up."

Protective anger heated his blood and singed hot at his cheeks. "Well, she was wrong to do that. You're her child and she was wrong to rely on you for anything."

Silence.

He glanced at her. "Shout at me. Tell me I'm wrong. Deep down inside can you ever imagine you doing that to our kid…I mean, your kid?"

The heat of her gaze bored into his temple and he cursed the slip of his tongue. If she hadn't wanted to run and never look back before, she certainly would now. Silently cursing, Jay pulled into the road leading to the station. Time was running out.

"Chris? Oh, thank God. Where are you? You're with her?" Her voice cracked.

Jay looked across to see her drop her head back against the headrest, her cell phone at her ear. The tension left her body in a rush of air. He pulled into a vacant parking spot in front of the train station door and cut the engine. Without thinking, he gripped her hand as it lay limp on her leg. Relief pumped into his heart when she squeezed her fingers tightly around his, her eyes closing.

"She's okay? Uh-huh. Well, what does the doctor say?" A long pause. "Okay, well, I'm at the station now. I'll be home in a couple of hours or so. Did the police find her?" Another pause. "Uh-huh, yeah, well, I won't forgive you for this. She scared the crap out of me. What? No, Chris. Not now."

She snapped the phone shut. "Can you believe he wanted to talk about rehab? Now?"

"She's in the perfect place to talk about it."

"What?"

"The hospital can deal with it for you. If we can convince—"

She inched back against the door, held up her hand. "We? What's all this 'we'? There is no 'we,' Jay. I'm staying with Mum."

She scrambled from the car, yanked opened the back door and dragged out her case. She ran toward the station doors before he had time to draw breath.

"Shit." Jay leaped from the car and, slamming the door, raced after her.

She took off at a sprint and was through the sliding doors of the station like a cat through a narrow alley. Her body skimmed through the crowds of travelers, leaving Jay feeling like a bounding, clumsy rhino chasing a red-headed gazelle.

He darted his gaze around the crowded platform. He couldn't let her go without him. She needed him now more than ever even if she was too stubborn…or scared to see it.

He rushed forward to the ticket office. The woman behind the counter flinched and inched back. Jay tried to soften his scowl but the desperation ripping through his blood at ninety miles an hour was too intense.

"When does the next train to Reading leave?" he panted. "Which platform?"

"It leaves in three minutes, platform six." She stared at him, wide-eyed. "You'll never make it now. I can get you a ticket for the next one at—"

Jay took off, leaping and jumping through people like an out of control jack-in-the-box. His blood roared in his ears as he took flight after flight of stairs, gathering speed, yet knowing he was too late. He was chasing the fittest, sexiest cop on the planet. He was an ex-drug addict with a once-a-week gym attendance. The woman would most likely leave him standing if they were to run track together.

He burst onto platform six just as the whistle blew and the train, carrying the woman he loved more than life, drew out of Templeton Cove. Jay sank to his knees.

THE HOSPITAL'S METALLIC smell of antiseptic and cleaning detergent hit Cat's nostrils with the same overwhelming force it always did. She exhaled through pursed lips and rushed straight to the Emergency reception desk. She bounced from one foot to the other, waiting for a woman telling the receptionist her "cystitis was burning like hell" to move out of the way. When no end seemed in sight, Cat pushed forward unable to contain her self-control. She whipped her badge from inside her jacket and flashed it.

"Excuse me. Sorry." She looked at the exhausted-looking receptionist. "I'm here to see Julia Forrester, attempted suicide brought in a few hours ago."

The woman glanced at her badge before scanning the screen. "Room forty-two, second floor."

Smiling her thanks, Cat pocketed her badge and hurried toward the stairwell the receptionist indicated. The smell might have been familiar, but the hospital layout wasn't. Every time her mum had been brought here, Cat had sat beside her in a curtained cubicle in the emergency room while Julia's wrist was plastered or her head bandaged. Then they'd gone home. This was different. This was a suicide attempt. This time she'd have a room. A bed.

Cat took off at a jog. She found room forty-two at the end of the corridor and stopped. Her hand shook on the door handle. Her feet welded to the tiles.

The past few days with Jay passed like a video behind her closed eyelids. Their time in the forest, their arguments, their kisses…their lovemaking. Did any of it really happen? Right now, her time with him felt little more than a dream. A pipedream. Opening her eyes, she blinked back her tears and opened the door.

"Mum." The single word left her mouth on a soft breath.

Chris came forward and went to take her hand but Cat brushed past him to her mum. Against the stark white of the sheets, Julia looked like a ghost. Her skin was dove-gray. Her eyes were hooded and vacant, two bruises showing charcoal beneath. Her lips were the palest pink. Cat came closer.

"Mum." Cat picked up her hand from the bed.

Her mum turned to her and two tears shone like crystals beneath the harsh light above them as they slipped down Julia's cheeks. Cat blinked and her tears broke, too.

"What did you do?" Cat leaned forward and pulled her mum into her embrace as Julia's body wracked within the circle of her own. "What did you do?"

Aware of the door opening and closing behind her, Cat was suddenly grateful for Chris's absence. She needed this time alone with her mum as they'd been alone for the seven years leading to this day. A day, Cat realized with deep and sudden clarity, that she always knew would come. Guilt and hopelessness whirled inside of her as she clung to her mum's skinny frame, seeking comfort as she had when she was a child.

"I'm sorry, baby." Her mum's words brushed over Cat's temple and lifted her hair. "So, so sorry."

Cat squeezed her eyes tightly shut. The immediate response burning on her tongue was to tell her it was all right, that everything would be all right. Jay's face filled her mind's eye. Everything wouldn't be okay, not anymore. His strength and determination seeped into her blood and her courage burned brighter. So he wouldn't be there for her. What did it matter? She could face down criminals. She could handle Bennett's betrayal. She had brought Sarah's killer to justice…and she could get her mum into rehab.

So her love for Jay would fade. She swallowed. *God, please let it fade.*

Gently, she eased her mum back and looked into her sad hazel eyes. "It's time, Mum." She brushed her hair back from her face and cupped her jaw. "It's time to stop."

She nodded. "I know. I can't—" Her breath caught on

a sob and she put her hand to her mouth. "I can't do this to you, to Chris…to me anymore. I'm tired, Cat. So tired."

Tentative hope poured into Cat's heart along with the fear, distrust and desperation she felt for so long. "Do you mean it this time? Really mean it?"

Cat thumbed away Julia's tears as they poured down her face, their significance neither lost nor dismissed. It was the first time she had seen her mum cry since her husband's coffin squeaked and trundled away behind a curtain the color of freshly drawn blood.

Julia nodded.

Pulling her mother into her arms once more, Cat whispered, "Then it's time for the professionals. I can't do this on my own anymore."

Her mum's trembling intensified and Cat held her tight. Tried to absorb the terror that clearly gripped the woman who gave birth to her and provided so many years of laughter and piggybacks, cookies and cheers before her father died.

"It's okay," Julia whispered. "It's going to be okay."

"Then I need to hear you say it. I need to hear you say the words."

The creak of the door behind her had Cat dropping her arms from Julia and turning around, ready to cuss Chris out for disturbing them during such a momentous step forward. When she turned, Cat's breath left her body in a rush. "Jay."

He stood in the doorway, his broad frame filling the space, his gaze not on Cat but on Julia. Her mum stared at Jay as though not really believing what she saw. Cat imagined she had the exact same expression of horror and embarrassment on her face, too.

"Julia." He came into the room and walked to the other side of the bed from Cat and sat down.

A knot of tension formed in Cat's stomach as her mum's arms fell away from her body and went around Jay. Her mother closed her eyes and dropped her head onto his shoulder, her eyes shut, silent tears slowly trailing down her cheeks.

Jay met Cat's gaze over her mother's shoulder and his eyes were steely with determination—yet edged with a tenderness that told Cat in no uncertain terms he was there for her, and her mum, whether she liked it or not. Exhaustion settled like lead around her and Cat slumped beneath its weight.

"I guess you got the train after me."

"I told you I wasn't going to let you do this alone. Now, I'm telling you we'll get through this, through anything. Together."

She opened her mouth to respond but any words of protest or acceptance dissolved on her tongue when he turned his gaze from her and focused his attention fully on her mum. He eased Julia back from his arms, his hands sliding gently down her arms to clasp her hands. He raised them to his lips and met her eyes.

"A lot has happened in seven years, huh?"

Protectiveness rose in Cat on a tidal wave. "Jay, now isn't the time—"

"I'm a drug addict, Julia."

Cat's breath caught in her throat and her gaze shot to her mum. Julia's widened as she stared at him. "Oh, Jay."

His smile was soft, barely whispering along lips Cat loved with all her heart. "I know, quite the pair, aren't we?"

A small whimper or maybe a laugh escaped her mum as she ran her fingers over his forehead and down the side of his face, letting her hand drop limply into her lap. "You look so...handsome."

He smiled. "Four years ago I resembled an extra from a certain Michael Jackson video."

Another giggle. Cat's lips twitched as her heart swelled painfully inside her chest. Hope and gratitude swept through her not only for what he said and did but also for his forgiveness, his pursuit of her. The fact he had traveled all this way without a bag or even a change of clothes to carry out what he promised he'd do. Be there for her. For her mum.

"Jay, this is madness," Cat said quietly. "I told you I have to do this alone."

He kept looking at her mum. "Can you hear this stubborn daughter of yours?"

Julia smiled, nodded.

Jay shook his head. "She doesn't get it, does she?"

Julia shook her head. "No."

Blowing out a breath and rolling his eyes, Jay turned to look at Cat. "I love you, Cat Forrester. I've always loved you, and whether you marry me here or in Templeton, I don't care. You will marry me. Whether it's this year, next year or ten years from now. The rest of the plan is up to you, but now, today, we do what I want."

Happiness swirled in her abdomen as Cat tried and failed to drag some of her authority to the surface. Nothing came. It was deeply buried beneath the torrent of relief and hope rushing through her; she might never feel the sense of isolation that plagued her for the past seven years ever again.

"You are insane if you think I'm getting married—"

"Catherine." Her mum's voice sliced Cat's words in half. "I am an alcoholic. I need help, and while I'm getting that help, Jay's going to love you like I should have." She turned to Jay. "Aren't you?"

He grinned and put a hand to his head in a salute. "Yes, ma'am."

Cat's tentative smile erupted into a grin and she pulled her mum's frail body into her arms. "Do you realize what you just said?"

"What?"

"You just said...you just said—"

"I'm an alcoholic." Her mum pulled back and her eyes shone with unshed tears. Her lips trembled. "This time it's for real. I'm tired but not tired enough to sleep forever."

"You're going to do this. You're going to get better."

Julia swiped at her tears and gestured for Jay to come closer. She took his hand. "I can do this. I can do this for you two. When you walked through that door just now, I was reminded of the life Richard wanted for Cat."

Cat swallowed. "What Dad wanted?"

Julia smiled, cupping a hand each to her and Jay's jaw. "Yes, my love, he said you two would marry one day, come hell or high water, and he swore so on his life. I thought when he died..." She stopped, exhaled. "When he died, I thought I'd never see you together again. Then when I started drinking, I didn't care one way or another. Now? Now I can feel him. I can feel your father. He's going to help me through this. He brought you and Jay back together to make me see, make me realize Sarah is dead.... Oh, God, Sarah is dead and she had her whole life ahead of her." She shook her head and cast her gaze toward the ceiling. "He's had enough. He brought Jay here to show me how I need to get a grip. My God, I'm scared beyond belief."

Cat brought her mother's hand to the bed and squeezed. "Mum, don't cry." Raw emotion and need for her father flowed on a suppressed avalanche of grief. "You can do this. I know you can."

Jay took her other hand. "If I can recover, so can you."

Cat stared at his profile and, even though her love for him grew like an expanding balloon behind her rib cage, she shook her head. "I want to be with you, Jay, but I don't think I'm strong enough to be with you and be what I need to be for Mum at the same time."

He opened his mouth to respond, but Julia got there first. "Not strong enough?" She dropped back against her pillows, exhaustion showing in the deep premature lines on her face. "You're the strongest woman I know, Catherine. The strongest and the most wonderful."

"Hear, hear." Jay winked.

Never able to resist her mum, or Jay, Cat laughed. "This is insane."

"But totally possible." All three of them turned to the sound of Chris's voice at the door.

Melinda stood beside him and Cat's emotions bubbled over as the weight of her burden split four ways. It would be all right. They would help her mum through the hardest months of her life, harder than losing her husband, harder than losing control in the first months of her addiction. She would get better.

Chris came forward and Cat stood to embrace him and then Melinda. Turning, she watched Jay shake Chris's hand and then kiss Melinda's cheek. Cat smiled when Melinda's cheeks flushed pink. No woman reacted any differently when Jay came within five feet of her.

Jay slipped his arm around Cat's waist and she turned to him. "We need to talk."

He stared at her, his eyes full of complicated desire, control and questions. "Uh-huh."

Her brother and Melinda made Julia comfortable as exhaustion showed in her face and her eyes grew heavy.

"I'll be back, Mum."

Julia's head was already turned into the pillow, slumber inching into her body.

Cat gripped Jay's elbow. "Outside. Now."

He smiled. "After you."

The second they stepped out of the room, he slipped his fingers into hers and led her toward the stairwell. They walked in silence back through the reception area and outside into the parking lot. It was early evening and only a few cars were dotted around in the immediate area. They were as alone as they were ever going to be in a city hospital. He led her to a vacant bench and they sat.

"So," he said. "What's next?"

"What's next, Garrett?" Cat quirked an eyebrow. "What's next is we'd better find a clothes shop and then a bed-and-breakfast if you intend to stick around awhile."

"A bed-and-breakfast? But—"

She raised her eyebrows. "But what? Who said anything about you staying with me? I'm a good girl. I have zero intention of living in sin."

His eyes shone with amusement as he inched closer, his hand stealing onto her thigh. Cat cursed the arousal that shot to her center like he touched her there rather than her leg. "Oh, I see." He kissed her neck and her eyes fluttered closed. "Not living with me, just sleeping with me. I can deal with that."

He nibbled at the sensitive skin at the curve of her neck and a sigh whispered from her lips just as her phone vibrated in her pocket. She snatched the phone from her pocket with a shaking hand.

"Hello?" She cleared her throat. "Hello. Sergeant Forrester speaking."

"Forrester, it's Harris. Are you running?"

Heat singed her cheeks. "Um, no, sir. I'm—"

"Listen, I have good news."

Cat met Jay's eyes, her arousal evolving into an excitement of a different kind. "Bennett?"

"Indeed, Bennett." Inspector Harris spat out his name. "Glad you didn't say *Inspector*. The man's a parasite who doesn't deserve the title. If you can guarantee the statement of your star witness, I think your actions will be deemed warranted. Especially considering you were protecting a civilian."

Cat closed her eyes and raised her hand to fist her hair back from her face. "Leave it to me, sir. Believe me, Kyle Jordon has a lot to gain from cooperating." She snapped her phone shut.

Jay frowned, his eyes searching hers. "What did he say? Was it about your investigation? Is he still on your side?"

Adrenaline, relief and love that her mum took the first step to recovery whirled inside of her. If they got Jordon on board in the same day…

She stood and pulled Jay to his feet, her hands slipping from his to hold his biceps. "Harris wants Kyle to testify to ensure my name is cleared."

"We have to rely on scum like Kyle Jordon to do the right thing? This is not over, Cat. He might have given us Bennett's name, but the chances we'll get him to stand up in court…"

She grinned. "Oh, ye of little faith. Unless he wants to spend the rest of his life in prison, he'll testify. I might even promise him a lower sentence for all his drug offences…if I feel like it."

Jay smiled. "And, of course, it can't be helped if Harris outranks your decision later on down the line, right?"

She winked and gave a theatrical sigh. "Right. What else can I do?"

Jay laughed and lifted her off the ground and into his arms. "I love you, Sergeant Forrester."

She brought her lips down on his and kissed the man she once dreamed of spending her life with and now knew she would. Their lips took, claimed and promised. After a moment, they pulled apart and Cat brushed her hand over the side of his face. "So, do you think Templeton will welcome a new inspector in a few months' time?"

"After everyone finds out about Bennett, I expect they'll be ecstatic about someone new taking the helm."

"Good. How about a female inspector?"

"I'm sure they'd love it. Why? Do you know... Are you kidding me?" Jay's face broke into a smile that damn near melted Cat's heart to mush.

She grinned. "I'm going after Bennett's job." She leaned forward and pressed a lingering kiss to his lips. "I want you to fight it all with me. Every problem that comes in the future, every setback and upset. I want us to grab this. I want it to work for us...and Sarah. When Mum comes out of rehab, I'm moving to the Cove and she's coming with me."

"Seriously?"

"Seriously."

He spun her around and Cat laughed as her entire life fell into place.

* * * * *

An Act of Persuasion

By Stephanie Doyle

She was here. Ben Tyler felt a deep satisfaction watching her walk through the country club.

It had been twelve weeks since he'd last seen Anna Summers. Three months since he'd heard her voice. He preferred not to think too much about the fact that he knew down to the minute when she'd last spoken to him.

"Hello, Ben." Anna looked different to him. Softer maybe. Her red hair still shifted about her face, and her freckles were still scattered across her face, but there was a change. Or maybe he'd simply missed seeing her.

"You changed your cell-phone number." The words were out of Ben's mouth before he could stop them. He hadn't meant to start with accusations. He'd intended to be agreeable before asking her to come back to work.

She shrugged. "I guess I didn't want to talk then."

"But you do now?"

"Now I have no choice."

No choice? "Are you in some kind of trouble?"

"You could say."

"Whatever it is, I'll fix it," he said.

"Oh, you're going to fix it. Just like that. Snap and it's done." There was no mistaking the edge in her tone.

Ben sighed at his strategic misstep. "Can we go someplace more private to discuss this?"

She nodded. They left and were halfway to his house when she finally broke the silence.

"So what did you want to talk to me about?"

He'd hoped she would start. But that smacked a little bit of cowardice to him. He was a grown man who fully accepted his actions. "I wanted to apologize."

She shot him a look. "Exactly what are you sorry for?"

He struggled to find the speech he'd prepared, the one that recognized he should have taken her feelings into account, that admitted he'd been wrong to shut her out. But she spoke before he could say anything.

"I'm pregnant."

**Will the baby bring Anna and Ben together?
Or will it drive them apart permanently?
Find out in AN ACT OF PERSUASION
by Stephanie Doyle, available March 2013
from Harlequin® Superromance®.**

What if you desperately
wanted a family but had
given up hope it would
ever happen?

Award-winning author

Mary Sullivan

presents the follow up to

IN FROM THE COLD

Home to Laura

AVAILABLE IN MARCH

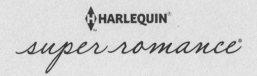

Try a new author!

From debut author
Colleen Collins

The Next Right Thing

When attorney Marc Hamilton offers suspended
private investigator Cammie Copello a chance to
reclaim her career, she must weigh her secret love
for him against following her lifelong dream.

AVAILABLE IN MARCH

H HARLEQUIN®

super romance®

More Story...More Romance

www.Harlequin.com

REQUEST YOUR FREE BOOKS!
2 FREE NOVELS PLUS 2 FREE GIFTS!

H HARLEQUIN®

super romance®

Exciting, emotional, unexpected!

Love the Harlequin book you just read?

Your opinion matters.

Review this book on your favorite book site, review site, blog or your own social media properties and share your opinion with other readers!

Be sure to connect with us at:
Harlequin.com/Newsletters
Facebook.com/HarlequinBooks
Twitter.com/HarlequinBooks

HARLEQUIN®

A *Romance* FOR EVERY MOOD™

**Stay up-to-date on all your
romance-reading news with the
Harlequin Shopping Guide,
featuring bestselling authors, exciting new
miniseries, books to watch and more!**

The newest issue will be delivered right to you
with our compliments! There are 4 each year.

Signing up is easy.

EMAIL

ShoppingGuide@Harlequin.ca

WRITE TO US

HARLEQUIN BOOKS
Attention: Customer Service Department
P.O. Box 9057, Buffalo, NY 14269-9057

OR PHONE

1-800-873-8635 in the United States
1-888-343-9777 in Canada

Please allow 4-6 weeks for delivery of the first issue by mail.

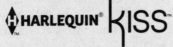